# WOLF'S CHANCE

USA TODAY BESTSELLING AUTHOR
## EVE L. MITCHELL

# WOLF'S CHANCE

# Foreword

This series is set in the same world as **The Blackridge Peak Series**. While you don't need to read *The Blackridge Peak* series first, doing so may enhance your experience of this series, as there are cameo appearances from its characters in *The Shadowridge Peak Series*. However, these appearances won't spoil the Blackridge Peak Series for you if you haven't read it yet.

This is Book 1 in a three-book paranormal romance series. This book is not a standalone.

Willow Harper has spent most of her life alone; after all, it's easier to be alone when you've already lost everything. Content in the quiet town of Whispering Pines, she immerses herself in her art.

Then Caleb Foster shows up. Tall, handsome, and *annoyingly* intrusive. Willow wants nothing to do with him.

Caught between curiosity and caution, Willow finds herself watching Caleb and wondering where he goes at night. He sticks out like a sore thumb during the day, but after sundown, he vanishes without a trace.

When fate throws them together, bringing supernatural threats and urban legends to life, Willow has no choice but to trust the mysterious stranger who dogs her days and hounds her dreams.

As their connection becomes increasingly difficult to ignore, they find themselves relying on each other to brave the approaching storm.

Willow didn't ask for his help...Caleb seems reluctant to offer it.

And both are completely unprepared for what lies ahead.

# ONE

# Caleb

The town of Whispering Pines was quiet under the evening sky. The streets were bathed in the golden hues of the setting sun. Soon the streetlamps would light the paths for the townsfolk as they walked the sidewalks, hurrying home or heading out to meet friends and loved ones.

Standing under the canopy of an old oak tree, I watched the gentle bustle of the people as they went about their business. I'd been in the town for a few days, chasing a *feeling*, hunting down a sense that something wasn't right, trying to unravel the puzzle that haunted my nights.

Whispering Pines held no sense of mystery. Nestled at the base of the Rockies, the town was aptly named, its natural borders the pine trees that enveloped the community, leading up to one of the many peaks of the Rockies. Whether the town or the pines came first, I wasn't sure; no doubt a town history would be available if I cared enough to look.

I didn't.

Whispering Pines held my interest for one reason and one reason only: the mystery of one inhabitant.

If *mystery* was even the right term.

Letting out a derisive huff at my inner musings, I cocked my head to the side as I heard the low thrum of electricity before the soft glow of the streetlights came on. Shadows formed, giving the street a slightly eerie promise of darkness.

Watching the stores along both sides of the road, I waited quietly, watchful for the one I was here for.

No one paid me any mind. In a town used to tourists, another stranger taking their rest after a long day was nothing new. The mountains closest to this town were popular with hikers all year round, so foot traffic was high.

Rubbing my hand over my jaw, the scratchy stubble reminding me that I needed a trim, I watched the door to the farthest store at the end of the parade. The store only had one display window, and while it was large, the viewpoint was still limited.

I didn't need to see inside; I was familiar with the layout, even though I had never set foot in it. It was an art gallery come art studio. One half of the store was a gallery. It held local artists' paintings and sculptures, while the other half had a workbench and a handful of easels scattered around.

It should reek of art and pretension.

It didn't.

The ones who frequented the store were mostly there for the studio. I hadn't seen a buying customer yet. However, in my research, I discovered the store's website had the same content, and more, available to buy online.

Even so, I had seen no sign of a courier dispatching sold

goods. My initial impression was that the store couldn't be profitable.

My opinion hadn't changed in the days that I had been here.

What had changed was my perception of the store clientele and the store owner, or more importantly, the object of my curiosity.

*Willow Harper.*

I didn't know what drew my attention to her, I just knew that when she walked past me on my first day here, her scent caused me to sit up and take notice.

She wasn't a shifter.

I knew shifters, and she was not one of my kind.

Her scent was human. Yet, the pull to her was undeniable.

Which was the puzzle I was faced with.

Who was she?

Who was Willow Harper and why did she hold my attention so?

Three days in this town had uncovered no answers. The only thing I'd learned so far was that I wasn't leaving until I knew why I was drawn to her and why my wolf snarled whenever anyone looked at her.

There was something about her, and I was going to find out what.

***

"You staying at the lodge?"

Looking up from my breakfast as my coffee cup was refilled, I tried not to scowl. The people of Whispering Pines may not care too much about tourists, but they still asked questions.

"No, ma'am." I took a bite of my toast. "Camping." Pointing to the full plate of bacon, eggs, and sausage, I grinned at her, ensuring I was showing my full mouth of food. "Like my first meal of the day to be cooked by someone else."

My poor table manners worked. The server failed to hide her reaction to my half-chewed toast and scurried away quickly.

Turning back to my breakfast, I ate my eggs and sausage quickly. Stuffing my bacon onto my toast, I folded it over, making a sandwich, and with a final swig of coffee, I placed my money on the table and left the diner, continuing to eat my sandwich on the way out.

I heard the low murmuring from my waitress complaining I had the manners of a dog as I left, which caused me to grin for real this time. Chewing, I wiped one hand on my jeans as I headed north, turning onto Main Street just as Willow was approaching the art store.

Her tall slender figure would have caught my attention anyway. Today, she was wearing loose light-blue jeans, a hole ripped out of one knee. A brightly patterned floral scarf was looped casually around her neck, sitting over her plain white tee, breaking up the solid white with a splash of color. Ash blonde hair hung to just below shoulder level. Today, it was loose in light waves that framed her face.

A large bag that carried her drawing pad and materials was on her shoulder, and I watched as she turned to greet a fellow "artist." The guy picked up his pace, rushing to meet her before they went inside. Willow pushed her hair behind her ear, a trait I noticed she did when she was nervous.

Taking the last bite of my makeshift sandwich, I saw her weight shift to her other foot. The creep reached forward and pulled her into a reluctant hug in greeting. Willow stepped back quickly, but it had been enough for the loser lusting after her. When he walked ahead of her, I couldn't hold back my scoff of contempt as she held the door open for *him*.

Willow looked up the street and our eyes met.

She hesitated as we stared at each other, and even from here, I could see her swallow. Her tongue flicked out quickly to wet her bottom lip as she looked away with uncertainty. She glanced into the store, she looked back at me, and then with narrowed eyes, she let her hold of the door go and started walking towards me.

As she advanced, I leaned against the wall and waited. Seeing my reaction caused her to slow down, but determination willed her onward. When she was a few feet from me, she stopped, her hand holding tight to the strap of her bag as she looked me over.

"You keep watching me."

"Do I?" At my denial, her eyes widened slightly in disbelief, and a faint blush spread over her pale skin.

Squaring her shoulders, Willow lifted her head slightly. "Yes. You do."

"How do I know you aren't watching me?" Scratching my jaw, I looked her over one more time. Her sneakers were scuffed and marked, and the cuffs of her jeans were frayed and torn. Looking back up, I met her surprised stare.

*Green eyes*. I hadn't been this close to her to note the color of her eyes before. The green was soft and muted. Scattered throughout the green iris were small, shimmering flecks of gold, brightening the color of the soft green. Her eyes were dull, framed by dark lashes, the opposite of vibrant, yet still, they captivated me.

"You're doing it again." The soft murmur of protest broke my reverie.

Blinking, I realized I *had* been staring into her eyes like a moonstruck fool. "I could say you were too."

Willow huffed out a soft laugh, with a shake of her head. She looked over her shoulder, back to the store. "I need to go..."

"I wasn't keeping you. You came to me," I reminded her. Slipping one hand into my pocket, I waited for her to turn and face me at my mocking tone. She did and I bit back my smile when I saw her determination had returned.

"I did." With a sharp nod, she took a step towards me. "You've been watching me, and—"

"It's a small town." Straightening up, I still looked down at her. She was five eight, maybe five nine, but I had the height advantage. "I've seen the guy who owns the bakery every darn place I go. I haven't been in the bakery once, but since I've been here, he's been at the diner, the bar on the corner of Pine, and the grocery store twice."

"How do you know he owns the bakery, then?"

I smiled at the question and the matching quizzical stare. "Because he wears a *Baked with Love under the Pines* T-shirt all the time." I shrugged. Lowering my voice, I leaned in slightly. "I think he may sleep in it."

Her soft laugh shouldn't have stirred my wolf like it did. "So you're not watching me?"

Glancing over her once, I dropped the teasing tone. "Well... I am now."

Willow's playful smile faded as we looked at each other. "Um..."

"Yo! Harper, you plan on flirting with Mr. Handsome some more, or are we gonna make some art today?"

Willow cringed and whirled to face her friend, who had just brought attention to us from everyone else in the street.

"Shut *up*, Lily! I'll be there soon!"

Facing me again, she was bright red and flustered, and I watched with amusement as she tried to make this less awkward while almost shrinking in front of me from the weight of all the curious stares.

"Harper?" I asked.

"Willow," she corrected. "Willow Harper." She fidgeted again. Pushing her hair behind her ear, she looked apologetic and pissed off at once. She was so out of her depth I wanted to laugh. "You're not telling me who you are?"

"You need to work on your flirting."

"Fli—" Anger cleared any awkwardness she may have been feeling. "I'm *not* flirting with you! I want you to stop watching me!"

I sniffed. "Why not?"

"Wh-what?"

I lifted my shoulder in a half shrug. "Why aren't you flirting with me?"

"I..." Confusion was back. Willow's mouth opened and closed twice, and her gaze dropped to her feet. She relaxed when she looked up at me again and saw me fighting back a smile. "You're playing with me." Pushing her hair off her face, she looked me over again. "I need to go..."

"Again, I wasn't keeping you."

Her brow furrowed while she figured out what to say. "I..." With a deep breath, she leveled me with a look. "I know you're watching me." Her will faltered when I raised an eyebrow at her statement, but she continued. "Please stop it, it makes me uncomfortable. I don't want to date you, and it's kind of creeping me out."

Holding her stare, I waited for it to become uncomfortable once more. When she started to fidget again, I spoke softly. "Conceited little thing, aren't you?"

Willow's eyes widened at the accusation. "I am not!"

"Course you are. You harass me in the street, demand I stop watching you when I've given no indication that I was, and then tell me you don't want to date me. Did I ask you out? No. So yeah, *Willow*, I'd say you have quite a high opinion of yourself."

"You're a dick."

"And now name-calling." Giving a low whistle, I pushed a little more. "You're not winning me over with your charm."

"I'm not trying to *win* you!" Her voice rose several octaves, no doubt causing more attention, a fact she was very much aware of as she winced. "I want you to leave me alone!"

Rolling my eyes, I gestured to the street. "I was. I was minding my own business. *You* approached *me*."

"To stop you from watching me!"

"I've never noticed you, darling. You're looking a bit desperate and, sorry to say, pathetic now."

"I am *not* your darling!"

Moving to walk past her, I grunted out a laugh. "*Finally*, you're right about something."

"You're walking away?"

"Look at that, right again. I've got things to do." I left her behind me, listening to her swearing under her breath as I strolled away. When her friend came out of the store to look for her again, I winked as I passed her. "Morning."

"Hey," she greeted me with an easy smile. "*Willow*! Butt, here, now! Class doesn't teach itself."

Willow was the teacher? I hadn't known that. Interesting.

I didn't look back as I carried on down the street; I was too busy processing everything I had learned about her in our short encounter.

She had fire but she didn't have the confidence to use it. When she was nervous, she fidgeted, either by shuffling her feet or pushing her hair off her face. Her clothes were worn. She pulled off a bohemian art teacher look well, but if I were a guessing man, and I wasn't, I'd say that she was short on cash. Or she spent her money on more important things than her appearance.

Looking down at my own worn jeans, I smirked. Could we have something in common?

What we *didn't* have in common was the fact that she was definitely, with no shadow of a doubt, not a shifter. That girl hadn't a whisker of shifter in her.

So what the heck was I drawn to her for?

She was good-looking—I wasn't blind—she wasn't hurting in the looks department at all. Her skin was clear, and her hair smelled of honey and magnolia. She wore no perfume. Only the soft smell of soap lingered on her skin.

I liked that. As a shifter, my nose was extra sensitive, even in human form, and some of the perfumes and colognes that people wore were so overpowering they made me nauseous. Yet Willow had nothing to enhance her natural scent.

Her face had been clear of makeup too. The number of times she pushed her hair away from her face, I doubted she used any product on her hair.

She was all natural.

My wolf snorted, echoing my thoughts that the pull to her *wasn't* natural. I almost looked over my shoulder, but I already knew she had gone inside the store. There wasn't much I couldn't hear, and I had heard her whispered shushing of her friend as they went into the art studio.

Looking at my watch, I checked the time. How long did an art class take? An hour? Two? Was it enough time?

Aware of my surroundings, ensuring no one paid any heed to me, I headed to the end of town. Traffic was quiet here; I was more conspicuous. A six-three shifter found it hard to blend sometimes. Luckily, the streets were relatively quiet, but I knew that the few people I did pass would know me again.

At my height, there's not much of me that is hard to miss.

Because of that, I looped the neatly laid out rows of houses twice, appearing as if I was mindlessly wandering, caught up in the scenery, when in fact I was circling back to my target. When it was quiet, I quickly jumped the fence, scurried across the backyard, and pressed myself flat against Willow's rear wall.

Her house faced the pine trees. Having spent the last two nights watching her house, I was familiar. Thanks to the neighbor's son, I also knew where the spare key was hidden. They lived two doors down, and the young teenage boy unknowingly showed me the hiding place when he broke in yesterday.

I'd watched him as he let himself in, helped himself to a soda and some chips, and watched TV for an hour before leaving, taking his trash with him and returning home.

Was Willow so absentminded she wouldn't notice her soda and snacks were missing?

If I were a better man, I'd maybe find some way to let Willow know. Or let the kid know I knew and make him stop. But I wasn't a better man.

If she was stupid enough to leave a key under a plant pot, then I'd be stupid not to use it.

Which sounded like good enough reasoning as I slipped the key into the back lock and let myself into Willow Harper's home.

TWO

## Willow

"So? Who is he?"

I was still hovering at the entrance, something pulling at me to go back outside and demand answers from the man who had just completely scrambled my brain. Lily's sharp jab in my ribs made me flinch and grunt at the same time.

"Ow!"

"You're completely drooling here," she said with glee. "Who is Mr. Hottie?" She frowned as soon as she gave him the nickname. "No, not Hottie. Hotcakes."

"Hotcakes?" I grumbled with an eye roll as I moved past her and headed to my easel. "Aren't we too old to be calling guys nicknames?"

"We're twenty-six, not old." Lily's eye roll was far more dramatic than mine, but then she always did manage extra emphasis on most things. I was quiet and subdued, and Lily Summers was the exact opposite. It's why we made such good friends.

Her reasoning, not mine.

I didn't think it mattered *what* made us friends other than the fact that we *were* friends. I'd earned another eye roll the day I said that too. Lily was the queen of the eye roll. Until I met her, I'd never known there were so many interpretations of a simple roll of the eyes.

"So?" She looked at me expectantly as I pulled out my tin of pencils. "Who is he?"

Trying to be casual, I shrugged. "I don't know." Keeping my head down so she couldn't read me too well, I knew I hadn't fooled her when I felt her move closer.

"You don't know?" Her voice dropped into a whisper. "I saw you walk to him."

"Yeah, I did that."

Glancing up, I saw her dark eyes watching me curiously. "You approached him. And he's a stranger?" My quick nod caused her to grin mischievously. "So, you *do* think he's hot?"

That brought my head up to look at her. "What?"

"Oh, come on, girl, you wouldn't have approached a stranger for no reason." Lily ran a critical eye over me, frowning slightly. "You could be better dressed."

"It's nine in the morning."

"So?" She pointed at her black jean skirt, her shapely, toned legs bare underneath. "This skirt is perfectly fine for a Monday morning but still shows off what the good Lord gave me."

"You do have amazing legs," I conceded as I considered my friend. Her skin was a rich deep brown color with a natural warm undertone. Her skin was smooth and luminous, emanating a natural glow. Another contrast between us—where she was dark, I was pale. Lily loved spending time in the sun, where I preferred the shade, or more honestly, the solitude of my art studio.

"And had *you* been showing a bit more of what God gave you, you may have kept Hotcakes' attention longer."

Swatting my best friend's arm, I gave her a stern look. "Firstly, I don't want his attention; secondly, it shouldn't be what I'm wearing that *keeps* his attention; and thirdly, I do *not* want his attention."

"You said that twice." Lily didn't care that I'd scolded her. She was watching me, enjoying my discomfort. "So, Miss I-Don't-Want-His-Attention, why did you go up to him and *get* his attention?"

Looking around the room at the other two occupants, who were over at the far end of the room, talking about their weekend, I still lowered my voice in case they overheard. "I think he's been watching me."

Lily's almond-shaped eyes widened fractionally. "Oh my God, really?" she whispered excitedly.

Stunned, I stared at her. "It's not a *good* thing!" I whisper-hissed. "I mean like *watching* me."

Lily gawked at me in confusion, causing a frown line to appear. "How do you know?" Checking to see the whereabouts of Peter and Lorna, she moved closer to me. "I've never seen that guy in my life. Where did you see him before this morning?"

"Saturday." Tucking my hair behind my ear, I tried to avoid her eyes as I spoke. "I was at the farmer's market, and he was there. I saw him because, well, he looks like *that*," I confessed with a blush. "I didn't think he saw me, but after I got some things, I looked and he was behind me, and just...watching."

Lily's nose scrunched up as she listened. "So...you saw him and liked what you saw?" When I made eye contact, she let out a small murmur as she thought about it. "Then he saw you... and maybe he liked what he saw?"

"Yeah. I thought that too." Opening my artist's A3 sketch pad, I placed it on my easel. "Then I saw him yesterday, and this time, he was trying not to be seen." I recalled the feeling of being watched as I went on my morning walk. "It wasn't until I was coming back from Josie's that I caught a glimpse of him, and I dunno, Lil...I just *knew* he was following me." Sitting on my high stool, I let out a sigh. "And then this morning, there he was, at the top of the street, just...watching."

"You went for a walk and got a coffee from Josie's and walked home?" Lily didn't look convinced as she summarized the last two mornings. "And then today, you see him again."

"You're making it sound like I'm overreacting," I muttered, straightening up as Peter and Lorna walked over to join us.

My best friend wasn't one for pulling her punches. "Because I think you are. We live in a small town. We have lots of tourists who come here to hike and *walk*. You live a few streets over from Main Street where all the stores are and where the coffee gets sold. Especially to someone who may be camping."

"So...you think it's a coincidence?" I saw her nod and I thought of my brief conversation with him this morning. "When I spoke to him, he said he hadn't been watching me."

"Well, duh. Even if he is a serial killer, he isn't going to *admit* it." Lily saw my what-the-fuck look and shrugged it off. "Girl, I said it was probably a coincidence; I didn't say don't trust your gut."

"You girls okay?"

We both turned to Lorna as she took her seat. Lorna was a woman in her fifties, her two kids were in college, and she had severe empty nest syndrome. She'd signed up for art classes to get her out of the house before she drove her and her husband to divorce. That was what she'd told me when she came in for the first lesson. She'd also signed up for Zumba classes, and baking classes at the community center, and I was sure I heard her tell Lily she was thinking of learning Spanish.

Going from a mom supporting two kids who had full extracurricular activities to a stay-at-home mom with no one to rely on her had been a culture shock she wasn't prepared for. Now she was filling up her days with classes, learning skills she hadn't had time to learn when she had her kids at home.

I'd learned all that from her within the first five minutes of meeting her. Within the first three, I knew what she wasn't saying: she was lonely. Lorna was also one of the sweetest women I'd ever met. Terrible painter, but she gave it her all and enjoyed it, and that was all that mattered.

"All good, Lorna," I told her with a smile. "How was the weekend?"

Lily huffed but said nothing else as I turned my attention from the mysterious stranger to my two students, well, three if you included Lily.

The morning flew by. I'd bought some wildflowers from the market over the weekend, and I had them arranged in a vase for my students to draw for this lesson. Still art was an acquired practice. So many thought it was about replicating what was in front of you. Many forgot that it was an *interpretation* of what you saw. I walked amongst the three easels now and again, giving pointers and admiring their efforts.

Lorna, straight and true, saw nothing but the flowers. Her brow creased with concentration as she did her best to match the shade of the paint on her palette to the color of the wildflowers.

Peter, middle-aged and slightly too generous with his hugs, concentrated more on the effect of light and shadow than the flowers themselves, creating a more sinister effect than I think he was hoping for.

Lily...well, Lily had drawn two stick figures holding hands. "What is that?" I asked, fighting my smile as I pointed at the odd-shaped square in one of the figure's hands.

"Picnic basket." Her tone betrayed her disappointment that I hadn't guessed that.

"Mm-hmm. And the flowers you're supposed to be concentrating on?"

She gave me a flat stare. "I'm setting the scene! The flowers will come later."

"Of course." Going back to my seat, I hid my laughter. She didn't need to come here. She had no interest in drawing or painting—she told me that herself—but she liked the quiet, and the fact I only had two paying customers made me her very own charity case. Lily's father owned the lumber mill just outside of town, and another three in the state. He was quite happy that his daughter didn't want to rush into finding a job after four years of college. He said she'd find something eventually.

My classes were twenty dollars for two hours, three times a week. I wasn't breaking anyone's bank with the cost of my classes, a fact Mr. Summers, Lily's father, liked to remind me of every time he saw me.

An entrepreneur I was not, but it paid towards my mortgage, so there was that.

Sitting back on the seat, I looked at my sketch pad. His face stared back at me. The wildflowers were no more a part of my sketch than they had been in Lily's.

He was a strikingly handsome man with a rugged yet sophisticated appearance. I knew exactly why Lily had called him *Hotcakes*. With long golden-blond hair that was pushed back from his face, cut to just below his ears, he had an effortlessly windswept look. His skin had a warm, sun-kissed tone, suggesting an active, outdoor lifestyle, which made sense that he was here in this town. He was most likely a hiker. The trails up the Rockies would appeal to him, I had no doubt. His strong jawline was accentuated by a thick layer of stubble that added to his masculine appeal, and his deep brown eyes were warm and intense, so dark they reminded me of high-quality dark chocolate.

Broad shoulders hinted at the strength that lay under his simple neutral-colored shirt. He was definitely eye-catching. Sitting back, I considered his portrait as I thought about what Lily had said. He was good-looking. It would be easy to believe that *I'd* been the one watching *him*, yet even as I stared at his lifeless portrait, I could feel the sense of *something* from him that I'd yet to put a name to.

His overall demeanor had been confident and charming, but he had shared nothing with me, not even his name, and I frowned as I considered the art in front of me. Did that sense of mystery add to his allure? I recalled the way he had spoken when he'd called me conceited.

*He also called me desperate and pathetic.*

I was glaring at his portrait now. Maybe the air of mystery I had created around him had erased my memory of him being *charming.*

Squinting at his picture, I tilted my head slightly. No, something was missing from this. It looked like him, but it wasn't *him.* How I knew that, I wasn't sure. Yet I knew something was lacking.

Taking my sketch pad off the easel, I turned to a new fresh page, quickly sketching the flowers in front of me. No good would come of sketching the handsome, *arrogant* man. A man who I knew was watching me. I was certain of it, and if I saw him again, I wouldn't confront him; I would do what I should have done to start with and avoid him.

Confrontation wasn't my style. I'd surprised myself this morning when I approached him. It was so out of character.

Gritting my teeth, I scolded myself for thinking about him. *Again.*

Glancing at the clock, I reminded my students that they had thirty minutes left in class, and I gave the vase in front of me my undivided attention for the next twenty minutes.

As Peter and Lorna said goodbye, Lily helped me tidy the store.

"It's better than yoga," she told me with a smile as she stacked the easels. "I get more zen playing at nothing than I do in the warrior position."

"You love yoga," I reminded her. Her comment about *playing at nothing,* I chose to ignore.

"Who doesn't like yoga?"

*Me. The uncoordinated.*

"What are your plans for the rest of the day?" I asked instead.

Lily toed her sneaker as she avoided looking at me. "I know it's a ploy, I know it is, but dad left the account ledgers on the kitchen counter when he left this morning."

Grinning, I watched her try not to squirm. "Ahh, that old trick," I teased.

Exasperated, she threw her hands in the air. "He *knows* I'm going to look at them, I know I'm going to look at them, but does he *ask* me to look? No. I'll balance his books, and he won't mention it, and then we'll do the whole dance again in a month."

"Why don't you just take his job offer?"

"Because then I'm the girl who could only get a job working for her dad!" she wailed.

"But you want to work for him," I countered reasonably.

"But he doesn't *need* to know that, Willow!"

Shaking my head, I switched the store computer on. "You two make my head hurt. You did accounting at college, you want to be a bookkeeper, he wants you to be his bookkeeper, you get along great—I don't understand why you aren't working at the mill."

Lily groaned loudly. "Because then he has all the power."

"He's your dad." Rubbing my forehead tiredly, I met her sullen frown. "You both confuse me," I admitted. "If my dad were here, I'd jump at the chance to work with him every day."

Lily snorted. "You don't even know who your parents are. For all you know, he could be some child-abusing alcoholic and is probably dead or in jail." Her snort turned to a disdainful sniff. "You told me you were found outside a church in a cardboard box. Abandoned. Why would you want to know those people? They *left* you."

She would never understand. She had her father, a man who doted on her. Her mother had left them both a long time ago after a sordid affair with her father's best friend, and while I knew her mom had tried to reach out a few times to Lily, her efforts had been in vain. Lily Summers was the most caring person on the planet until you wronged her, or her dad, and then God help you because she didn't believe in forgiveness for betrayal.

But still, Lily *knew* where she came from. Despite her relationship with her mom, she still knew her.

I didn't have that knowledge regarding my birth parents. I'd spent my life in an orphanage until I was ten.. Then I was fostered by a nice couple, who kept me until I was sixteen. They died in a car crash, and I was back in the foster care system, spending time in three different homes until I hit eighteen.

My original foster parents had left me a sizable sum when they passed, which had taken seven years to pass through the legal system when my "aunt" had contested the will. It was with their money I'd bought my home, a simple two-bed bungalow, in a small town at the foot of a mountain, surrounded by fresh air.

A fresh start in a new town.

One where I was surrounded by nature and felt at peace. I'd met Lily in my first week, and we'd hit it off. In her way, Lily had adopted me more solidly than any foster parent before her, and when days were hard and I struggled to get out of bed, Lily was the one who made sure I was taken care of.

It was the knowledge that I had of how loyal she was as a friend that made me not start the old disagreement about the reasons why I was left. Instead, I simply listened as she listed the reasons why working for her dad was a bad idea.

When she was gone, I found myself back at the sketch pad, the page turned to the stranger's portrait.

Unease sat low in my belly as I stared. He was so familiar, but I knew I'd never seen him before the market on Saturday.

"What mystery do you hold?" I asked the sketch, my finger trailing over his jawline, imagining the feel of his short beard under my finger. "And why do you scare me?"

The sketch had no answers, and as I closed the cover, I knew I had none either.

THREE

# Caleb

LOOKING AROUND THE KITCHEN AS I WALKED CAREFULLY through Willow's living space, my first impression was how clean it was. Not just surface clean, but *clean* clean. The smell of chemicals lingered under the fragrance of fresh flowers and, from a glance around the room, possibly six different aromatic candles.

This room was an allergy sufferer's worst nightmare.

Her furniture was a bland neutral. There was a *lot* of beige. As I moved towards the hall, I couldn't help but think that this was not the house of an artist. I expected splashes of color. Bold prints with garish contrasts. Instead, I was faced with...beige.

The first bedroom faced the street and was utilized as an art studio. Which made sense, since she spent so much of her time at the store on Main Street. But again, the room lacked personality. White walls with distressed white weathered hardwood flooring, and a simple gauze curtain that shut out the curious passersby. Two easels sat center stage, and an L-shaped workbench was the only other furnishing.

Some canvases sat facing the wall, while others of muted landscapes dotted the room. None were mounted onto the wall, and I wondered if that was another trait of her self-confidence. Or lack of it. More frustratingly for me, this room told me little about Willow either.

Conscious of the thin covering between me and the street outside, I moved to the next room.

The bathroom was pristine white, featuring a sleek washbasin, a spotless toilet, and a bathtub with a modern shower overhead. The simplicity and meticulous organization of the space told me as much about Willow as anything else in the house.

Which was little.

Other than the fact she obviously had too much spare time to spend cleaning.

Pushing open the door to the remaining room, I stepped into her bedroom and let out a low chuckle. *Here* was where she spent most of her time, which took me by surprise, considering she had a home studio. While by no means messy, this room was just more lived in. I could tell from the slightly rumpled bedspread, still in neutral tones, but it looked worn and well used.

Her bed took up most of the space. Pushed up against the corner of the room, it faced the pine trees. Her drapes were pulled wide open, allowing an uninterrupted view of the woods behind her house.

I knew she closed them at night while she slept, but I appreciated the simple view nonetheless. A desk sat in the opposite corner, again facing outwards. She seemed to spend a lot of her time looking *out*, if the positioning of her furniture was anything to go by.

The walls were covered with sketches, paintings, and a few portraits. Nothing was framed or even looked professionally finished, but her personality shone through, revealing more about her than anything else in the house. The landscapes were mostly of local scenery, one of Main Street in winter, which had an impressive amount of detail. The sketches were mostly done in pencil. One seemed to be charcoal, but most of them were black-and-white abstracts of familiar landmarks created by clever use of light and shadow.

I paid more attention to the portraits. An older couple was predominant throughout, sometimes together, most times apart. Her friend from this morning was also scattered about, her face sketched at varying angles. I recognized the woman from the diner and the guy from the bakery—he really did seem to be everywhere I went.

As I absorbed her artwork and admired her skill, I noticed a common thread to it all. The same was true for her house. She wasn't featured in any of her art, and I hadn't seen a single framed photo of her either.

Yet, this room, it was *her*. From the skewed sneakers at the entrance of her closet to the half-empty water glass by her bed. The drapes were pushed back so far they couldn't be seen from outside. The scattered artwork may have been capturing moments in her life that she wanted to keep close to her.

The small adjacent bathroom held a washbasin, toilet, and shower. White walls, white ceiling, white floor.

I'd seen hospital wards with more personality.

A mirrored cabinet over the sink revealed the normal hygiene items, for a woman who lived alone. The condoms were the only thing interesting. Tapping the lid of the unopened box, I looked around, checking that I had missed nothing.

Back in her bedroom, I opened her closet and stepped into the small space. Immediately I was enveloped in her scent. And something else. Something I couldn't quite identify.

Her drawers held no secrets apart from the very unsurprising fact that her taste in underwear was as bland as her taste in home decor. Plain white tees were only broken up by a handful of black T-shirts instead. Three pairs of jeans hung harmlessly in the corner, and being no fashion connoisseur myself, I wouldn't put my life on it, but they all looked exactly the same: same fit, same color, same unremarkable jeans.

She had two hoodies, one gray and one black.

This woman could be a spy for all I knew. She'd blend in a crowd, and if anyone ever broke into her home—myself not included—they'd be so bored they'd leave.

She owned nothing of value. No jewelry. No laptop, no tablet. It seemed she chose to isolate herself from technology. I'd seen one TV in the living room, but that was it.

When I came out of the closet, I got down on my hands and knees and looked under the bed. I found a pencil. Considering how spotless the floor was, under the bed was almost a chaotic mess with its lone wayward pencil.

I turned on the spot as I soaked in the room, taking note of the art, the bed, the drapes, taking in everything that the room told me. If there were mysteries in this room, they were well hidden.

"Who are you?" I mumbled as I began to lift her drawings

off the wall to see if they were masking Willow's secrets. They weren't. The walls were bare behind them.

Still, I couldn't shake the feeling that this was her space. More than just her room, this was where she was comfortable. I felt it when I walked into the room, and I still felt it now.

Picking up her pillow, I inhaled deeply, my wolf nose picking up a scent I wouldn't associate with Willow. Sour almost. Bitter.

"Now what's this?" Pulling off the pillowcase, I pushed my nose into the soft pillow. The bitterness was deeper, stronger.

"Sickness?" Drawing my head back, I looked around the room once more. "What am I missing?" A small drawer in her desk revealed a diary, which contained coded letters and numbers, and the more I looked at it, the more I saw the pattern. "You're ill." Frowning, I flipped through the pages again. The code was unique to Willow, but a pattern was there. I just needed to know what the pattern was for.

Returning to the kitchen, I opened the refrigerator, my lip curling in disgust at how little meat there was. The shelves were filled with fruit and vegetables, and the only meat she had was two skinless chicken breasts.

Almond milk, bottled water, and one bottle of wine rounded off the contents of her fridge.

A search through her cupboards revealed nothing more exciting than some crackers, canned soups, and protein bars.

Nothing indicated she was sick. But now that my nose had the scent, I could smell it everywhere. Faint in the kitchen and on her couch, but it was there. Lingering.

She wasn't diabetic. She had carbs and candy, more than an emergency stock if she dipped in blood sugar. There was no medication, except one bottle of Tylenol, but most homes would have some form of painkiller in them.

In her bathroom, there'd been nothing to note except that she chose regular tampons, not plus. The only other thing worth noting was her choice of condom was the ribbed kind in regular size.

"I know less about you than when I walked in," I grumbled, returning to the fridge. Yesterday, I'd watched the teenager eat chips and drink soda, yet I'd seen nothing that hinted at that in my recent search. "You don't eat someone's last bag of chips and think you won't get caught..." Looking through the cupboards again, I frowned. "Unless you know he's here and leave them *for* him."

That made sense.

Why though?

Did he need somewhere safe? Was he in danger? Chewing the inside of my cheek, I again scoured the place, hoping I missed something.

"She's a bleeding heart?" Rolling my head on my shoulders, I shrugged off the feeling of irritation. I'd never come across a blank slate before.

This woman could be anyone.

I didn't like it.

Walking back to the room she used as a studio, I stayed close to the wall as I entered, hoping to remain undetected from any prying eyes.

There was nothing here except her art. I compared a landscape to the one I had seen in her bedroom. In comparison, this one was...flat. It was still very well done, but now that I had seen her personal drawings and paintings, I could see the differ-ence. A commission?

A canvas facing inward had caught my eye before, and now that I was back in the room, it drew me to it. Curious, I lifted it and turned it around. I almost dropped it in surprise as my face stared back at me.

My eyes narrowed as I took in the drawing. My hair was away from my face, the waves that sometimes irritated me were pushed neatly away from my forehead. My hair was darkish blond, with lighter strands throughout that had many a woman ask me if I colored my hair. The nose was straight, too long in my opinion, but in the portrait, it was evened out with full lips. A thick scruff of stubble coated the face, hiding a strong jaw and giving some definition to the cheekbones. My hair curled slightly under my ears, drawing attention to the slight scar that ran from the bottom of the right ear to the collarbone.

Staring at myself, I felt slightly unnerved as my portrait watched me back. Leaning closer, I scoffed at the exaggerated length of the eyelashes. With everything else so precise, it amused me she had used artistic license on this.

Placing the portrait back where I'd found it, I went through every canvas to see if there were more.

Finding three, I arranged them in front of me. In one, I was half-hidden in shadow, a hoodie worn under a jacket. In another, my face was turned away, looking over my shoulder to the trees and mountain behind me. In the third, I was leaning against the wall, under the shade of a tree on Main Street, a familiar smirk on my face as I appeared to be waiting.

Flicking my eyes over each portrait, I didn't know what to

think. I'd been here three days. She only spoke to me this morning.

I hadn't worn that jacket since I'd been here.

I wasn't beside *that* mountain.

*And she hadn't been home since this morning's encounter.*

"She's psychic?"

Psychics were a money-grabbing farce. *Actual* premonition was rare, almost a myth.

"Myth? Says the wolf shifter," I muttered. Pulling out my phone, I snapped pics of all the pictures of me. Putting the canvases back in place, I hesitated. On one, there was a date penciled in the bottom corner. It confused the hell out of me until I realized she'd written it British style, day before month.

Two things creeped me out about this. One, she wasn't British, and two, this was drawn two months before I got here.

"What the fuck are you?" Quickly, I took a picture of the date, and then I cleaned up after myself, ensuring the room looked like it had before I went snooping.

Unease settled on my shoulders. In the kitchen, I grabbed one of her candy bars and bit into it as I thought about everything I didn't know about Willow Harper. Like the important information, such as where she was from. Who were her parents? Why the fuck was she drawing me? Who the *hell* was she?

*Why the fuck was she drawing me?*

My senses suddenly alerted me to the sound of someone approaching from outside. Checking my watch, I saw I'd overstayed my welcome. Stuffing the candy wrapper in my jeans pocket, I crossed the floor on light feet, easing the back door open just as a key slid into the front lock.

While she opened the front door, I closed the back one, masking any noise with the sound she made. I heard a long exhale just as the latch caught on the back door.

Crouching low, I used the wall to hide my presence when Willow walked into her living space and came to a sudden stop.

I could hear her heart racing from here, her adrenaline kicked in, and I pressed myself against the wall.

"Who's there?" Her voice was quiet, almost like she didn't want the answer. "Someone's been here. Are you still here?"

The floorboard creaked and, tilting my head down, I listened closely. She was turning in a circle? I heard her walk away and knew she was checking the rooms in her house. She was brave. I'd known a lot of women in my time among humans, and I was certain at least half of them would either be outside by now or at least on their phones, calling for help. That reaction wasn't what I expected *just* from women either; I knew a few men would react the same.

While she was gone, knowing just how few rooms she had to check, I eased along the wall to the corner of the house, ran to the fence separating the properties, and jumped over it quickly. Keeping low, I waited, and sure enough, only moments later, the back door opened.

Knowing it was risky but chancing it anyway, I turned my head to see between the narrow cracks in the fence.

She was on the back step, not looking around her space or her neighbors'. Her attention was fixed on the woods in front of her. Reaching up, her fingers pushed her hair behind her ear, and I caught the slight tremor of her hand. With an uneven step, Willow went back inside her house.

I waited until I heard the lock turn and then waited some

more. When I was sure she was no longer at her kitchen window, staring out at the trees, I ran to the teenage kid's backyard, hopped the low fence, and within a few strides, I was enveloped by pine trees.

I didn't stop, moving back further into the woods before I looped back and approached her house, knowing that the shadows of the pines hid me well.

Her kitchen window was clear. The drapes were pulled across the bedroom window. Did she think someone would be watching? Or was she already sure it was me?

Willow remained home for the remainder of the day. Each time she was in the kitchen, she never looked up. She never looked outside once.

It was for that reason I never moved from my spot all night.

She knew someone had been there, and she was probably sure they were observing her, so her act of defiance was to show herself to them as she stayed in her home, unafraid, but not *quite* brave enough to raise her head in case her hunch was true.

She didn't want to see who it was. She didn't want to be proven right.

My gut was also telling me *who* she knew she'd see.

*Me.*

Watching.

Waiting.

Waiting for what? I was no longer sure.

# FOUR

# Willow

I HELD HIS GAZE AS HE STARED STRAIGHT INTO MY SOUL. I could feel my heart beating faster, and my palms grew sweaty as the heavy look saw past every defense I had.

"Jesus," I muttered as I leaned back in my seat. The man from this morning watched me from my large sketch pad. "You shouldn't be so darn life-like."

Hearing my critique, I fought the smile. As an artist and a teacher, I always said that we wanted the portrait to look life-like, and instead, I was criticizing the effect. Reaching out, I smudged the charcoal at the edge of his face, which had been intended to create a shadow, and as I smoothed it out, the aura of danger he exuded was blended out, creating a more rounded cheekbone than the sharp line I had previously.

"You were in my house," I spoke to the portrait as if he were in the room with me. It'd taken several hours of being at home before I *stopped* looking over my shoulder to check if I was alone. "You've seen Alistair use the key, haven't you?"

The sketch did not reply, but I knew. I *knew* he had been in my home. Nothing was out of place, there was no foreign smell in the rooms, but I could sense it. A sense that someone had been here. Someone I didn't invite inside.

"He's not a vampire, Willow," I scolded myself. "He's just a man."

*Just a man?* Licking my lips, I studied his face. He was *quite* the man. He was freaking gorgeous, but that didn't mean, just because he looked like an angel, that he was a saint.

Having met him this morning, I would say he was the *exact* opposite of angelic. Reaching out, I corrected the slight crease at the corner of his eye. Sitting back, I nodded as I took him in. Yeah, the slight smirk, the crinkle at his eye, that was how he looked this morning. Barely concealing his amusement as I spoke to him.

Not amusement.

*Mockery.*

He wore the air of arrogance effortlessly. It contrasted with his casual clothing, but as I studied the face in front of me, I knew this man was much more than the simple clothes he wore.

"What do you want with me?"

I'd thought about calling the police, but really, what could I do? Say that a guy I don't know and have never met before was in my house today? But I can't prove that he was. Also, I've been drawing him for the last couple of months but didn't suspect he was real until Saturday. Oh, and I think he's stalking me.

"I look like the stalker," I muttered as I stood up. "*I* approached *him*. I saw *him* first. Would you even have spoken to me if I hadn't confronted you this morning?" The image stared steadily back at me. "Yeah, I know, you think I'm an idiot." Pulling my hair off my face, I twisted it into a knot, using a hair tie from around my wrist to secure it at the nape of my neck. Walking over to the door, I looked back at him as he watched me leave. "If it's any consolation, I think I'm an idiot too."

My bed beckoned. It'd been a long day, but I was hungry. I'd tried to avoid the kitchen as much as possible, sure that he was out there, but the growl of my stomach told me what it thought of that idea.

In the kitchen, I put the kettle on the stove, emptied a can of soup into a mug, and placed it in the microwave. A few minutes later I took the cup of tea and the mug of soup to my room, the corner of a bag of chips held firmly between my teeth.

Once I was changed into pajamas, I grabbed my laptop out of my tote, snuggled under the blankets, fired up Netflix on my laptop, and did my best to forget about men with chocolate brown eyes and thick wavy hair, as I focused on the Winchesters and their drama.

I couldn't relax. It was impossible. My mind kept drifting to him. The few words he had spoken to me had not been kind. But then, why would he be? I accused him of stalking. "He *is* stalking you." Pausing my show, I put the laptop aside. "Is he?" I thought about what he said. "It is a small town," I reminded myself. "You do see everyone at least twice if you're in town, and he seemed to be in town a lot." Sitting up, drawing my legs to my chest, I rested my chin on my knees as I thought about it. "You have absolutely no way of knowing if he was in here. It could have been Alistair and one of his friends."

There was a candy bar missing. One bar. I'd seen that kid eat candy; he wasn't sharing his sugar snack with anyone else.

Restless, I got out of bed and took my empty cups to the kitchen. Using the cover of darkness, I peered out into the trees beyond my backyard. The trees were so dense that it was hard to see anything, which was slightly unnerving. However, they hadn't bothered me for the last two years that I lived here, and I refused to let them bother me now.

I shouldn't leave a key under a plant pot. That was the obvious answer. I didn't feel safe in my home, and even before Mr. Mysterious, it bothered me that I left access to my home out in the open.

Alistair knew I did it, and utilized the fact, and if I was honest, it was *because* of him that I left it outside. His dad was gone mostly for work, and his mom didn't hide her multiple affairs. I'd never snooped too closely into their relationship. Lily had told me that Alistair's dad knew about his wife's trysts, and what people did behind closed doors was their business.

But Alistair was just a kid. I'd been his age once, and I knew how it felt to feel like a stranger in the place you called *home*. Six months ago, I told him I was putting a key under the plant pot. I told him I was counting on him not to take advantage of my trust, but if he needed to step outside of his house once in a while, there was a space for him two doors down.

He'd never abused my trust. I left snacks in the house, and he thanked me by eating them and not making a mess. We didn't talk about it, and I think he appreciated that more than the chips and candy.

Parents were hard.

I'd been lucky-ish. I had good folks who cared for me for a chunk of my life—this house proved that. When they passed, they left me a large portion of what wealth they had. Once the courts ruled that it was my inheritance, I had taken that money and invested it in this house. Still, there were days that I didn't believe that it was mine. A part of me was still waiting for the lawyer to phone and tell me the decision had been overturned and this house didn't belong to me.

It was probably why I kept everything neutral. *Bland*, Lily called it. Personality-free.

Movement in the shadows snapped me out of my daydream. The night air was still, and that was more than the wind. Standing still, I watched with wide eyes the shadows of the night. The trees didn't move again, but the uneasiness grew. The soup I had earlier sat heavy in my belly.

The sense of being watched became so strong that it was almost unbearable, and I fought the urge to turn and run into the bathroom and lock the door.

Slowly, I backed away from the window, alarmed at how close I had moved to the front of the kitchen, clear to anyone who would be looking in, even under the cover of darkness. I didn't dare blink, and when I reached the arch that led to the other rooms, I turned and sprinted to my bedroom.

Wedging a chair under the handle, I clambered into bed, pulling the covers over my head like a three-year-old child terrified of the monster in their closet, ears straining for the sound of the hunter looking for its prey.

"You look like death."

Looking up, I watched as Lily approached, balancing a cup holder with two coffees and a bag of what I hoped was doughnuts.

"And you look disgustingly cheery." Lily didn't care that I was grouchy. Her sleek shoulder-length dark bob bounced as she walked, the lighter brown highlights catching the sunlight that streamed through the window, adding dimension to her fashionable hairstyle. "Tell me it's doughnuts."

"It's doughnuts," Lily confirmed, dropping the bag carelessly on the small counter. Peering at me, she grasped my chin, tilting my head to the left and right. "You look terrible. Did you sleep?"

Jerking my head free, I ignored her, choosing to pick up a coffee instead. "Zero percent?"

"No, full fat, I decided to fatten you up."

I hesitated for a second before I took a welcome gulp. "You'd never do that to me."

"Meh, depends if he was hot."

Grinning, I accepted the offered sugary fried breakfast treat. "You most definitely would not do bodily harm to me for a guy."

Lily sniffed before taking a bite of her doughnut. "True. Maybe a cat?"

"I don't like cats," I reminded her.

"Which is why you need me to knock some sense into you. Cats are awesome."

"They're arrogant."

"They're fluffy."

"They have a superiority complex," I countered.

"They deserve it."

"We're not arguing about cats again," I warned her.

"We're not arguing. It's called a friendly debate."

I rolled my eyes. "We are not *debating* about cats again. I like dogs."

"Dogs lick their own balls."

I fought to control my laughter. "So do cats."

"Cats do it with class. Dogs are just sloppy." She shuddered. "I mean, have some pride in your work, you know?"

"This is ridiculous."

"*You're* ridiculous."

We stared at each other before we both started giggling. "So..." She set her cup down. "Why do you look like shit?"

"Slept funny."

"Flare-up?" Her face was serious as she gave me a quick once-over.

"No, just a bad night's sleep."

"You've been doing too much," Lily scolded, the mother hen in her taking over. "I told you that early morning classes were a bad idea."

"I'm fine, and early morning classes *would* be a bad idea for me, but it's ten in the morning. The *morning* is almost over," I reminded her.

Lily wasn't to be deterred. "You're not getting away with being sassy," she scolded. I watched her carry one of the high-backed chairs across the small store.

"What are you doing?" Instead of answering, Lily took hold of my wrist and pulled me towards the chair, her intentions clear. "Lily! I don't need to sit."

"Yes, you do, you look exhausted."

"I'm just tired," I protested as she pointed at me and then the chair. "Don't point at it like I'm a pet! I don't need to *sit!*"

I watched as she drew herself up to her full height, a lofty five three, but the woman's personality made her so much more of a presence than you bargained for. "Do you want to be sick for the rest of the week?"

It was no use. I knew I'd buckle under her uncompromising glare, so I took the easy way out and sat down, ignoring her pleased murmur of approval. Silently I took the coffee she handed me, and my half-eaten doughnut.

Lily patted me on the head as I sullenly looked out the window. "Such a good girl," she teased. "Now, see, if you were a cat, you'd have left by now."

Snapping at her hand as she pulled it away, I growled. "If I were a dog, I would have bitten you."

Lily ignored me while she checked the itinerary for today. "How are you really feeling?"

"I'm fine. I'm not overly tired. I had a bad night's sleep, that's all." I'd had a bad night's sleep because I was waiting for the stranger to attack me in my bed. I had no recollection of falling asleep, but I knew that I had caught some sleep, but not as much as someone like me needed.

Lily watched me with concern once more. "You can't afford a bad night's sleep. Do you want to go home?"

"And do what? Lie on my couch and nap?"

"Sounds like bliss," she sighed theatrically.

"It sounds boring. And *weak.*" Standing up, I picked the chair up to put it back in its proper place, avoiding her narrow glare.

"Willow, you know better than I do how to treat your illness, so when I tell you that I think you should rest, then it must be because *I think you should rest*."

"Are you sick?"

Both of us turned to see Peter standing in the doorway. "Is class canceled again?"

Sharing a look with Lily, who thankfully had her back to Peter so he couldn't see the face she made, I shook my head vehemently. "No, Lily's just being overly dramatic."

"Mm-hmm, how unlike her," he murmured as he took his seat, and I leapt forward to grab my best friend's arm, pulling her back before she gave him an earful.

"No," I warned her quietly. "Just smile, remember?" Lily flashed her teeth at me, more of a snarl than a smile. "Or not," I added hastily.

Peter was an ex-employee of her dad's. I wasn't sure of the history, and I wasn't sure Lily was either, but she was fiercely loyal, and she protected her dad without question. Peter made a cutting comment about her dad once, and that was enough for Lily—his card was marked, and I wasn't sure he would ever redeem himself.

Peter was oblivious to my friend's struggle to keep quiet and was already settling into his chair to begin today's lesson. Lorna arrived not long after, and once she'd given a breathless recount of her morning, my three students quieted down for their lesson.

Lily paid even less attention than she had the day before, and her glances of concern soon grated on my already fragile nerves.

Pushing myself to my feet, I told them I was getting some fresh air and went outside. I knew I was overreacting. She was my friend and she was concerned, but I needed room to breathe.

The streets were busier than I expected, but I let the hustle and bustle of the morning wash over me. Leaning against the wall, I closed my eyes, enjoying the warm sun on my face.

A strong grip held onto me, and groggily I opened my eyes, staring into the dark eyes of the stranger who was haunting me.

"You?"

He was frowning, but I quickly noticed it was with concern. Trying to clear my head, I assessed him as he held me.

Not held me, he was *holding* me up.

"Do you normally fall asleep standing up?"

*More than I should.* "Um, sometimes."

The door to the studio opened, and Lily came out. She took one look at me, and the worry line between her eyes deepened. "Willow! I *told* you this would happen!"

"What would happen?" he asked, and I realized he was still holding me upright.

Stepping back, I tried to disengage from his hold, but he held tight. "I'm fine."

"You are so obviously *not* fine," Lily scolded me. "You need to go home and rest."

"Are you sick?"

My eyes closed as I struggled to process. "No."

"Yes!" Lily was full-on glowering now. "She has ME."

"I can see you're a good friend," he answered smoothly, which actually made me smile as he clearly misunderstood.

Lily's flat glare only made me smile wider. "No, I don't mean *me*. I mean she has myalgic whatever, chronic fatigue syndrome."

I felt his attention shift from Lily to me, but I didn't dare look up. "You're tired?"

I heard the doubt in his voice. Ugh, how many times had I been asked that skeptical question? Was I tired? Yes, I was freaking exhausted from people assuming I was lazy.

"A bit more weary than I thought," I conceded under my friend's warning glare.

"You need to go home." I watched Lily's gaze flick back to the man beside me. "I can't leave the store." Her ability to lie so carelessly was the one thing I resented about her, but she was already talking to him again before I could stop her. "Is there any way you could help?"

"Excuse me?" He sounded surprised. I wish she still could surprise *me* with her boldness.

Looking at my feet, I wanted to be far away from here. "I'll manage. Lil, stop," I pleaded, hoping she would get the message.

"Well, you won't manage to walk by yourself."

I knew what she was thinking. She was relentless in her determination. "I'll be fine."

He decided to be helpful by being *not* helpful. "You were just sleeping against the wall."

*Yes, I'm aware, thanks.* "It happens."

"It does?" His incredulity was worse than the *tired* comment. "Like narcolepsy?"

That actually made me laugh. "No, nothing like that."

His finger slipped under my chin, and he tilted my head back to look at him. "You stare at my feet any longer and I won't be sure you haven't fallen asleep again."

Looking into those molten pools of chocolate had me swaying on my feet for the wrong reason. He held my stare, and I saw him searching my face for...something. Lily cleared her throat, causing us to react differently. He stepped back as if he was scalded, and I jumped like a startled rabbit.

Both of us watched Lily try to cover her grin.

"So..."

"You want me to take Willow home?"

The dryness of his tone was lost on Lily. I, on the other hand, was painfully aware of it. "You don't need to do that. I'll be fine."

"She really shouldn't be alone," Lily told him with an exaggerated level of concern. She winked at me, and I knew I was going to throttle her. "I'll get your purse." She disappeared, my shout of protest falling on deaf ears.

His low chuckle made me turn to him. "It's not funny."

He nodded. "She's subtle."

"She really isn't." He had a dimple on his left cheek. It was a feature I hadn't noticed before. Maybe because I hadn't seen him smile.

"You're staring," he murmured.

"You don't need to walk me home."

He shrugged. "It's not far." We held each other's stare. Did I call him out on the fact he just told me he knew where I lived? "Unless you live outside of town?" he added. "Otherwise, the town's small, won't take long."

His stare never wavered as he lied to my face.

I had ME, I wasn't weak.

"You can stop with the pretense." My voice was soft, but he heard the challenge.

His eyes got darker as he watched me. "Well all right then." He held his hand out to me. "You ready?"

Was I?

# FIVE

# Caleb

WILLOW WATCHED ME, HER GAZE DROPPING TO MY HAND once before she took a step back, rejecting my offer. Her friend was back, chattering away like an annoying little yappy dog, but Willow listened and nodded in all the right places.

When those green eyes met mine, I realized the other girl had stopped talking.

"You ready?" I asked her again.

"What's your name?"

Turning my head, I looked at her friend. "Caleb."

"Caleb," Willow repeated quietly. "I see that." She saw my curious look, and the familiar blush spread over her cheeks. "It suits you." She wouldn't meet my eyes, and I turned my attention back to her friend, who was talking *at* me again.

"I don't have a phone."

I knew that would have silenced them both, and I relished in the merciful quiet at my little white lie.

"You don't have a cell?"

Had I announced something truly shocking, I might have

understood the look of horror on the girl's face. But surely not owning a mobile tracking device wasn't that appalling? "Never needed one."

"Who doesn't need one?" she asked incredulously. "Are you normal?"

I almost laughed. "Define normal."

Willow reached out and pushed me slightly. "If we're going, we should go." I saw her pointed look at her friend. "I'll phone *you* when I'm home."

The *safe* was unspoken, but we all heard it.

Willow walked slightly ahead of me as she set off in the wrong direction, and with a wry grin, I followed her, knowing her game too well. We walked in silence, but her glances soon turned into stares, which morphed into annoyed frowns.

"Do you often let men you don't know walk you home?"

"No." The frown deepened.

"What makes today different?"

"You know why."

"If I knew, do you think I would've asked?" She was full on scowling now, but the brisk pace she set off with had turned into a slow walk.

"I don't know much about ME."

"Changing the subject?"

"Or making conversation?" I countered. When I was met with silence, I thought about what I knew of illness. "What causes ME?"

"There are many factors that are attributable to the cause of it," she told me with a sigh. "But honestly, I don't think anyone knows." She held up her hand. "I'll save you the trouble. I caught mono when I was younger, not long after turning sixteen. ME is an illness that is believed to involve a combination of things, from genetics, environmental influences, and biological factors." Willow turned her attention to the sidewalk. "I'm an orphan. I don't know if either of my parents had it, never met them to ask." Her hand circled in front of us. "I've moved around a lot, foster families and stuff, so when I was able, I moved out here. Clean air, freshness, better than a city."

"Can't argue with that," I agreed as I took in the mountains that surrounded the town. "And the biological? From when you had mono?"

Willow nodded. "Yeah, it can weaken the immune system. I don't know if it *was* the reason I got ME, but I also don't know it *wasn't*."

"Cure?"

"No. Manageability." Her hands slipped into her jeans pockets.

"And how does that work for you?"

Willow stopped walking and glared at me. "Do you actually care, or are we going to talk about how you were in my house yesterday and have been watching me?"

I feigned surprise and I knew she saw right through me. "I was in *your* house?"

Throwing her arms in the air, she let out a small scream, spun on her heel, and started walking briskly back the way we came.

Jogging slightly to catch up with her, I took a light hold of her arm, pulling her to a stop and turning her towards me. "Are you okay?"

Her anger shone out as she scowled at me. "No. Why are you lying?"

"I don't remember you asking me anything."

I watched her eyes flare wide with temper before she pinned me with a glower. "You are full of shit, Caleb. Caleb what?" When she saw my blank face, she let out an exasperated sigh. "What's your last name, *Caleb*?"

"You think my name isn't Caleb?"

Willow's glare narrowed so fast I wasn't sure her eyes were still open.

"You awake?"

She kicked me in the shin. I started to laugh as she had a meltdown in front of me. "What is your last name?" The way she ground out the question, I could practically hear a period punctuating each word.

"Foster."

"Caleb Foster?"

"Yes, ma'am."

Willow resumed walking. "Don't call me ma'am."

"Yes, ma'am." I heard her huff of displeasure and followed behind her, noting when the steam left her sails once more. "So, ME. Chronic...tiredness?"

Willow sniffed. "Chronic *fatigue* syndrome. It's an illness, extreme exhaustion. It doesn't get better with a simple nap. The fatigue is rarely gone, to be honest, and no matter how much rest I get, I'm always fighting fatigue."

"I didn't know that," I admitted.

Willow shrugged and I could tell she was uncomfortable. "Physical and-or mental exertion makes me worse."

Nodding, I watched as she drooped in front of me. Scooping her up in my arms, I ignored her protests as I carried her along the sidewalk. "Drawing helps relax you?"

"I never said I draw."

"You had charcoal on your hands earlier."

Willow looked at her hands, studying the dark smudge under the nail. "Did I?"

"You did."

I didn't meet her searching stare and carried on walking. "Can it be cured? Your illness?"

"No. Managed."

"You said that earlier, how do you manage it?"

"I pace myself, I keep a well-balanced regime, not too much of one thing. I eat well and healthily. I try to stick to a sleeping pattern. Basically, I have a routine." She plucked at my sleeve and snorted. "And I do everything I can to avoid stress."

Glancing down at her, I grinned. "How's that working out for you?"

"I'm failing."

*Yeah, me too.* "Medicines?"

"I don't take anything." Willow returned to studying her thumb. "I've been low," she admitted softly. "But I haven't depended on medication for my low moods, not saying that was the right thing, maybe I should be taking something more regularly, but for me, I don't. I sometimes take Tylenol for the headaches, but if I stick to my routine and patterns, I get by."

*She got by.* It didn't sound like living to me, and I must have shown what I was thinking, as I heard her sharp intake of breath.

"I don't need your pity." Her voice was quiet but hard.

"I don't give out pity," I corrected her. Setting her down on her feet, I steadied her as she regained her balance. "I'm also not a mind reader and don't know where you live."

Willow tilted her head back to look up at me. "You must be shit hot at poker."

A sliver of amusement slipped out. "Why is that?"

"You lie without blinking," she told me as she placed her hand over my heart. "Do it again."

"You're very free with touching."

"Says the man who just swept me off my feet. Literally swept me off my feet."

"You were failing."

"I've failed before."

Watching her, I took in her features, a hardness in her firm stare. Her determination was so strong an illness like hers must be frustrating for her. For anyone.

"I don't." When she blinked, I clarified. "Fail. I don't fail."

"Never admitting it doesn't mean you're winning."

"Never *losing* means you're winning."

"Does it?"

It was my turn to look away. "Do you want to tell me where you live?"

"No." Looking back down at her, I raised an eyebrow, but she remained steadfast in front of me. "Why tell you when you already know, Caleb?"

I could deny it, like I had been, but she was determined and so sure. What was the point?

"Why don't you tell me what *you* already know?" I countered and saw her falter. Her hand dropped from my chest. "What? Suddenly you have no words?"

"You looked at them."

"You know I did."

Willow nodded. Closing her eyes, she blew out a breath.

Pushing her hair behind her ear, she rocked back on her heels. "I don't know how," she admitted as she studied her sneakers.

"How long?" I swallowed hard, dreading the answer. "How long have you been drawing me?"

"A while."

"A while? A week? A month? A year?" I floundered as she remained mute. "A lifetime?"

Willow chewed her lip, finally meeting my eyes once more. "A month, maybe more."

"How much more?"

"I don't know. I thought you were a dream." She looked around, and it took me a moment to realize she was looking for something to rest against. "I never saw your face until recently; I didn't know it was you."

Stooping, I lifted her back into my arms and resumed walking, in the right direction this time. "You need to sleep."

"I need a lot of things," Willow acknowledged quietly, her head resting against my shoulder. "I can tell you one thing," she carried on. "I've never done this before."

"Drew someone you've never met?"

"Well, okay, two things." Willow's eyes were closed. "I've never done *that*, and I've never been carried home by a stranger."

"Am I a stranger?"

I hadn't realized I'd spoken out loud, but I felt her stiffen slightly in my arms. "I don't know."

Her eyes were open once more, and she was looking up at me as if I were the puzzle that needed to be solved. I didn't have the answer either, and for the rest of the walk to her house, neither of us spoke.

I was lying on her couch when she came out of the bedroom. Willow had been so out of it by the time we reached her house, I'd simply put her in her bed and left her there. I didn't know anything about her illness, but holding her phone to her face and peeling her eyelids open while she mumbled about strangers in her dreams had allowed me to gain access to her phone.

I'd used the phone to reply to her friend's text message, who I now knew was named Lily, to let her know I was home and safe, and in bed. I deleted the reply Lily sent that told me to give her all the "gory details" later.

I'd then used the internet access to find out about ME. I'd quickly learned it was much more than feeling tired, and another common misconception was that it was just in the sufferer's head. No amount of exercise could cure it, and it had absolutely nothing to do with being lazy.

Some of the articles had surprised me. After seeing how quickly Willow had deteriorated beyond "simple" tiredness, it wasn't clear to me why people may think it was a fake illness.

I heard her before I saw her approach. Slow but steady as she walked into the room.

"You stayed?"

"I did."

"You're on my couch."

"The floor wasn't comfortable."

Willow looked me over. My boots were on the floor, and my jacket was on the counter in the kitchen. "You seem comfortable."

"I'm not on the floor."

"Why are you here?" Willow looked down at her clothes. "Did you undress me?"

I gave her a flat stare. "I took your sneakers and scarf off. You're hardly naked."

"I feel naked."

"Can't help with that." Turning back to the TV, I waited for her to speak again, knowing I was pissing her off.

"You can't stay here."

I was on my feet so quickly that she stepped back in alarm. "I'm not staying; I was waiting to make sure you were okay." Crossing to the kitchen, I picked up my jacket. "Job done."

"You don't have to leave."

Straightening from picking up my boots, I watched her as she fidgeted, uncomfortable in her own home. "Giving me mixed signals here. I can't stay, but I don't need to leave."

"I have questions."

"You and me both."

Willow gestured to the kitchen. "Do you want a cup of tea?"

It was a peace offering. I think. Warily we watched each other before I dropped my boots. "Yeah." I followed her to the kitchen, noting how she still looked exhausted. "You need help?"

Willow shook her head without making eye contact. "I feel better."

"You should never play poker," I told her easily. "You'll lose."

Glancing over her shoulder, I saw the first hint of a smile. "Maybe you can teach me to lie so fluently."

I held her stare until I saw the smile fade. "Who says I'm fluent?"

Willow turned her attention to putting the kettle on the stove, getting two cups, and rummaging in her cupboard for a box of tea bags. She put the bags back and, reaching up, took out a teapot and a tin of tea leaves. "It's a little treat," she explained as she spooned three carefully measured servings into the pot. "Darjeeling."

"Nice."

Squinting at me, she looked unsure. "Are you teasing?"

"Never."

At that, she laughed. "Yeah, *that* doesn't surprise me."

When the kettle began to whistle, she took it off the heat, waiting a few moments until the boiling water cooled down, and then poured the water into the teapot. Bringing the pot over, she set it between us, returning with two cups and a tea strainer.

The silence grew awkward as she waited to pour the tea, and when we both had a steaming cup of black tea in front of us, she raised her head to look at me.

"Who are you?"

"You know my name."

"I do." Willow nodded. "If that is your name."

"It is."

"How long have you been here?"

"Saturday."

She looked down at her hands in...disappointment? "Really?"

"I have no reason to lie about that."

"You have reason to lie about other things?"

I hesitated. "Some things."

"What?"

"If I told you, I might be lying."

Willow rolled her eyes, raising her cup to take a sip of tea. "You're hardly James Bond." Seeing my confusion, her eyes widened. "Tell me you know who James Bond is?" When I shrugged, she gulped tea, forgetting it was hot, and I almost wore the finely brewed Darjeeling.

Placing my cup aside, I leaned forward onto the breakfast bar. "My turn." Willow mimicked me, putting her cup to the side. "How have you been drawing me?"

"Um, charcoals, sometimes paint, um...pen—"

"*Not* what you've drawn me *with*, I mean *how*? How have you seen me?"

Willow was already shaking her head. "I don't know. I thought you were a dream."

Jabbing my thumb at my chest, I glared at her. "Do I look like a fucking dream?"

She stifled her laughter, but I could see the amusement in her eyes. "More like my nightmare."

"*Exactly.*"

The humor vanished and her scent changed to wariness. "Who are you?"

"It doesn't matter who *I* am, Willow. It matters *what* you are." She shook her head but said nothing. "Am I the only thing you've drawn you can't explain?"

Her look of confusion answered my question. "Aren't you enough?"

I nodded but internally my nerves calmed a little. The last

thing I needed was her drawing my wolf. *Any* wolf. "Doesn't it worry you that you're drawing men you've never met?"

She turned her head away. She needn't have bothered; I could almost taste her fear. "Are you going to hurt me?"

"No."

Willow gave me a look that quite clearly told me she didn't trust me. Which was fine, because I didn't trust her either.

"Then why should I be worried?" It was an attempt at bravado, but it fell flat. I could hear her heart racing, I could see the bead of sweat on her brow, and her lips were so dry that her tongue no longer provided any relief, no matter how many times she licked them.

"Because as you pointed out...I lie."

# SIX

# Willow

*I* LIE.

Two words that had been rattling around my brain the rest of the week. He told me himself. Caleb hadn't stayed long after he dropped that bombshell.

If the idea had been for me not to trust him...he'd already won.

My ME was causing me great fatigue this week and, loading my brush with color only to tap it off again, masked the real reason for my snort of derision. I was glad I was alone today, because Lily had been watching me like a hawk. Hovering too close in case I needed support.

I didn't need it.

Well. I didn't need it a *lot*. I was grateful for her, in so many ways, but she needed to stop hovering. I was picking up on her anxiety, and it was making me worse.

I hadn't even told her about Caleb or our conversation. She would have been uncontainable if she knew he'd been in my house. All she knew was that he walked me home as she tasked him to do. As far as she was concerned, he'd lived up to her expectations, making him a decent guy. She *was* pissed off he hadn't been seen since.

I hadn't seen him either, but I was under no illusion that he wasn't *seeing* me.

I'd searched the woods behind my house for signs of his campsite. Not-so-subtle inquiries had revealed he wasn't staying in town. People had seen him during the day, but no one had seen him once it got dark. The general consensus was that he was a hiker, just passing through. The trails up the peak were challenging. It was perfectly natural that he couldn't do each one per day. He was most likely camping as he hiked.

Only, I had a feeling that he wasn't.

Caleb Foster had more questions than I had answers, and I knew he wasn't happy about it. He had been accommodating in that he saw me home. He had been respectful in that he had stayed with me until I was feeling better.

He had *not* been courteous. He had *not* been kind. He was *not* a gentleman.

"But is he bad?" I asked the painting in front of me. I was sick of seeing Caleb, sick of painting or drawing Caleb, so I was forcing myself to paint something different this afternoon. A meadow of wildflowers, kissed by the first rays of the morning sunshine, was supposed to bring me peace and relaxation.

Instead, as I added color to my artwork, I resented the bright cheerful painting. Dropping my brush to my palette, I turned my attention to the window to look outside at the quiet street.

Today was a store day for me. Meaning that instead of painting with students, I painted alone. My store was never really busy. Rephrase, my store was *never* busy. I made a few sales a month from online customers, but it was never going to enable me to retire early.

It was a depressing thought, but also, if I retired early, what would I do all day? Paint? Draw? I did that now.

Pressing my lips together in annoyance at my lackluster nature, I glared at the opposite side of the street. There was nothing to see there—just an empty bench that was hardly ever used. But still, it bore the brunt of my frustrated glare as I thought about Caleb. "Where are you?"

The bench remained empty and silent. Weariness weighed heavily on my shoulders as I picked up my paintbrush. I needed to focus on relaxation.

A positive mindset was a good thing for people with my illness. At least that's the lie I told myself.

Forcing myself to breathe slowly, I resumed my painting, tiny yellow dots placed randomly to depict buttercups or dandelions. Forcing myself to focus on *anything* other than the man on my mind worked for a short time.

When I raised my head again, I looked outside toward the bench, and Caleb was sitting there, staring back at me.

I wasn't even surprised. It was as if I manifested him into being.

He knew I saw him, and with casual indifference, he stood, and within a few strides he was opening the door and walking into the store.

"Where have you been?"

A smirk pulled at his lips. "Keeping tabs on me?"

Wiping my brush on a folded paper napkin, I scoffed

loudly. "An impossible task since you seem to disappear as easily as smoke."

He was beside me now, his earthy scent tingling my nostrils. He smelled of freshness and pine.

"Looking for me that hard, were you?"

I could deny it, but what was the point? "We have more to talk about."

Caleb sniffed, looking to the door. "Do we? You don't have the answers I need."

"I could—"

His dark look made me shut my mouth. "Woman, you don't even understand the questions."

"Then *help* me understand."

He raised his hand to push his hair back, and I scolded myself for noticing how large his hands were. The man was just...big. My mind took that step. My eyes flicked downwards just below his belt buckle, and I looked away before he noticed that I had just checked him out.

Caleb wasn't looking at me. He was paying particular attention to a framed sketch I'd done last winter. It was a simple piece, the top of a mountain, scarce of vegetation in winter, and a lone deer tearing the bark from the trunk of an old, withered tree.

"You see many deer around these parts?"

"There are enough. They come down off the mountain if the winter is harsh."

Our eyes met briefly when he shot me a skeptical look. "You look tired."

"The day must end with a *y*." The corner of his mouth

turned up, but he said nothing else. "Why are you here?" I asked him as I watched him study all the art on the wall.

"Your customer service skills are lacking," he admonished, reaching forward to straighten a framed landscape, this time in oils.

"I have excellent customer service when I have a *customer* in front of me."

"We can agree to disagree." He'd moved to the farthest painting on the far wall. He studied it for a long time before turning his head and fixing me with his intense stare. "You see many wolves?"

"They're there."

"Where?" His sharp stare unnerved me.

"On the mountains." I shrugged. "I can hear them howling sometimes." I'd known him for such a short time, and using the term *known him* was an exaggeration, but the alternative was to refer to him as the man who gate-crashed my life. Watching him watch me, seeing that he doubted me—again—I got off the chair and went to stand beside him.

"Never heard wolves down here."

"Then you're not listening with your ears," I snapped at him. "Why do you think the deer are rarely seen?"

Caleb turned to face me, his expression unreadable. "Why?"

"The wolves hunt them." His snort of laughter only irritated me more. "Why are you here? Again?"

"Passing by."

"Another lie."

Caleb fixed me with that stare of his. "That's bothered you, hasn't it?"

I wanted to lie down. He exhausted me, and I already felt emotionally drained from this man. "*You* bother me."

Caleb returned to his study of the wolf scene. A simple painting of woods and a clearing with a black wolf emerging from the shadows. "As I said, no customer service skills."

"As *I* said, you're not a customer."

"How much is the picture?"

He was looking at me expectantly, and I didn't have the words to tell him he was making my head hurt. The man fluctuated between hot and cold more times than I could count.

"Willow? The price?"

God, he was an impatient prick. "Two fifty."

It wasn't. It was a simple painting that I had done one morning. To anyone else, I'd feel guilty for asking for a hundred. Him, well, he could pay it or leave it.

"I'll take it."

All right...it seemed like he was taking it. Shit. I wasn't expecting that. "Um...you sure?"

Those dark eyes were on me again. Inscrutable. Secret. Penetrating.

Caleb walked towards me, his hand pulling his wallet out of his back pocket. "It's not my place to say it—it's your business —but really, you need sales help, because you're bad at it." He put three bills on the counter. "When can I get it?"

"Sales help?" My eyes were glued to the bills. He just dropped two fifty in front of me like it was nothing. I'd spent the week thinking he was homeless; now he was Mr. Let's-Drop-Cash-Like-It's-Hot?

"Good God, you're worse than I thought." Caleb's scornful

muttering brought me out of my fog. "No wonder nothing sells."

"Hey!" He'd been gazing back at the painting, but he turned to face me when he heard my protest. He said nothing, but I could feel his mockery. "Quit it." Grouchily, I went over to the painting, and careful of the hooks, I lifted it off the wall. I forgot the frame I'd put it in was heavy, and given my current weariness, I almost dropped it. Caleb was there to catch it. "Um...thanks."

"Do I still need to pay for it if you break it?"

"It's yours now," I told him, following behind him as he took it to the counter. "It breaks in my store, tough."

"Wow. Stellar sales skills, yet again."

"Maybe I just don't like you, Caleb."

"Maybe you're full of shit, Willow." He smirked. "I think you like me just fine."

The painting lay between us as I glared at him, and then, remembering I *was* a professional, I opened the cupboard under the counter and pulled out the brown paper wrapping. "I'll just get this wrapped."

He said nothing as he watched me first wrap the framed painting in bubble wrap, tape it half to death, and then wrap it carefully in brown paper. I was rummaging in the cupboard for a postage label when he spoke, breaking the silence. I was so absorbed that I almost forgot he was there, and I jumped, accidentally banging my head on the cupboard's roof.

"Whatever else you need to do to that, it's fine. I can take it from here." Straightening, I rubbed the top of my head, and Caleb didn't hide his amusement. "Thought I heard an echo."

"Shut up." Slapping the label down, I snapped at him.

"Postage label, so you can ship it home." Pointing out the window, I gave him directions. "Postal place two blocks over. You can't miss it. It's right beside the printer shop."

Picking up my painting—no, *his* painting—he handed me back the label. "I don't need this."

It hung between us like a tentative peace treaty. One that neither party fully trusted.

"You have your own shipping labels?" I didn't hide the doubt in my voice.

"Does it matter?" He placed it back on the counter. "You should rest, you look tired." He said it so matter-of-factly it couldn't even be described as concern. "You've made a sale, close up shop. Go home."

He was halfway to the door when I spoke again. "That's what this was? It's a *pity* sale?"

He didn't even look back. "It's a *sale*, Willow. That's all that matters." Opening the door, he turned to glance at me before he left. "Hire a salesperson. You need one."

The door was barely closed behind him when I heard a familiar laugh, and seconds later, Lily came bounding in. "Oh my gosh! Did Loverboy *buy* something?"

"Not loverboy," I corrected her. I endured the happy hug anyway because hugs were nice, and Lily's were the best. "Yes, he bought a painting."

"He must *really* be lusting after you," she declared loudly.

"Lily! Lower your voice!"

"There's no one here!" Her laughter was infectious, and when I smiled, she hugged me again and hurried over to the space on the wall. "Oooh, he bought the creepy wolf one." Her smile grew. "Why aren't you happier? You hated that painting."

Tucking the bills into a money wallet and ignoring Lily's eye roll at my old-fashionedness, I shrugged. "I didn't hate it. The wolf just...it just creeped me out."

Lily climbed up onto one of the art stools. "You're adorable." Stretching her arms over her head, she looked at me fondly. "You drew the wolf and then you were scared of the wolf. It's too cute."

"I wasn't scared, it was creepy. Foreboding."

"It was cute. And fluffy."

"It's not a puppy." Shaking my head, I sat down too. My legs felt too weary to keep me up. Lily noticed and her playfulness vanished as concern washed over her.

"Hey, you okay? Do you need to go home?"

*Yes.* "No, I'll be okay. Just going to take it easy."

I held in my sigh as she jumped off the stool, coming over and collecting my purse. "You're closing. I'll take you home. I have the car today, and you can sleep."

"I don't need to sleep." I really needed to sleep. "I'll be okay." Chances are I wouldn't be.

With her hands on her hips, Lily glared at me. "Not only are you lying to yourself, you're lying to me." Wide-eyed, she looked at me like I'd just stabbed her. "Why would you lie to me? Why? Why, Willow?"

"You missed your calling in the theater." My dry tone earned me a grin, and I was too tired to protest anymore. "Fine, have it your way. You can take me home."

She stuck her tongue out at me triumphantly. Could a tongue be triumphant? Groaning, I searched for my keys. I definitely needed home; I was jabbering about triumphant tongues.

A slim arm wrapped around my waist. "Hey, girl, you look

close to passing out. Come on." Gently, she held me up, propping me against the doorway as she locked up. "You're swaying."

I think I nodded. I could feel how unsteady I was. It was all Caleb's fault. Each time I was with him, he drained me even more.

"You want Caleb?"

I jolted in surprise. What? No! "Nuh-uh...no."

"Phew, I would have for sure known there was a story there that you were keeping from me."

I was halfway to comatose, and she was worried she'd missed out on gossip. If my eyes would open and my mouth weren't so dry, I would tell her she was an idiot if she thought there was ever going to be a *story* to tell that involved me and Caleb.

With the shop locked up and a sign up saying "back tomorrow," we got into Lily's car. I loved my best friend. She was kind, funny, charming, all the things. Beautiful. Her skin was flawless, a dermatologist's wet dream, I was sure. Yet, for all her brilliance, she was, quite possibly, the worst driver on the planet.

"Now remember to buckle up," she told me with false cheerfulness. When my arms didn't cooperate, Lily leaned over and strapped me in. "When you're feeling better, I am going to scold you so bad for neglecting yourself like this."

I might have nodded in agreement, or I might have just let my head drop, as it was getting heavier to hold up.

I must have been asleep when we got to my house, because being practically dragged from a car was enough to wake anyone.

"Lily, I got it." Struggling to my feet, I swayed until I felt her steady me. I tried to open my eyes to focus, but it was a battle I wasn't winning. "The neighbors are gonna think I'm stoned or something."

"Your neighbors are probably stoned, and also, fuck them."

"Lil! Shh, they'll hear you!"

"Who cares?" The front door took a long time to get to, or so it seemed until I heard a cry of protest as I was placed against the wall. "Why's your spare key been moved?"

"Caleb."

"You gave him your spare key?"

I just knew her eyes would be like saucers.

"No, he found it."

"He found it? Why? Was he in your house? Did you tell him where it was? Why was he in your house?"

I raised my hand to stop her barrage of questions. "Girl, shhh. Enough with the questions, I need sleep."

She muttered the whole time, but soon I was in bed, nestled under my blankets, and the door closed as Lily left me alone. I had no doubt I would be interrogated when I woke up, but for now, I could sleep.

I just needed to sleep.

# SEVEN

# Caleb

I CARRIED THE PAINTING EASILY, TUCKED UNDER MY ARM, and made my way to the edge of town. The folk used to seeing me now never batted an eyelid. Walk with purpose and confidence, and very few people will challenge you, even if you don't belong.

*Especially* if you didn't belong.

I had been here for a week and dined at three establishments. Each one had gathered information about me, noting that I was a hiker with a campsite near town. It was a familiar story for this town. Whispering Pines had so many hikers passing through that my story wasn't unusual.

I kept to myself. I made the small talk but divulged nothing. What was I going to say? That I was a wolf shifter, and a local girl had drawn me here because she kept sketching me? Yeah. While I stood out as a stranger to this town, I still blended enough not to draw attention from the local cops. If I were to tell them the truth, I would be in a mental institution quicker than I could blink.

I used the trail to move farther away from the town. I passed no one else, and with my senses alert to any unfamiliar noise, I left the trail and entered the woods. It wasn't the most favorable walk through the woods, and I hoped that the uneven ground, low-hanging branches, and dense vegetation kept even the eager hikers at bay. Any scratches I sustained healed quickly. When I was far enough, I stopped, pulling off my jacket, shirt, and T-shirt and loosening my belt. Taking off my boots, I tucked my socks into them. Stripping off my jeans, I folded them, placing them on top, rolling my head on my neck as I stretched. My wolf was restless, and I was eager to run. But first I needed to deal with this painting.

Uncovering my rucksack, I put my clothes away, ensuring the shirt and T-shirt could pass one more day before I needed a laundromat.

Crouched over the painting, I tore through all of Willow's careful packaging. Rocking back on my heels, I took in the wolf she had painted.

It was the side profile only. I liked how she had captured the blackness of his thick coat emerging from the dark shadows as if the wolf was morphing into existence from the very darkness it came from. The bright blue of the wolf's eyes wasn't diminished just because I could only see one.

The wolf was large. Imposing.

An alpha.

Sucking my teeth, I stood over the painting and brought my foot down heavily on the frame, snapping it.

Pulling the painting from its encasement, I dug in my rucksack, finding my lighter, and with no preamble, I set the painting alight. As it burned, I undressed fully, and as the painting curled and burned under the flames, I shifted into my wolf.

Stepping back from the fire slightly, my wolf waited patiently for the painting and frame to burn out. Satisfied that nothing remained, I let the wolf run.

Ponderosa pine towered over me as I ran, weaving through the dense woods as I climbed the mountain. The higher I ran, the more the trees thinned out, and soon I had vast open areas to run in. While I ran, my mind puzzled over the enigma that was Willow.

Was she human? She definitely smelled human. Her frailty was human. Shifters rarely had sickness. Our Goddess Luna made us strong. She could see perfectly well, so that ruled out being a shaman, and even then, she would still be a shifter.

Willow was human. I would bet my life on it.

Movement at the corner of my eye had my wolf banking, and after a brief chase, I enjoyed a juicy rabbit. The sky was darkening, and with a full belly, I climbed higher up the mountain, taking shelter between a large fallen rock and the mountain. With my head resting in my paws, I watched the night awaken as darkness fell.

Content in my solitude, I wondered how many others were like me, who preferred life away from the pack.

Wolves were not solitary creatures.

We thrived in packs.

Communities.

I couldn't think of anything worse. I liked it here. Alone. Just me, the quiet, and the open sky.

A black crow settled nearby, squawked at me when I snapped my jaws at it, ruffled its feathers, and then it too, seemed content to settle for the night. So I wasn't alone. But since the bird really wasn't going to bother me at all, I lay back down.

Thinking of packs encouraged my mind to wander back to when I was younger. My father was a strong wolf, and my mother was the perfect loving wife. I had been happy. Loved. Our pack was small but content. In my older years, I had seen many packs, ones where stores and businesses were the norm. Where pack paid for goods and services.

Our pack hadn't been like that. No one had more than the other. Not even the alpha. Everything was shared, everything was equal. There was no "less than" in our pack.

The way it needed to be. The way it should be.

My wolf whined and I pulled the feeling of sadness back into me. Holding onto the past only kept you looking back. The way forward was to face what was in front of you and not look back. The past was the past and needed to stay behind me. No good came of thinking what could have been; we only had what was.

Lifting my head, I watched a shooting star fall across the sky and automatically said a prayer to the Goddess Luna. It was an old tale my mother would tell me when I was a child. A shooting star was the sign from Luna that an alpha had been born.

Having known a few alphas, I could only hope this one was a better one than most. The crow snapped its beak, and I snapped my jaw. I wasn't fond of crow—I preferred chicken— but I'd snap its neck if it kept annoying me. It hopped up higher on its chosen resting place, and when I saw it wasn't going to fly away, I returned to watching the stars.

In the morning, I woke to a light drizzle of rain. The crow was still sleeping soundly, and I left it undisturbed. A night on the mountain, under the stars, and undisturbed had refreshed me.

Thoughts of Willow still lingered, and I wasn't sure how I was going to solve the mystery that she presented. I should probably just leave Whispering Pines and leave her behind me. She drew my picture, but it was hardly sinister.

*At the moment.*

Even in wolf form, the huff of disgruntlement was loud. For now, it was simple sketches of my face, but what if she drew *more?* What if it became shifters she drew? I would need to tell the Pack Council.

I hated the Pack Council.

They did nothing when my family was killed.

They did nothing when my home was destroyed.

They did nothing.

No. The only person I could count on to solve the riddle of Willow Harper was me.

Whether I liked it or not.

---

THE HALF-DRUNK COFFEE CUP SAT FORGOTTEN IN FRONT of me as I stared out the window of the small café, watching the movement across the street. Behind me, the two young servers whispered, debating whether to approach me again to ask if they could get me anything else. My coffee had gone cold a long time ago.

In the far corner, a new mother's baby hadn't stopped

mewling since they came in, and the mother's sighs of growing despair echoed around the room.

But my focus was on the woman who should have arrived in the store across the street. She was late, and I wasn't prepared for the feeling of disappointment that hit me. I'd stayed away for a few days after burning her painting, and I expected Willow to be at work today, but it was Lily who was opening the store, while the two regular students hung back uncertainly, and while I couldn't hear her perfectly, her body language was telling *everyone nearby* how unhappy she was with their questions.

As I got ready to leave the café, my attention shifted to the male walking down the sidewalk. Tall, dark-haired, with an imposing frame and stoney face, he was undoubtedly an alpha with something on his mind.

And if I were to take a guess, I'd guess that the some*thing* was some*one*, and that someone...was me.

He pushed the door open, and with barely a glance at the two servers, he headed straight to me. He pulled out the chair opposite me and sat down. His dark gray T-shirt accentuated the power in his arms and chest. Green eyes pierced mine as he leaned back in the chair.

"Alpha," I greeted.

"Cannon is fine." He turned his head to the servers. "Two coffees." I didn't say I didn't need another; he wouldn't care. He was an alpha and alphas got what they wanted. When he turned back to me, his expression hadn't changed. "Why are you here?"

No build up. No more of an introduction other than his name. Nothing. It wasn't the alpha way. "Why are *you* here?"

If he was surprised by my tone, he didn't show it. "I ask the questions."

"Says who?" The stare-off was broken when the coffees were delivered to the table. I murmured my thanks, while Cannon simply nodded and drank half of his drink in one gulp.

"I needed that." His quick once over of me didn't bother me at all. "Why are you here?" He cut me off before I replied. "Don't do that. We don't need a dick-measuring contest. I asked a question. You will answer."

"I'm not your pack."

"I don't give a fuck."

Amusement flickered in his eyes as he watched my reaction to his bluntness, and I hated that his no-bullshit attitude impressed me. "A straight-talking alpha, that's new."

"Is it?" Cannon's eyebrow arched and he finished his coffee. He said nothing as he reached across the table, picked up my untouched cup, and took a drink. "They always assume that 'two coffees' mean for me and another."

So he hadn't ordered for me; they were both for him. He was holding my interest, and I wasn't sure how I felt about that. "Caffeine junkie, I see."

He smirked slightly. "I have a demanding mate."

Of course, he did. His whole aura was power. His mate would be worthy of such a strong alpha. "I'm just passing through."

"You've been passing through a town of this size for about three weeks." He drained his coffee. "How many times do you plan to pass through it?"

It wasn't three weeks, maybe two at most. I spent a few days watching the town before I walked in as a human. "There are no packs near here," I spoke quietly. There were too many people faking indifference now. "I do not disturb any shifter with my presence here."

"You've been alone too long, Caleb." Cannon also kept his voice low, but his posture was hard. The fact he knew my name bothered me, but I tried not to let it show. "Lone wolves are still governed by Pack Council. You know the danger of having no pack." I did know. No pack could be dangerous for some. They went wild, untamed; it was said that they turned rogue. "There have been changes that you may not be aware of," Cannon carried on.

"I don't need to know," I replied bluntly. "I break no laws with how I choose to live. I bring no attention to myself."

The alpha gave a long exaggerated look around the room where most eyes were on us. "You're right, you're positively blending."

The smirk escaped before I managed to school my face. "A walk then?"

Cannon stood, his hand reaching for his back pocket, and I didn't bother looking as he paid. I didn't think he looked at the bills he laid down. Money wasn't something most shifters worried about. We didn't come into towns and cities without it.

Shifters provided for the pack, and the pack provided for them.

Outside, I hesitated, torn between following an alpha or asking Lily where Willow was. Cannon missed nothing, his attention flicking towards the art store. "A woman?"

His slight tone of surprise should have grated on me, but I knew if I were in his shoes, I'd be questioning myself too. "It's complicated."

His smile had no humor. "Simplify it for me as we walk."

We walked in silence to start with. Neither of us discussed it, but both of us headed to the tree line. Cannon dropped back slightly and let me lead as the trees enveloped us. The alpha knew how long I'd been here. I didn't bother trying to deceive him with where I had left my stuff.

When we reached the small area I'd been using, Cannon didn't even bother looking around.

"You've already been here," I realized.

"I do my homework." Cannon nudged the remains of the charred frame. "This?"

"A painting. I changed my mind about liking it."

Cannon watched me. "That's a lie. What was it?"

My stomach turned slightly as I felt the power of the alpha in front of me. I wasn't expecting him, a walking lie detector, to turn up. I hadn't been expecting *any* alpha to turn up.

"A painting."

"Of?"

The silence grew between us. With a sigh, I turned my head when I answered. "A wolf."

"A wolf or a shifter?"

"Shifter."

Cannon frowned, stooping to pick up part of the ruined frame. "You?"

"No."

My answer was too quick for the sharp alpha in front of me. "Who?"

Fuck, I didn't want to answer this. "Why are you here, Alpha?"

"Who was the shifter, Caleb?"

"How do you know who I am?"

Cannon leveled me with a look but blew out a breath. "Things have changed since you last checked in with a pack." I almost told him I never checked in with a pack, but I was aware that this alpha already knew that. "There's a lot of shit that's happened before, there's a lot still to come, but the Pack Council knows that."

"Things really must have changed," I scoffed. "Those old farts know fuck all usually."

It was the first time the man in front of me genuinely smiled. "As I said, things are changing." Cannon's gaze swept the area where we were standing. "You're a lone wolf," he said, his voice softened. "It's admirable to go it alone."

"But?" I knew it was coming; it usually did when I met another of my kind.

"But how long before *lone* becomes *rogue*?"

"I like my own company," I told him simply. "I'm alone by choice."

"Not by choice," Cannon corrected me. "The death of your family, your pack, you never chose that."

"Fuck you."

Cannon's mouth twitched in a semblance of a smile. "Your fire fuels your temper."

"You have no right to talk to me about my family."

"You're right, I don't." The piece of charred wood tapped off his palm. "Who was in the painting?"

"Why are you here?"

"Who is the woman in the store?" Cannon cocked his head to the side. "Who is she to you?"

"She's no one."

"Another lie." His humor was gone. Instead, he looked ready to take me out, and I did not doubt that he could. "Start speaking truths, Caleb, or the next person I speak to will be her."

My instinct was to attack, but the movement behind me was the first time that I knew that we weren't alone. Turning, I saw the sharp watchful gazes of the two shifters who emerged from the trees.

"Luna, you guys are good," I complimented them as my wolf prowled closer to the surface.

"We're pack," Cannon reminded me from where he stood behind me. "And you look ready to run," he added dryly. "Why are you here?"

The fight left me. He was an alpha, his pack was with him, and although I knew I could defend myself, I also knew I couldn't beat them. Him. I wouldn't beat an alpha like him. "I don't know," I admitted. "Something drew me here."

"The woman?"

Why deny it? He probably already knew. "Yes."

"She made the picture?"

"Painting," I corrected. "She did."

"And the shifter she painted?"

I held his steady gaze. "It was you. She painted you, Alpha Cannon."

## EIGHT

## Willow

I felt better.

I was treating feeling better with caution because I wasn't sure when the last time I actually felt better was. However, I wasn't dead on my feet like I had been when I last saw Caleb.

Caleb.

God damn that man. The man had up and left.

Or that's what I assumed had happened because no one had seen him for days. He'd been here longer than I thought he would stay, and now that he was gone, I felt...bereft.

"This won't do at all," I scolded myself. "He was just a guy. He wasn't even a *nice* guy." I nodded to myself at the reminder that he was a colossal dick. "A dick who broke into your home."

Lily was out of town for the weekend. One of her college friends was getting married, and she was excited to be attending the wedding. Lily, the hopeless romantic that she was, was convinced her future hubby was to be met at a wedding. I told her that as long as it wasn't the groom, then there was no harm in dreaming.

Ha. Says the woman who had dreamt of Caleb every night since I saw him last. I didn't remember the dreams, but I couldn't shake the sense of foreboding when I woke up. It was almost as if something had happened to him, but I still had the sense that he was okay.

Safe.

*Why would he not be safe?* Shaking my head at my nonsense, I focused on packaging an order. I'd sold that painting to Caleb, and now, not even a week later, I'd made another sale. The painting that had sold was actually one of my favorites. Another meadow, covered in wildflowers located high on a mountain. The peak cast a shadow over the meadow but not in an opposing way. It gave a gentler impression, as if it was cradling the meadow, keeping it safe. There was that word again...*safe.*

I'd painted this on canvas, so it was easier to box and package. I just liked to take better care of my products than I probably should.

As I worked, my attention wandered too often to the bench across the street or the café I'd seen him come out of a few times.

The door opened and two men walked into my store. One was big, as big as Caleb, but older. The other was slight in stature, but there was an air about him that made me nervous. Warm smiles greeted me, and any feeling of unease I had quieted.

"Welcome." I smiled back at them, Caleb's nagging voice in the back of my head reminding me that I had poor sales skills.

"Afternoon," the older man spoke to me. "It's cooling down."

I was already nodding in agreement. "Thankfully! I'm ready for autumn." The smaller man watched me for a moment and then started studying my artwork. "I'm Willow," I told them, waving my hand at the wall behind me. "Look around. If I can tell you anything about a piece, just ask."

"You did them all."

It wasn't a question; it was as if he already knew. "Not all, most." I pointed at Lily's misshapen vase. "There are other local artists that display here for either attention or sale. Except that, that's one of a kind and not for sale."

The larger man's answer was too low for me to hear, but judging by the way the smaller guy covered his mouth, I think I was better off not hearing it.

I moved my position so I could watch them as I finished the packaging. I wasn't a jumpy woman. Men didn't make me nervous usually, but there was an air about these two. Even the scrawnier man set my teeth on edge. I didn't want to have my back to them, which surprised me. I wasn't usually this way.

They spoke so quietly to each other that I couldn't hear them. They studied each painting and drawing like it was worthy to be hung in the Louvre. I liked what I created, but even so, to have that level of intensity while my art was being scrutinized was making me feel awkward and nervous, so when the big guy turned to me and told me they would take six of my paintings, my jaw was on the floor.

"Pardon?"

The smaller one looked me over as he came closer. "You don't sell them?"

"What?" I was standing with packing tape in my hands. Quite clearly having sold something. "Of course I do."

"Great." He smiled like he had when he came in. "How much?"

"Um." Caleb was right, I was a bad salesperson. His reminder gave me the boot I needed to remember this was my store, my art, my job, and my livelihood. "Show me which ones again."

Five minutes later, I was being handed more cash than I was used to holding at any one time.

"How long have you lived here?"

"A few years," I answered. The big guy was called Royce, and the other man, I had learned, was Mal. He watched me too intensely to be considered polite, but the other man made up for his weirdness, so I concentrated on Royce.

"What made you move here?" Mal asked. "Scenery? Hiking?"

I laughed. "I don't hike."

"Why?"

"There could be bears." I hoped my playful tone would make them stop asking questions. "Or wolves." Their attention seemed to sharpen, and I had no idea why I thought that, but they were both just...more. Clearing my throat, I forced myself to remain positive. I *had* just sold six pieces after all. "I really appreciate your business," I said with complete honesty. "You sure you want to take them all today? I can easily ship them if you need."

Royce shook his head. "Nah, it's fine. We have the truck."

"Right." I watched as he picked up three of the pieces easily off the counter. Mal held the door open for him, but my gut twisted in anticipation when he didn't follow his partner out the door. Mal walked back to the counter and didn't even pretend to pick anything up.

"I'm a doctor."

That, I hadn't been expecting, and I knew I hadn't hidden my surprise very well. "Ah." Not much else you can say to that.

"I'm telling you because it makes what I say next less creepy." He grinned, and I had a feeling that this was the first time he had been genuine with me. "Your skin is clammy, your coloring is off. The darkness under your eyes tells me you don't sleep well."

"And I thought I looked quite good today." My sass made him smile wider.

"What is it?" His head tilted. "Fibro? Lupus?"

"Nothing as sinister as that. I have ME." I felt the usual discomfort when I spoke about my illness.

"You moved here for a better quality of life." Wisdom and understanding were evident now that I was looking at him. Really looking at him, taking him in. He hadn't been getting ready to dissect me and eat my liver with a nice chianti; he was a doctor analyzing a patient.

Wait...wasn't Hannibal a doctor?

"I mean you no harm."

Brilliant, he was also a mind reader.

"Pretty sure that's the line every killer tells their victim right before they kill them." I'd meant it as a joke, but the flat way in which I said it made us both falter.

Royce walked back into the store, and his sure step slowed as he picked up the tension between us. "You two okay?"

"Yup." I was relieved he was back. "Mal was just telling me

he's a doctor." I didn't miss the sharp look Royce gave his companion.

"Was he? That's interesting." Funny, Royce didn't seem to think it was interesting at all. He picked up the other three pieces. "We got everything?"

"Yeah." Mal was looking around the room, distracted, and missed the other man's frown. His gaze fell on me once more. "Keep hydrated," he told me. "Your sleep pattern has been disturbed. Fix that." Like it was that easy. "More veg, less candy." He nodded toward the open counter door where a solitary candy bar lay. "Three meals a day, less snacks."

Jesus.

"I know how to look after myself." *Why did I sound so defensive?*

The doctor raised an eyebrow. "Then why are you so fatigued?"

"I have ME."

"You have an illness that is controllable. Using it as a crutch only makes you weaker." His simple head nod on the way out floored me as much as his harsh words had.

"He forgets himself sometimes," Royce told me apologetically. "Thank you for these. Bye."

The door closed quietly behind them, and they left me wondering what the hell had just happened.

"Strangest two weeks of my life," I muttered, starting to clean up.

It was mid-afternoon, the sun was shining, and whether I'd wanted it or not, I took the doctor's advice and closed the store early. The walk home was sluggish but enjoyable. My step slowed as I neared my house.

"Should I be surprised you're on my front step?" I asked Caleb as I walked up the path.

"You're home early. Going anywhere?"

I ignored him as I opened the door. I didn't bother telling him he couldn't come in. I wasn't sure I could keep him out, and despite his obvious dislike of me, I didn't feel unsafe around him.

I didn't feel safe either, but I was curious about where he had been.

"No, I just decided to come home."

"Sick?"

Repressing the sigh, I shook my head. "I am perfectly fine." I recalled what the doctor had said. "Apart from being clammy, having a poor diet and I don't sleep enough."

Caleb looked me over slowly, and my heart rate picked up despite my brain screaming not to be affected by him. "You look okay to me."

Okay. I looked *okay*. It's what every woman craved to hear. *How do I look? Okay.* Ugh. Kill me now.

"Thanks," I snapped, and I saw him frown. "Why are you here? To what do I owe the pleasure?"

"Have you painted me this week?"

This day was just full of surprises. "Wow. Now you just come out and ask?"

He was still frowning. "Why would I not?"

Excellent question. "It's personal."

"Yes. To me."

He had a point, but that *wasn't* the point. "Don't you think it's not personal to me?" Stuff the doctor, I needed chocolate. I reached into the cupboard for the emergency candy bar and found it missing. *Damn it, Alistair.* Fighting back the scream of frustration, I turned to face him. "And no. I haven't."

"Show me."

I gaped. He looked unfazed. "No!"

He rolled his eyes and then went and looked anyway. "Caleb!" Hurrying after him, I tried to stop him at the door to the studio, but he merely swatted my hand away like I was an annoyance.

On my easel sat the sketch pad, and on the open page sat a picture of Caleb crouched over a fire. He appeared to be naked. The accusatory look he shot my way made me look away. But if anyone had the right to be angry, it was me.

"You burned it."

"It's not what you think."

"Isn't it?" We were in a proper stare-off. "You bought it. You burned it. Why?"

"Changed my mind, the composition was off."

"Liar."

He shrugged, moving to the wall and flicking through canvases. "Anything else?"

"No."

Caleb smirked. Walking past me, he entered my bedroom. "Right."

I wasn't even fighting. He was taking over. This was my home, so why wasn't I fighting? Because I was exhausted. Slowly I followed him, and in my room, I lowered myself to my bed.

"What is it?" he asked, flipping through my notebook, looking at all my recent drawings of *him* like the narcissist he was.

"You." Closing my eyes, I rubbed my temples. "You're exhausting."

"You were fine when you came home."

When I opened my eyes, he was crouched in front of me. "Why did you burn it?" Sure, I hadn't liked the creepy wolf either, but there was no need to damage it.

He didn't answer as he watched me carefully. Concern gave way to the hardness I expected of him, and I wasn't surprised when he stood. Disappointed, but not surprised. "I drain you."

"No. It's my ill—"

"No. It's me."

Looking up at him, I saw how much he believed it. "Caleb..." As I reached out to take his hand, he stepped back. The sting of rejection pierced my heart.

"I make you ill." He sounded bitter, and I didn't under-stand it at all. "How long has it been since your ME left you this wasted?"

"I'm always like this," I started to tell him, but as I spoke, I realized I was wrong. I *had* been worse since I met him. Since I started *drawing* him. When he saw that I'd reached the same conclusion, he gave a derisive snort. "What does this mean?"

"It means they were right."

"Who were?"

"The alpha. The others." His sneer was ugly, and I didn't like how angry he was.

My head was reeling. My body was craving energy that I could only give it with sleep. "Alpha? Others? What are you talking about?"

"Look at you." He sounded disgusted, but something deep

inside me knew it wasn't at me. "You're so drained. I can *see* how much I affect you." Strong arms lifted me, and I was placed further up the bed. "Rest. We'll talk when you wake."

I hadn't been tired. I had been *good*. I had been fine. But the two men from earlier and then Caleb, and I could barely open my eyes.

"They're like you..."

I heard him curse and then mutter something that sounded a lot like he was accusing them of not waiting. Waiting for what, he never said. I knew when he left the room because my energy leveled out, and while I was still so tired, I wanted answers.

I could get up and demand them. I could. I really, really could, but I wanted to sleep. Caleb wouldn't leave, not when I was like this and he blamed himself. He had stayed before, and he would stay again.

When I woke up, he was in the backyard, sitting on the lowest step, watching the tree line. "Better?"

"I have so many questions."

"I don't have answers."

Lowering myself carefully, I joined him on the step. "You must have some."

Caleb rubbed his forehead, finally turning to look at me. "Trust me when I say that I have no answers as to why you were drawing me before you met me or why being in my presence makes you weaker." He looked back towards the trees. "If I knew the answer to any of this, I would be a happy man."

"That must be nice to see." He threw me a look and I smiled. "Where have you been?"

"I was trying to find answers."

"Did you find any?"

"No."

"Maybe you weren't asking the right questions."

"Okay, let's see if you can help me out. How long have you been psychic?"

I laughed. He didn't. I stopped laughing as he waited for an answer. "You're serious?"

"You see me when you sleep. Right?" I nodded. "You're either a psychic or a witch."

My elbow dug into his side, hitting solid muscle, and he didn't move an inch. "I'm not a witch!"

"I don't think so either," he mused. "Which brings me back to psychic. Or prophet?" His look was assessing. "No, not prophet, Luna doesn't need them."

"Who's Luna?"

"My Goddess."

Whoa, I was not expecting him to be religious. "I think that's blasphemy."

Caleb's lips twitched. "Not to me, it isn't. You keep your God, I'll keep mine."

"Are you a monk?"

His burst of surprised laughter made me smile. I didn't think he had laughed since I met him. "I'm no monk."

Yeah, he was too...*manly* to be celibate. "Minister?"

He frowned. "Is that the same thing?"

"I think they can get married."

"Huh. No, I'm not that either. I'm just a man."

Turning on the step, I faced him, looking at him so closely I was bordering on invading his personal space, before I drew back, putting some space between us. "And yet again, you lie."

## NINE

## Caleb



I DIDN'T HIDE THE SMIRK AS WILLOW MET MY GAZE fearlessly. She was so slight, so frail, and yet here she was, ready to challenge me.

"You doubt that I'm a man?"

Willow flushed, her gaze automatically dipping down, and I knew she remembered checking me out the other day. She thought I didn't notice. I noticed everything.

"I know you're a man," she grumbled. "Your pig-headed arrogance goes hand in hand with the levels of your testosterone."

I laughed. She was funny even when she meant to insult me. She kept me entertained at least. "Ouch, you wound me," I teased.

"I'd like to wound you," she muttered as she got to her feet. "Come inside. I feel exposed sitting out here."

I could have told her there was nothing to worry about. I could have told her there was no one listening that shouldn't be.

I could have told her many things, but instead, I stood and followed her inside.

"Tea?"

"No."

She hesitated, then she set about making herself tea. We didn't talk as she went through her routine, and this time instead of tea leaves, she settled on a bag in a cup instead. When she had her beverage, she walked past me, taking a seat on the couch.

"Where do you want to start?"

The fact that Willow was taking control of this conversation shouldn't have surprised me, but it did. Her calm steady look was deceiving, or maybe she was genuinely more in control than I was. As my life had turned into a shitshow I wasn't expecting, maybe she had picked up on that.

I stayed low on the radar of the packs. I avoided alphas. Now I had an alpha, his beta, and a fucking human on my ass. And Willow.

Another human.

I no longer wanted to be here, but I knew I couldn't run. I couldn't walk away while she was bringing attention to herself.

I couldn't leave while she was a danger to herself. Or my kind.

"How long have you been drawing people you've never met?"

"A month or two." She held my gaze as she sipped her tea. "You're the first." Her lips twitched. "Hopefully my last?"

It was framed as a question. A question...as if I had the answer.

"Lucky me." I sat opposite her. "Why me?"

"Your charm?"

Her eyes were dancing with amusement. "This isn't funny," I snapped at her, and I watched as her mirth dispersed. "Do you have any seers, witches, or psychics in your lineage?"

Willow shrugged. "No idea."

*Maybe if I snapped her neck, then we wouldn't have a problem anymore?* The ferocity of my anger surprised me, and I pushed it down, along with the surge of panic I felt at the feralness of my anger.

"Can you ask?" I strived for calm.

"No." She carried on, cutting off any protest I may give. "I'm an orphan. Or more correctly, I don't know who my parents are. I was left at a children's home."

She was abandoned? I studied her once more. Could she be a shifter after all? She didn't smell like my kind, but then if she didn't know *how* to shift, she may never have done so. But she was weak. Was it a side effect of her never having shifted?

Willow froze when I stood and crossed the room, dropping to a crouch in front of her. "Wh-what are you doing?"

She didn't resist me when I picked up her hand, turning it over in my hold until her palm was facing up. Her sharp inhale was the only sound as I ran my nose along the faint veins that showed at her wrist. My tongue flicked out and tasted her skin.

I could hear her racing heart and the shallowness of her breath, but I tasted nothing other than the vanilla body wash she used.

"Caleb?" Willow's voice held no strength now, and I ignored her as I let my fangs out and bit into her soft flesh. "Ow!" Willow scrambled away from me, clutching her wrist to her chest protectively. "What the *fuck*, Caleb? You bit me?"

My head was bowed as I tasted her blood. The heady scent of fresh blood caused my body to react, and desire pulsed through my veins as the coppery tang of Willow's blood danced across my tongue. I knew she was talking to me, but I was fighting for control from my wolf.

Desire scorched my veins as I fought the impulse to grab her and fuck her. Shaking my head, I struggled to regain control. My control was slipping. I knew my eyes had changed color. Fuck, I couldn't let her see me like this, and I couldn't leave. She would have more questions if I left than she did now.

Questions I was forbidden to answer.

"Give me a minute," I growled as I pulled my wolf and my lust back under my control.

"Give you a minute? Give *you* a minute?" She was angry, and she had a right to be. "You bit me like you were some kind of wild animal!"

She sounded further away, and I guessed she'd climbed over the back of the couch to get away from me. "I didn't mean it."

It hung between us like the lie it was.

"You didn't mean it." Her scoff was loud. "Get out. I don't want you here anymore."

I stood, and a quick glance at the mirror confirmed my eye color was back to normal. "Did you ever want me here?"

Willow had a cloth pressed to her wrist. Her eyes watched me warily as I approached her. "I don't know what's going on," she told me carefully, "but this is no longer funny. I want you to leave. Now."

I ignored her, reaching for her arm. She resisted, even going so far as to hit out at me, but she was no match for my strength.

Taking the cloth off her, I inspected the two puncture marks I'd left on her wrist. "It won't scar." Pulling her to the cabinet in her bathroom, I got a large Band-Aid and wrapped it over her wrist. "You'll be fine."

Willow was struggling to accept my calmness. Her scent was scared, confused, and...something that was dangerously close to arousal. Or maybe it was anger.

"We still need to talk," I told her.

"Get out of my house."

Sucking my teeth, I cocked my head as I considered her. "I said sorry."

"You didn't say sorry!" Anger overrode all her other scents. "You don't even *sound* sorry. You bit me. You made me *bleed*, and you stand there as calm as you like."

"I said I didn't mean it." She was right, I hadn't said sorry. "It was a moment of weakness."

"A moment of weakness?" Her skepticism was warranted. "How often are you *weak*?"

"You're acting like a scared virgin." I looked at her more closely. "You're not, are you?" That would explain my reaction to her blood.

"No, I'm not a virgin!" Her face was scarlet. "Jesus Christ, Caleb, what is *wrong* with you?"

"If you're not a virgin, then why the fuck are you clutching your pearls at a little blood?" Her eyes were as wide as saucers. "Okay, so you like vanilla sex. Got it. Can we get back to the point?"

Willow barged past me and stormed back to the kitchen. I followed, fully prepared for her to attack me with a knife or something. Instead, she was facing the window, her back to me.

"Why do I see you?" Her voice was tight with fury. She watched me in the reflection of the window, and I could see the unshed tears.

"That's what I was hoping you'd tell me."

"I don't have any answers for you, I told you that."

"You've never had any visions before me?" She shook her head. "Do you see anything else?" She almost turned but shook her head. "So you don't see, like, a scene or a vision?" Her head shook quickly. "Do you actually see me, or do you just wake up with my face or something in your mind?" She did turn at that, and I half shrugged. "It's new to me too," I reminded her.

"But biting people isn't."

"You're the first human I've bitten," I answered without thought. Her eyes were wide again, and I inwardly cursed my stupidity.

"You bite animals?"

"What the hell, Willow! Of course I don't bite animals!" I thought about it. "Not live ones. I have no problem biting into them when they're cooked and on my plate." It was an effort at lightheartedness that fell flat. "Okay, I think we need to revisit this tomorrow or something."

"I don't want to see you again." She wasn't looking at me, but I could see the determined set of her jaw as she glared outside. "That means I don't want you hanging about the woods either. I want you gone. I don't know why you're here, I don't know why I see you when I sleep, but I know I don't want to see you again."

"If I leave, do you think the visions will stop?"

It was her turn to shrug. "This is fucked up. You are..." She made eye contact before turning her back to me. "You're too much. You think you make me weak. It sounds preposterous, but it *feels* right. Those men from earlier, they weren't a coincidence, were they?" I shook my head, and she nodded, her shoulders slumping. "Just leave me alone. Leave town. Please. I don't have what you're looking for."

How did I tell her that she was the answer, and she just didn't know it? But she was right. From the sound of it, she had been fine before. No paintings of men she'd never seen.

"I'll be gone by morning."

"Thank you."

She was looking at me from the reflection in the window. We held each other's stare for a moment, and then I turned and let myself out of her house. I was at the gate at the edge of her small garden when I heard the lock turn and a deadbolt slide home.

"I'd lock me out too," I mumbled as I headed up the sidewalk, away from her house. I didn't want her to see me enter the woods; she already thought I was peeping on her. I entered the woods and made my way to the small area where I'd made my base these last few weeks.

Cannon rose to his feet as I joined him and his beta. The wiry human was nowhere to be seen.

"She knows nothing. We agreed it was better if I leave here."

"Why?" Cannon looked me over. "What did you do?"

I huffed out a laugh. "You assume it was me?"

"Your scent is guilty," Royce confirmed. "Plus, I get the impression she may like you."

"Trust me, she doesn't." Tipping my head back, I looked at

the darkening sky as I tried to sort my jumbled thoughts. "I bit her."

Cannon's cough of surprise made me look at him. He was fighting a grin. "What the hell would you bite her for?"

"She was abandoned as a child," I explained. "I wondered if she was a shifter and just didn't know it."

Royce and Cannon exchanged a look before the alpha spoke. "That's stupid."

I tended to agree. This wasn't the first time I hadn't been thinking straight when it came to Willow Harper. "So we agreed if I leave, she is unlikely to have any desire to draw me."

"But it's not just you she's drawing," Royce reminded me, exchanging a look with his alpha. "As long as you're here, you can watch her."

"I can't." I avoided looking at either of them. "She has an illness, it's—"

"ME." Royce's voice was gruff. "Explains the scent of her, but that's not your fault."

Blowing out my cheeks, I rocked back on my heels, shoving my hands into my back pockets. "Well..."

"Caleb." Cannon's low commanding voice made me raise my head. "Explain."

"When I'm with her, her energy depletes. She gets sicker when I'm near."

"You drain her?" Cannon was watching me thoughtfully. "I've never heard of our kind having that effect on humans."

I said nothing.

"Has she noticed?" Royce asked me. When I nodded, he scratched his jaw. "Bonded?" he asked Cannon, who was watching me steadily. "What affects one may affect the other."

"Bonded to a human?" Cannon mused. "I've never heard of it."

"They're linked in some way," Royce spoke, looking me over curiously. "Do you feel anything when you're near her?"

"Agitation." They both grinned, and I cursed my loose tongue. "But physically, nothing like that."

"I'm curious as to why you bit her." Cannon tilted his head to the side. "Scenting her skin would have been enough." He looked to Royce. "You smell anything other than human on her?" His beta shook his head.

"I figured if she was even part shifter, with her age, it could have been suppressed, and I needed to make sure."

"Fair point," Cannon conceded. "Next time, I recommend asking." His lips twitched and I flipped him the finger. "Well, you can't leave," he declared. "We can't take her. Too many people would notice."

A stab of alarm twisted my gut. "Take her?"

Cannon nodded. "Doc wants to run tests on her, but we can't exactly do that here. We need her back on Blackridge Peak."

My wolf prowled too close to my skin. "She isn't going anywhere near your Peak," I burst out angrily. "Stay the fuck away from her."

Cannon's eyes shifted to turquoise. "You seem to forget your place, *rogue*. If she's a threat to me or mine, she gets dealt with."

"She can barely function!" I snarled back. "She's no threat to anyone!"

Cannon gestured to his beta who turned and picked up paintings that had been lying behind him. He handed them to his alpha, who took them easily despite them being different sizes. Cannon picked up the first one and showed it to me.

"This is the clearing above my packlands," he told me. "This is the view from the top of the peak that shadows the next highest mountain." His gaze pierced mine. "You're familiar with that mountain." He showed me the next painting. "This is the place of the Luna Ball last year." He tossed it to the ground. "This is the abandoned mine at the base of the mountain." He held up the final piece. "And that is where your parents were murdered. Am I right?"

When I said nothing, Royce took a step towards me. "You haven't seen these in her art store?" I shook my head. "She was wrapping a package up when we were there—the post office 'lost' it." He turned and showed me the piece, and my heart stuttered. "It's not just *you* she paints," he told me softly. "It's places where you lived when you were pack."

Swallowing down the pain, I tried to appear as though I wasn't affected as they showed me paintings of my past. A past that I had left behind, but here it was, following me. Painted by a woman who didn't have a fucking clue that she was ripping my heart out with each brush stroke.

"How much longer before she sees more than you?" Cannon spoke quietly. "She's seen where you come from; she's seen *you*; how much longer before she sees you shift?"

"She won't."

"Caleb, you aren't stupid." Cannon's reprimand was warranted. "I don't think distance will make a difference," he told me bluntly. "Either you stay here and figure it out, quickly, or we take her to the Pack Council and damn the consequences."

"I say we put her in front of a shaman anyway," Royce muttered.

"I say, you put one hand on her, and I will cut it off." They both looked at me, neither of them surprised by my outburst.

"Fine. You have two weeks."

I looked at the alpha as he pulled his shirt over his head. "Two weeks?"

"Two weeks. You have no answers by the time I return, then she comes with us." Royce was already undressed and ready to shift.

"I'll have answers." Cannon nodded and then the black wolf was in front of me, his beta at his side. I stepped aside as they moved past me, a lone wolf giving due respect to an alpha and his beta. When they were gone, I sat on the ground, my eyes on the paintings.

How the fuck was I going to unravel the mystery of Willow Harper in two weeks when she never wanted to see me again? I had no idea.

I should have kept moving. The first time I saw her, the first time her scent called to me, I should have kept moving.

"Luna guide me," I pleaded to the Goddess in the heavens above. "I need a little help, and a lot of luck." The wind whistled through the trees, but no answer came. Standing, I gathered the discarded paintings, intending to break and burn them like I had done before.

My thumb grazed over the rocks of the mountain I used to call home. "What are you, Willow? What do you want with me?"

Placing the paintings gently against an overturned log, I

turned them so they were facing away from me. I didn't need to look at them to know what I'd lost.

# TEN

# *Willow*

"WHY ARE YOU SO DOWN?" LILY ASKED ME, HANDING ME A bottle of water from the grocery bag that had our lunch in it. "You're telling me that you're not, but every time I look at you, I see sadness."

"I think you're exaggerating." I tried to smile, but I knew it was flat. Tucking my hair behind my ear, I tried to lift myself out of my low mood. "Maybe it's because I never got a slice of wedding cake brought home."

Lily rolled her eyes, but the distraction worked as she launched into telling me again why the wedding cake was so hideous and why she couldn't possibly bring me a slice. In truth, I think she ate mine on the way home, but the cake was elderflower and lavender, which sounded like a tea blend I would avoid, never mind eat.

Lily sighed dramatically, unwrapping her vegetable panini absentmindedly. She hadn't met anyone at the wedding. She had flirted plenty from what I had been told, but there were no sparks. Not even a flicker. I wanted to commiserate, I did, but whenever I thought of "sparks," I remembered the feeling as Caleb bit into my wrist.

"Do you think vampires are real?"

Lily stopped midchew, her eyebrow arched in question. "No. Maybe?" She shrugged. "Would you rather an Edward or a Lestat?"

"Neither," I told her honestly, feeling stupid for my question.

Lily took another bite of her sandwich. "Of course, you're team Jacob."

"I never understand why anyone *isn't*," I pointed out. "And anyway, who wants to drink someone's blood?"

"So they live." Lily opened the bag of chips she'd brought for us to share. "They feed to live, it's all very—"

"Parasitic."

"Romantic," Lily countered. "Oooh, okay, how about Damon? You *have* to admit he's better."

"Than what?" I opened my sandwich. Simple cheese, lettuce and tomato. "A leech?"

"Girl, you cannot diss Damon. He's hot and way better than the options I gave you before." Lily ate a few chips. "Okay, okay, I got it! Dean or Sam?"

"Dean."

We shared a look and both grinned. "Totally," Lily confirmed. "And he'd kill all the vampires."

"And the werewolves," I added. "All the creepy things go night night when Dean's around." We ate in silence. As much as I tried, I couldn't stop looking at the bench across the street.

"So, Caleb just left?" Lily was really bad at feigning indifference.

"You're as subtle as a brick." She merely winked at me, drinking from her water bottle. "Yes, he left."

"And he never said *anything?*"

"What were you expecting him to say?" I looked down at my sandwich, losing my appetite as I thought about the man who was gone in person but who, in my dreams, still very much had a starring role.

"Goodbye?" Lily's disappointment would have been amusing if I wasn't still torn about Caleb leaving like I'd asked him to.

"He was just a guy, Lil," I admonished, standing up and walking to the small storage area where I sometimes kept new pieces that I hadn't dared to showcase yet. With trembling fingers, I reached out for the newest piece and took it out of hiding. "What do you think?"

Lily quickly put her sandwich down and wiped her hands on her jeans before joining me to study my latest piece of art. "Oh wow, Willow," she exclaimed, the admiration clear. "It's beautiful." I nodded. It was. A pool, perhaps a spring, was surrounded by trees with two flat boulders close to the water. However, it was the soft waterfall that drew the eye. "The light on that waterfall," she breathed. "Is it real?" She reached out to touch the painting. "I can almost feel the coolness of the water." She beamed at me, and I knew I blushed at the praise.

"Thank you."

"Where is this? We need to go."

"I don't think it's anywhere." But the lie tasted heavy on my tongue. I knew it was real because I knew it was connected to Caleb. While Lily gushed over the painting and helped me place it on the wall for sale, I didn't tell her I hadn't painted all of the scene that I'd dreamed of. I didn't tell her that on the edge of the clearing, leading to the pool had sat a gray wolf.

I hadn't drawn it into my painting. I'd tried, but each time I'd attempted to capture the beauty of the majestic animal, I'd ended up starting over.

"I love it." Her declaration brought me out of my thoughts. "I might need to buy it."

With my back to her, I didn't have to hide my smile. "You have no more room for your pity purchases," I scolded, but she could tell I was joking.

"Well...I have an office now."

Looking over my shoulder at her, I saw her shift her feet uncomfortably. "No, you didn't," I said as I turned. "You gave in?"

Her head dropped into her hands as she groaned. "I gave in!" When she raised her head, she looked defeated, but she was fighting the smile. "He's unbearable to live with, you know."

"Which is a lie, and you know it." Reaching out to swat her on the arm, I missed as she danced out of reach. "Plus, you're working for your dad. It's not the same as living in the same house as him." Resting back on my seat, I shook my head as I watched her. "When do you start?"

Lily sniffed, inspecting her nails. "Monday."

Frowning at her indifference, I ended up gawking at her. "You started *today*?" She didn't meet my stare, deciding to tidy up our half-eaten lunches. "Oh my God, are you on your lunch break?"

"Shut up."

I laughed out loud. I couldn't help it. She looked so smug

and bashful at the same time. "Congratulations on your new job," I told her, hugging her. "How long is lunch?" The fact her phone started to ring made me laugh again. "You're already in trouble!" I wasn't hiding my glee.

"Shut *up*, Willow!" Lily's cheeks were burning as she answered the phone. "Hi, Dad!" I giggled when she rolled her eyes at me. "Of course I'm coming back this afternoon," she said, picking up her purse. She mouthed *goodbye* to me, and I waved, watching her hurry out the door. Only Lily would take too long a lunch break on her first day of a new job.

I spent the rest of the day cleaning the store. I'd had class this morning. Lily had told me she wouldn't be in class, but Lorna and Peter had turned up, eager as ever. Realizing that Lily wouldn't be returning as a student made me sad but also happy. Sad that I'd miss her student fees, and happy that I would no longer be taking charity from her.

Plus, I knew she was going to love working with her dad.

Around four, I decided I'd had enough and wanted to catch some of the afternoon sunshine. I'd been freaked out by the doctor that afternoon the other week, but despite that, I'd taken his advice. I walked to and from the store at a pace that suited me. I ate three meals a day, and I had banned candy, chocolate, and Alistair from my house.

I was going to cave when it came to Alistair, I knew that. It wasn't his fault his mom wasn't the best parent. I'd thought I saw his dad was home, which would keep Alistair out of my house too. For how long? I guess that was up to me.

I'd also been sleeping better, but before, I would wake up with an image in my mind of Caleb, but now I felt the dreams more. I was glad he wasn't here. I didn't think he would appreciate knowing he had a recurring role in my head at night.

I didn't know why I was so obsessed with him. I'd tried using a different adjective, but none of them felt right. I *was* obsessed. He was an enigma. Biting fetishes aside, he was someone I wanted to know more about. I just didn't know how or why.

The walk was slower than I hoped. I put it down to daydreaming about wavy dirty blond hair and eyes the color of a chocolate fountain. No, that was a terrible comparison. The depth of color in his eyes was deeper than the color of milk chocolate—it was dark chocolate—but no, that wasn't right either. It was milk chocolate with a hint of darkness. Or the other way around? Dark chocolate with a hint of lightness... Shaking my head at my nonsense, I tried to shake Caleb from my mind.

At home, I made a peanut butter and jelly sandwich, poured a glass of milk, and took my dinner to my studio with me, ready for an evening of painting.

The tray slipped from my hands, crashing to the floor, when I found Caleb sitting on my stool, facing the door, waiting for me.

"That will stain."

His easy, casual demeanor and his entire indifference at being in my personal space *again* made me finally react.

"Stop breaking into my house!" I yelled at him, and he didn't even so much as flinch. Stooping down, I picked up my dinner off the floor, glaring at Caleb the whole time. "Why are you here?"

"Would you believe I missed your charm?"

"Hell no."

"Yeah, I wouldn't believe it either." He stood up, brushing past me on his way out of the room. He returned moments later with a damp cloth. "For the floor." He must have seen the fleeting thought of violence that I had, imagining myself shoving the cloth down his throat, because he smiled. "Feeling feisty today, aren't you?"

"I thought I told you to leave?" Without waiting for his answer, I marched into the kitchen with my ruined dinner.

"I did leave." He had followed me and now stood with his arms folded and his hip resting against the counter, the cloth on the counter. "I came back." He watched me as I pretended to ignore him, dumping my sandwich in the trash and really hoping the milk wouldn't make too much of a mess. I snatched the cloth from where he left it.

"Give me that." Caleb held his hand out, and I placed the cleaning cloth and the paper towels I'd grabbed into his hand, careful not to touch him, hoping he wouldn't see the tremor in my hands. If he noticed, he pretended that he didn't.

I welcomed the brief chance to gather myself and find some semblance of composure while he cleaned my floor. It was his fault I dropped it, so it was only right he cleaned it. Huffing out a laugh, I rubbed my temples. I was being a child, and I had a man, who continually broke into my house, *in my home again*.

"You probably should call the police."

Turning around quickly, I gaped at him. "Are you a mind reader now?"

"No," he said, tossing the paper towels and the cloth in the trash. "It's what any sane woman who lived alone would do." He paused as he looked me over. "Never have understood why you haven't."

Truthfully, neither had I.

"For all your..." I waved my hand in front of me. "*That*, and the general level of 'stalkerishness' you seem to excel in, I don't think you would harm me."

Caleb resumed his earlier pose of folded arms across his chest, his hip leaning on the counter. "You haven't reported me to the cops because you think I'm good-looking?" he asked me doubtfully.

*What the actual...*

"What?" I knew I was gaping at him again. "No! I meant you're all...you, but you don't strike me as someone who would hurt me."

He rubbed his forehead. "I don't even understand what you say sometimes, do you know that? I cannot figure you out."

"I'm the easiest person to figure out. It's really not that diffi-cult." I felt like he insulted me, but I wasn't sure why. "Orphan, lives alone, paints a lot, has ME. See? Done."

"Has visions of people she's never met."

I gave him a flat stare. "That's only happened with you."

He was unimpressed. "I want to say I'm flattered, but—"

"You'd be lying. I know. I get it. You're Mr. Immovable." That so wasn't the right word, but whatever. He could deal with it. I had *him* to deal with after all. "Could you please stop breaking into my house?"

"Can't promise."

Why would I expect anything else? "Can you *try* to stop

breaking into my house?" He smiled and I knew he was laughing at me. "So, you left." I decided changing the subject was better. "You weren't gone for long."

"No." Caleb watched me intently. "When you have your visions or dreams or whatever you want to call them, what do you feel?"

"When I realize I've dreamt of you?" He nodded once. "Irritated mostly."

He was unfazed. "Willow, can you try to be an adult?"

"I can be an adult; you just bring out the rebellious side of me."

"You mean the teenage brat?"

I could continue throwing sass his way, but he was right, we were adults. Taking a deep breath, I squared my shoulders. "I feel drained like I haven't slept. I try to get solid sleep for my health, but even though I know I haven't woken up, I know that I'm not rested."

He watched me impassively. "And how long does that feeling last? Do you paint what you saw immediately?" I shook my head. "Do you wake up having painted or drawn me in your sleep?" Again, I shook my head. "What's the longest you've waited between dreaming about me and drawing me?"

"*Dreaming* about you?" I scoffed. "You sound like you're the man of my dreams," I snorted with contempt. "Trust me, you aren't."

"I am quite literally the man of your dreams," he corrected, his posture all stiff and judgy. "Trust *me*, I wish I wasn't. Now answer the question."

I wanted to swear at him. Quite colorfully. I wanted to call him names a respectable businesswoman shouldn't know. I wanted to act like the rebellious teenager he accused me of behaving like. Instead, I pushed my anger down and tried to smile instead.

He would not beat me. "I think the most—sorry, the longest —I've left it, maybe a day?"

"And how bad did your ME get that day?"

Frowning, I thought about it. "I...I don't know."

Caleb looked away from me as he thought over what I said. "I don't think it is being near me that causes you to be weak," he mused. "I've been thinking about this. I've been in your presence a number of times—"

"I noticed."

He ignored my interruption. "And only a few times have you been weakened so much I needed to help you."

He raised his hand, his fingers sinking into his thick hair, and he rubbed his scalp in frustration. I watched fascinated as the strands broke free of his normal pushed-back hairstyle, and a few curls fell loose over his forehead. It changed the look of him, softened him. My fingers itched to sketch him.

"Why are you looking at me like that?" His voice was wary as he pushed the stray hair back.

"Wondering why you're shaking your dandruff onto my floor." Oh my lord, yeah...I needed to control my mouth.

Caleb threw his head back and laughed out loud. "I don't have dandruff. You're safe."

"Well, I haven't gotten my tetanus shot after you bit me, so keep your*self* to yourself."

"You're being dramatic."

"You bit me."

"I apologized."

*Did he?* "I don't care."

"Fine."

"*Fine.*"

We glared at each other until Caleb let out a low curse and turned away, walking back to my studio. "Show me everything new," he called over his shoulder.

No *please* or *thank you*, just *show me*. I followed him because the quicker I showed him, the quicker he would leave. I hoped. When I was done, he pulled a crumpled-up piece of sketch paper from his pocket. Flattening it out, he looked up at me.

"And this?"

Swallowing hard, I didn't demand to know why he went through my trash. It was no longer a surprise the boundaries he willingly crossed. "I don't have a good flair for animals."

The wolf stared at me from the sketch. Even it seemed to know I was full of it.

"Looks good to me." His voice was gruff as he spoke. "Any more of these?"

"No. I...I can't get it right, so I left it off."

"Off?" He was suddenly alert. "Off of what?"

"The painting I put in the gallery this afternoon." He took hold of my elbow, steering me from the room. "Caleb!"

"We're going back to the gallery. You'll show me everything."

Wrenching my arm free, I spun to face him. "You can't boss me around like this, Caleb!"

"We either go together or I go alone. Which would you prefer?"

Grinding my teeth together, I glared at him, wishing it had the power to hurt him. "Together."

His scornful smirk set my blood on fire with temper. "That's what I thought."

*Asshole.*

# ELEVEN

# Caleb

Willow didn't own a car, or if she did, she kept it somewhere that wasn't near her home. I had no use for a car, as four legs were better than four wheels, so we walked back to the art studio.

I knew that she was self-conscious of being seen with me. Her furtive glances left and right gave her away, but the walk back to Main Street was quiet. It was early evening, and businesses were either closed or closing up. Too early for the few restaurants to be doing much trade.

"Why here?" I asked her as we walked. I wasn't particularly interested; I just wanted to make sure that if anyone did see us, she would look more willing to be with me if they saw her talking.

"I liked the name." She shrugged as she looked around. "How could you not like here? It's populated but quiet, it has a strong tourist trade who like to buy art of where they've been hiking, the property prices are decent... It all worked."

"It is a good spot," I agreed. "Mountains and forests on your doorstep, cleanish air."

"Cleanish?" Willow shot me a look that I'd come to recognize as she didn't agree with me. "It's so fresh and clean here."

She would never understand as she wasn't a shifter. "I've inhaled fresher." That earned me an eye roll, but she didn't pursue it. "You study art at school?"

"Yup."

Okay, so she was going to make it difficult. "Which school?"

"Am I to assume you don't already know?"

She really was feeling sassy today. "I know very little about you, Willow, and what I do know, I already feel is too much."

"Then why are you asking me questions!"

"I was trying to make the walk more enjoyable."

"I would *enjoy* my forced walk more if it was done in silence."

"Understood."

I never mentioned it when her stride got shorter or the fact that she was slowing down. I merely adjusted my own pace to match hers. If she noticed, she said nothing. I was lost in my thoughts when she spoke, surprising me.

"I went to school in Boulder."

"Colorado?"

"Yes."

"Nice." It was a town I was familiar with. "The Flatirons are a good hike."

"So I'm led to believe."

"You've never hiked?" She shook her head. "You told me before you've had your illness since you were sixteen?"

"No, I got sick when I was sixteen; I developed ME after that."

"Mono?" I tried not to laugh. "I forgot you said that."

"I caught an infection. I hadn't kissed anyone," she snapped at me, causing me to grin at the scowl she sent my way.

"What age were you when you first kissed?" I had no idea why I asked it, but she was so adamant the other night about not being a virgin, and now she was telling me she caught mono from *not* kissing, I couldn't help but poke the bear.

"That has nothing to do with you."

"I know. Humor me, I'm bored."

"It's not my job to humor you." Willow glowered at me once more. "If anything, I think I give you too much amusement as it is."

I wisely said nothing.

We finally arrived at Main Street, and I was as relieved as she was. Willow was perspiring, her breathing was forced, and I felt like a dick for making her walk back here tonight. Inside, she pointed to one of the stools, and I nodded as she made her way to it.

"You have water in that fridge in the back?" She nodded and I went and got her a bottle of water. I hovered while she gulped it down, watching her hold the bottle to her forehead. "You okay?"

"Yeah, I've been trying to increase my exercise, but it's been a day."

"Am I affecting you?"

Her eyes were closed as she cooled herself down, but I saw the twitch of a smile. "You are, but not in the way you mean."

I looked away from her, and the first painting that caught

my eye was hanging prime center of her gallery. Moving closer, I took in the waterfall, the pool below it, and the rocks that were large enough to lie out on nearby. Her attention to detail was to be commended, but it didn't stop the fury that rode through my veins as I looked upon this sacred haven.

"The wolf," she spoke from behind me, "it was sitting beside those large slabs of rock."

I nodded. I wanted to reach out and touch the water, it looked so inviting.

"I tried to place it in the scene, but it didn't fit."

"Because he doesn't belong there," I murmured. "He hasn't belonged there for a very long time."

"He?"

Turning, I hadn't been aware that she had moved, and she was behind me, within hearing distance. I'd been so caught up in the memories I never heard her moving. That was careless.

"You know this place?" she asked me curiously.

"I do. You need to stop painting."

Willow's eyes went from interested to outraged in seconds. "Why?"

"Because every time you paint something like this, it's dangerous."

"It's a landscape painting."

"It's dangerous."

"Why?" she demanded.

"I can't tell you why, just trust me."

"No." She crossed her arms, her face hardening. "Tell me why."

"I can't."

We glared at each other for a few more moments before

Willow turned away from me, seeking the support of a chair. "You exhaust me." I could see how heavy her exhaustion lay upon her.

"I know." Turning away from her, I took the painting off the wall. "I'll pay for this." Looking over at her, I saw her anger and frustration. "You need sales, I'm buying, you should be pleased."

"You're buying them to destroy them. It doesn't make me happy. I put hours of work into that."

"Name the price."

She shook her head sadly as she looked away from me. "You don't understand."

"I understand that you're painting scenes you don't know. I understand that your visions scare you. What I don't understand is *why* you'd *want* to paint them."

Her brow furrowed as she thought about it. Sniffling a little, she looked down at her legs. "Because they speak to me."

"Really? What do they say?" I asked her, knowing I hadn't hidden the sarcasm in my question.

"You wouldn't understand."

Pushing my hair back, I watched her, with my hands on top of my head. How could one woman be so completely aggravating? I *would* understand, but to push her might scare her away even more. "There's a lot here that neither of us understands. I don't really want to know more, do you?"

"The frequency with which I painted when you were gone increased." Willow was looking at her gallery wall. "Painting takes time, preciseness, but these...they flew off my palette onto the canvas." She looked at me and back to the wall. "I couldn't *not* paint them. Do you understand that?"

"Truthfully? No."

"Me neither." Slowly she walked over to the other side of the room, and I watched as she opened a door to a small storage cupboard. When she struggled to lift a canvas, I hurried over to help. When we were finished, there were six new paintings.

All landscapes, all of places she could never have seen.

"The two men who came here the other week and bought six paintings, I think they're linked."

Carefully I watched her. "What do you mean?"

"They bought six, you bought one, I made seven more." Her hand had a tremble in it when she waved it over them. "I don't know these places, but I *know* them." With a tired sigh, she rocked back on her heels. "These are my best work, and I produced them like I was rolling them off a printer." Willow pointed to one. "I don't think the paint is even dry on that one," she scoffed. She finally looked up at me. "What's happening to me, Caleb?"

"We need to figure that out."

"And how do we do that? Do you continue to break into my home?"

"I would like to stop having to do that," I admitted. "But I feel that—no, that's not right, I *know* that—I need to make sure I see what you're painting." I dreaded the next words that I would have to say. "I need you to meet someone."

"Who?" Willow waited nervously.

"A friend of a friend."

"What does this friend do?"

"It's complicated to explain." I also wasn't sure how I was going to ask Alpha Cannon for help from his shaman. If he even *had* a shaman. "If I can get them to agree to meet you, will you come?"

"Will they bite me?"

"For fuck's sake, Willow. It was a nip." She ignored my protest and waited patiently. "They won't bite you." I hesitated, and her eyebrows raised in question. "They may take some blood."

"Why would they need my blood?"

"Willow, you're having visions. You're dreaming about people you've never met and places you've never been to. Is this *really* the part you're going to question?"

Dipping her head, she stared at the floor. "I don't know, don't you think I, *we*, should be questioning it all?"

"Yes. I do. Hence *I want you to meet someone.*"

"Will they take blood from you too?"

I almost told her it wouldn't be necessary, but I lied and nodded. She seemed to relax then. She also looked ready to pass out.

"We need to get you home."

"Yeah." She tried to stand up but swayed. "Shit, you're doing it again."

"Or painting seven full-on landscapes in a week hasn't helped," I griped as I reached to steady her.

Willow smiled at the acidity in my tone. "Or that." She leaned into me, and I knew, had she been healthier, she would have wanted to put as much distance between us as possible. "I won't make the walk."

"You don't say." My hand circled the nape of her neck, my thumb hovering over one of her pressure points, ready to press down.

"You're even more sarcastic than I am." Willow looked up at me. "I think I'm going to pass out."

"You are." I applied pressure to the point I knew would incapacitate her, and caught her as she fell, then looked around the studio. "Now what?" Picking her up, I looked for a place to lay her down. "I should have kept moving," I muttered to myself.

The store had stools and a sales desk but no actual bench. Carrying her through to the small kitchenette, I had no choice but to put her on the short counter beside the sink. She was half slumped over in a sitting position, but I hoped I didn't need to wait too long.

Pulling the phone from the inside of my jacket, I called the one number I had stored in there.

"Caleb?"

"Royce...I need a shaman." I heard his unspoken question. "She's painted seven more. Places she should never know existed." My reflection looked back at me as I stared out the small window in the back of the store, grateful that no one passing by would see the store owner passed out beside me.

"She's human," Royce reminded me. "A shaman will be of no use for her."

"No, I don't expect him to be, but he needs to see these paintings. He needs to ask Luna for answers."

"Now you believe?" I understood the skepticism in his voice.

"I always believed. I just didn't accept the plan mapped out for me."

I heard him grunt. "Few of us rarely do."

The sound of the phone being covered followed, and when he came on the line, I was expecting him. "Alpha Cannon."

"We don't have a shaman," he told me bluntly. "We have a doctor and, well...it's complicated."

"Too complicated for an alpha?"

"What did she paint?"

"It'd be easier if you asked what she didn't paint." Tilting my head back, I looked at the ceiling. "She's been drawing my wolf."

Silence was my answer, and I waited patiently. "Forget the two weeks. Bring her and everything she's painted, sketched, or doodled. Bring them here."

"Everything?" I walked back into the store. "She has a *lot* of artwork."

"Then get a bigger truck. I expect to see you soon."

He hung up.

"Well, that went well."

"You told me you didn't have a phone."

*Of course she was awake.* Going back into the kitchen, I saw Willow sitting where I'd left her. Her look was once more cautious. "How much did you hear?"

"You were talking about how much art I had."

"Anything else?" When she shook her head, I opened myself more to my wolf. Letting the shifter magic ride close to the surface, I listened with my wolf senses. Her heart was rapid, but it wasn't racing. Her breathing was labored, a sign of her exhaustion. She wasn't lying. "I told you I knew someone who could help. Maybe. That was them." Willow didn't say anything, her gaze careful as she waited for me to finish. "Two problems we need to solve." Her eyes narrowed in anticipation of not liking what I was going to say, which was expected and a little amusing. "One, you have a lot of art, and we need to take it all with us." When she opened her mouth to protest, I carried on. "Two, we need to go to them, so you need to close the store for a few days."

"No." Sliding off the counter, she stood, her legs unsteady, but she backed away from my automatic offer to help. "Absolutely not. I can't leave here for a *few days*. Are you insane? I run a *business*."

"The air quotes weren't necessary," I mocked her slightly and was rewarded with a look of fury. "You need a break—don't argue with me. You're running yourself into the ground. Maybe, *maybe*, a break is exactly what you need. Maybe being with me, away from all this, will help."

"How?" Her expression was so skeptical that I knew I'd have to think faster on my feet.

"I'm basically your muse, right?"

"Wrong."

The flat stare was unyielding. "Humor me, okay?" *Think smart, Caleb, easy does it.* "What do we know so far?" I asked her, changing tactics. "About a month or so before I arrived in Whispering Pines, you started drawing me. Right?" She nodded once. "Then you meet me, confront me, really for no fault of my own"—the scowl was back—"and you move from painting just me to landscapes, scenes that you've never been to but I *have*." Willow's brow was creased as she waited for me to get to the point. I was eager to know where I was going with this myself. "I left, and your subconscious spread out from the..." I struggled for the right word, "contained area to a wider catchment area."

"Wider catchment area?"

"Not my best word choice. Just roll with it, okay?" Willow's huff of derision spoke volumes. "I come back, and you're back to me. Right?" She was going to deny it. "I was in your room; I saw them all. Honestly, it's a little creepy."

"I'm not obsessed with you or anything like that," she snapped, her face flushing.

"Really? Tell that to the two sketchbooks and the stumps of HBs that are in your trash can."

"You're arrogant."

"I'm stating facts. That doesn't make me arrogant."

"Okay then, you're a dick." She smiled sweetly at me. "Better?"

I shrugged. "Probably more accurate." She lost her smile. "But I'm also right."

Shaking her head, she looked away from me. "See? Arrogant."

"My *point* is, I think if you're with me, you'll draw less *and*"—I spoke over whatever she was going to say—"you'll rest better. You told me yourself, you're drained. You're dreaming, or the visions that you're having are eating into the time when you need your body to replenish itself. Instead, you are hurting yourself."

"So your best idea is for me to spend time *with* the person who may be making me ill to start with?"

"What have you got to lose?"

Willow gestured to the studio. "My *business*."

Ugh, she was a stubborn woman. "Look. You have ME. Don't stand there and tell me you haven't had this store closed for days before when you've had a bad spell?"

"That's different."

"How?"

"Because it was a necessity; it wasn't my choice."

"Is that all?" I grinned at her, and she took a slight step back. "Why didn't you just tell me to kidnap you if it makes it easier for you?"

"I...kidnap? *What!*"

"Relax, it won't even hurt." I turned away from her to look at the amount of art. "Help me pack this up first, and I'll tie you up first thing in the morning. Deal?"

# TWELVE

# *Willow*

CALEB WAS INSANE. HE HAD TO BE. NO ONE SUGGESTED that, did they? The problem was, I knew he wasn't joking, and I knew in his own weird way, he thought that threatening to kidnap me would help me.

I was going to pass out again.

"I'm going to faint."

Caleb pierced me with a stare. "Seriously?" His eyes ran over me briefly in a cold clinical manner. "For dramatic purposes or your ME?"

"Drama, obviously," I snapped at him. I never considered myself a violent person until I met Caleb, but since meeting him, and *talking* to him, I'd had the urge to punch him more than once. I was sure I heard him mumble a curse under his breath, and I almost, *almost* made him repeat it, but instead, he pointed to one of the stools.

"Sit there, hold on, and just direct me, okay? I can't have you passing out. I have a lot to do, and you slowing me down isn't going to help."

I knew my eyes were wide with disbelief. "I'm sorry, did you just say that your plan to kidnap me needs to be on your schedule?"

"Definitely dramatic," he muttered. "Willow, we both need this done. Remember"—he reached out and started taking art off the wall—"this is for you."

"Am I supposed to say thanks?" I retorted waspishly.

"Some gratitude would be nice." He wasn't looking at me, too busy removing my carefully hung paintings with zero consideration. He missed me flipping him off, but even so, the pettiness inside of me, which seemed to show up whenever he was near, was satisfied.

"Could you be more careful?" He was stacking up the pieces like they were building bricks or something equally as sturdy, and his carelessness was making me anxious.

"They're fine."

"They're not fine!" Getting off the stool, I went over and picked the first piece up. Carrying it over to the counter, I started to wrap it.

"Are you doing that for them all?" Caleb looked between me and the pile, his mouth a thin firm line. "Do we have time for that?"

"Make time."

"You're being unreasonable. These are never coming back here," he told me. When he saw my look, he sighed. "Willow, what did I just say? We need to take these to the people I know, and they won't care if they're bubble-wrapped. You're being unreasonable."

I stopped what I was doing and turned to look at him. "Do you have kids?"

Caleb's jaw clenched. "No."

"Me neither, but what I have is my paintings. These are my babies."

"That's not only stupid, it makes you sound like a crazy person."

"I don't care. I had a friend at college who was doing English Lit, and she wanted to be an author. She said every book she wrote would be her baby. Her characters were her children, and that's how she would treat them. With the care, love, and attention that each book, each character, deserves. Like a child. Her child." I pointed at my painting in front of me. "This is exactly the same, my heart and soul are in this painting, in *everything* that I create, so I don't give a damn if your *friend* doesn't care what condition *my* artwork reaches him in. *I* do. Until they are paid for, they are *mine*." Caleb's arms were folded across his chest, his face impassive. "Do you understand?"

Once more, those dark eyes swept over me. "Yeah, I understand that both you and your friend from college need therapy."

*Dick.* "The more I get to know you, Caleb, the more I don't like you."

He shrugged. "Not here to be popular."

*Oh my God, I can't even...argh! I will not scream.* "I'm not going until they are all wrapped." Stubbornness was a failing, they may say, but good grief, he made me this way.

"Fuck me." When he started wrapping them two at a time, I almost objected, but the look he gave me made it clear it was this way or no way.

I knew when to pick my battles. This wasn't the hill I

would die on. He was wrapping them at least, and that was a small win in itself.

Caleb stood back when he was finished. "Do you have a car?"

"Did you see a car?"

"A simple no would have sufficed."

I was annoying him as much as he was annoying me. *Good.*

"I need a truck." Caleb looked out the store window with a speculative look in his eye.

"You're thinking of stealing a car, aren't you?" Why was I surprised? "You are *not* stealing from my friends and neighbors!"

Caleb looked at me as if I was an idiot. Which I must have been as I was still standing here when he quite clearly told me he was going to kidnap me later. "Why the hell would I steal a car? I don't need the police tailing our asses for theft."

Valid point. I didn't tell him that, of course.

"You got anyone you can ask to borrow one?"

"No."

He nodded. "Uh-huh, so your friend Lily, her truck can't be borrowed?"

*I hate you.* "She needs it for work," I lied.

"Really?" He smiled and it held no warmth. "Willow Harper, you are a shit liar."

"Caleb Foster, you are a shit person."

"Never said I wasn't. Phone Lily."

"No." It was my turn to cross my arms and stand my ground. "What would I say? Can I get your vehicle to aid in my kidnapping?"

Caleb was not impressed. "If you think that will work, sure.

Or tell her you have a potential buyer who wants to see all your artwork, you're very excited, but you have to go to them, and you need a mode of transport to do it." He smirked. "It's not even a lie."

"I'm not excited about this."

"So a small white lie in a whole lot of truth." He walked past me to the kitchen. "Don't sweat the details too much."

"You're relentless, you know that, don't you?" I didn't receive an answer and, honestly, I didn't expect one. He came back with a bottle of water for me.

"Drink, you need fluids."

"I'm fine."

"Drink the water, Willow. Hurting yourself to be a stubborn ass doesn't make this easier for either of us." He watched me take a sip, then another drink. "Phone your friend. We still have your house to do."

"There has to be another way."

"Do you have a license?" he asked me.

"No. Why?"

"The other way was hiring a truck. You don't have a license, so we can't."

"Then we use yours."

"Don't have one."

He was piling the paintings for easier transportation, I assumed. "Then *how* are you going to drive a truck!"

Caleb glanced up at me. "I can drive; I just don't have a license."

"Who doesn't have a license?" I demanded.

"You, apparently."

When he handed me my phone, I snatched it out of his

hand. "You're going to regret this," I told him as I pressed call on Lily's number.

"I already do."

He was saved from my scathing reply when Lily answered the phone.

"Willow! Hi, are you okay, do you need me?" I felt worse than I already had for what I was about to lie about.

"Hi," I started. Conscious of Caleb watching and listening, I turned my back. "I'm good," I lied. Rolling my head from side to side, I stretched my neck, trying to loosen the knot of tension at the base of my skull. "I need a favor."

"Anything, you know that."

I startled when Caleb reached around and took the phone from me, pressing the speaker icon and holding the phone in his hand as he stood behind me. I could feel the heat from his body, his front almost touching my back. I quickly stepped away from him, turning to face him, and I saw how easily my reaction had amused him.

"Willow?" Lily's voice snapped my attention back to the phone. "What's the favor?"

"I need a car." I hesitated when Caleb made a hand motion to suggest bigger. "A truck maybe?" He nodded. "I need to borrow a truck."

"Um...why? You can't drive."

"I know, I have a..." I couldn't say *friend* when it came to Caleb; the word would choke me first. He saw me struggle and rubbed his finger and thumb together. "Buyer. I have a buyer for some artwork. He—"

*"Oh my God, Willow, that's amazing!"*

Caleb winced at Lily's shriek, and I couldn't stop my smile.

"Yeah, it's really exciting." The lie tasted like ash on my tongue. "But he's?" Caleb nodded quickly, confirming the sex of my *buyer*. "He's not from here and wants to see the paintings and a few drawings and things first before he commits. So I said I would take them to him."

"But you can't drive! And I just started my new job!" Lily wailed, and Caleb was too slow to hide his smug look. He knew she couldn't take me? How? He pointed to himself and then made a talking motion with his hand, pointing at the phone.

Asshole.

"I, well, um..." As I watched him, he raised an eyebrow, and I shook my head at his shit-eating grin. "I have someone who can help."

"You do? Who?"

"Well...remember the guy?"

"Hotcakes?" Lily was shrieking again, and this time, it was me who winced.

"Caleb," I stressed. "His name is Caleb."

"Oh my God, is it like a date? Wait! Are you dating? *How could you be dating and not tell me!*" I knew my face was on fire, and Caleb was struggling to hide his amusement as Lily went on...and on. "Have you kissed him? Was it good? I bet it was good. I bet he knows what he's doing."

"Lily! Can you *please* stop?" I had to shout to be heard. When I had silence, I continued. "It is *not* a date. We have not kissed. It's just that he knows the situation and offered to drive."

Lily was now quiet for so long it was unsettling. "Lil?"

"Is he kidnapping you?" Caleb failed to smother his laughter, and I heard Lily's gasp. "Is he there with you now? Oh my God, are you okay? I'm coming!"

She hung up on me, and Caleb burst out laughing as I looked at him helplessly. "I...I've got nothing." He was still laughing, and I could admit it was a little bit funny.

"She doesn't even know where to go," Caleb said, still chuckling. "Hopefully, she brings a truck with her."

I tried to call her back, but Lily didn't answer. With a frustrated sigh, I turned my attention back to Caleb. "We should start walking. Whispering Pines is small; if she misses us at the house or here, she'll pick us up halfway."

"Or we wait here. We need the truck. We don't need your friend, as amusing as she is, to overreact completely when she can't find you here or at home." He tried to keep a straight face, but I could see the amusement dancing in his eyes. "She seems the kind of woman to blow things out of proportion, and we don't need the cops' attention on us."

"We don't, or *you* don't?"

He gave me a level look, and I saw him assess me one more time. "You can't walk back anyway. You look ready to drop."

He was right. I was exhausted. I didn't have the kind of healthy body that coped well with a mixture of excitement and adrenaline, and since I went home today, my body had been in one mode or the other. Leaning against the counter, I watched as Caleb stacked everything for loading into the truck or car, or whatever Lily brought, and I prepared myself for that conversation with her.

It wouldn't be easy. She knew me well and could read me like a book. A really simple book, with pictures. "We need a lie," I blurted to Caleb.

"For someone so high and mighty about the moral high ground, you surprise me," he quipped, looking over his shoulder at me.

"Shut up." Walking over to him, I grabbed his arm for support when I swayed. "Lily knows me. *Really* well. She won't believe I'm just taking off with you, especially after I told her I thought you were watching me and it creeped me out."

"So?" He didn't seem bothered at all. "People's opinions change all the time. Simply tell her we've had a chance to talk more and you like what you see. This trip will give you a chance to explore that further."

"If I were interested in you, which I am not, I would have told her today." I paused. "And I told her earlier that you left, without a goodbye, so there's that."

Caleb looked past me to the front door of the store just before it was hammered on.

"Shit. She's here!" Hurrying over to open it before Lily drew too much attention to me that I didn't need, I welcomed my best friend. "Hey."

She brushed past me, stopping in the middle of the floor when she saw Caleb casually checking the wrapped paintings, and I saw her look at the empty wall behind him.

"Hi." Caleb smiled as he straightened. "Lily, right? We haven't been properly introduced, but I've heard so much about you."

My best friend was stunned for a moment, and then she turned to look at me, mouthing *what the heck?* "Lily." She told him, walking forward and extending her hand. "I've heard not much about you, and what I did hear wasn't good."

Caleb looked at me and I looked down at my feet. "Well, that's disappointing, Willow."

Now they were both staring at me, and I would have liked very much just to leave. "Yeah, it's..."

"Complicated?" Lily was drilling me with her stare, and I looked to Caleb for help.

"Not complicated," Caleb assured her with a smile I'd never received from him. I hated that I noticed that, and I hated it worse that I felt a stab of jealousy. "Willow and I have been... testing the waters, would you say?" I caught myself from snorting and simply nodded. "It's been a back and forth and all kind of new." The smile he sent my way would make a girl's knees weak.

Not my knees. I wasn't stupid. Or that's what I was telling myself.

"New?" Lily was laser-focused on my face now, and I had nowhere else to look. "I thought it was more *complex*."

"Well, there's that too," Caleb admitted with a low laugh, but Lily was in seek-and-destroy mode. He could flash all the bashful smiles he wanted, but she had me in her sights now.

"Willow, can I talk to you?"

I flicked my eyes to Caleb, and his head dipped slightly. "Sure."

"Would it be presumptuous to start loading the truck?" he asked Lily with all the charm of a trickster. Lily was caught off guard, and I watched in disbelief as he plucked the keys from her outstretched hand when she said sure. "Thanks."

He came over to me and led me carefully to the stool I had been sitting on earlier. "Sit while you chat. You look worn out." His look of concern was all for her benefit, but even knowing that, I would still be fooled. Lily was, and I saw the moment my friend softened and her guard dropped.

Manipulative bastard.

"Sooo..." Lily waited until the door was closed when Caleb left carrying some of my paintings. "What the hell, Willow?"

I needed to lie and lie well. "It's all been a bit—"

"Sudden? Yeah, you don't say?" Lily pointed to the other stool across the room. "I sat there today and spoke to you about him, and you said hardly anything. You said that he *left*, and now it's 'I'm going on a road trip with the guy!'" Rubbing her temples, she looked at me. "Tell me straight, are you or are you not being kidnapped?"

The burst of hysteria escaped before I could control myself. Lily watched as I laughed, and I knew I needed to regain control, but I couldn't. It was all too much. The door opened and Caleb walked in, looking between me and Lily.

"She's tired," he told her. "The ME has really been draining her lately, did she tell you?"

Lily shook her head, looking at me with concern. "She never mentioned it at all."

"Yeah, she's been working so hard on these paintings. It's really one of the reasons I want to help her with this. She needs to rest, really rest, and I know a road trip sounds the exact opposite, but I think once we get there, it'll be good for her."

As my hysteria ebbed, I watched in fascination as Caleb wrapped my best friend around his finger.

"You know Willow's been painting more?" Lily asked dubiously.

"Yeah, of course." He flashed another smile. "She's been through about a box of pencils, her studio at home is almost overflowing with work, and"—he shook his head as he looked over at me—"there's hardly any food. Even her stash of candy has gone, and it's not even Alistair's fault."

Lily looked at me, stupefied that he knew so much about me, and I couldn't even tell her it wasn't how it sounded. Because he made it sound *so* much more than it was, and I was simply lost on what to do next.

Caleb rubbed the back of his head as he looked at Lily, all shy and bashful, and I wanted to throat-punch him. "I know you're worried I'm some mad stalker or something, but honestly, I'm just a guy who sees someone who needs a break and can help her with that. When Willow said she got a call from a buyer and didn't have a way to make the meeting, how could I not offer to help her?"

Lily was nodding. "It's really kind of you." They both looked at me. One with concern, one with self-satisfied smugness. "And you're okay with Caleb helping you out like this, Willow?"

I cleared my throat, forcing a wide smile. "I couldn't be happier."

Lily looked between the two of us. "Well okay, who am I to intervene in you getting some sales!"

Who indeed, I mused as I watched her high-five my self-proclaimed kidnapper. Who indeed.

# THIRTEEN

# Willow

WE WERE IN MY HOUSE, PACKING MORE PAINTINGS AND sketchbooks. Lily had handed over her keys to her truck with no questions asked. Well, she asked one question about insurance, and Caleb told her that he had some kind of insurance that insured him for most vehicles if the car owner had comprehensive insurance. I was sure it was bullshit and Lily would see through it, but she didn't. She told him that was *so* convenient, and I began to question her intelligence, because surely anyone with a brain cell would see exactly *how* convenient it was.

But I said nothing. She'd given me a hug and a look with too much glee and a very unsubtle head nod to Caleb when she told me to *have fun.*

If I kept telling myself the sooner I had answers, the sooner it would all be over, then at some point, it would all be over.

Right?

"You seem...off. Moody."

Looking up from the box I was putting my sketchbooks in, I gave him what I hoped was a blank look and resumed my work.

"Okay." Caleb dropped the packing tape with a sigh. "What is it?"

"I don't know what you mean."

"Well, you haven't played the dumb card up until now, so I guess it was due?"

Straightening, I glared at him. "The *dumb* card? Really?"

"Look, I told you to lie down, you refused. I told you to rest, and you insist on helping. You know why we're doing this, so why are you being difficult?"

"I'm not being difficult," I said through gritted teeth, "I'm *helping*."

"You're as helpful as a wet paper bag in a storm," he snapped. "For Luna's sake, just lie down already and rest. We have a long drive ahead, and I don't want you to be even sicker through it."

"Spare me the caring crap. You sold enough of that baloney to Lily!"

He watched me shrewdly. "Ah, I see, that's why you're pissed. Your friend didn't rescue you?"

With hands on hips, I confronted him. "I thought I didn't need rescued?"

He ignored me. "You think she should have noticed how out of character this was for you and raised an alarm." Caleb resumed packing. "I admit, I didn't think she'd buy it either," he said, patting his pocket where the truck key was with a smirk, "but I guess we were both wrong." His look was condescending. "Stings a little though, am I right?"

"Fuck you, Caleb."

I left my bedroom and went into the kitchen, leaving the

light off and running the tap to fill a glass of water. He didn't follow me, and I was grateful for that. I just needed some space.

He was right. I never expected Lily to swallow his bullcrap, but she ate it up like a starving man. Okay, that was harsh. I took a sip of water. No, that wasn't harsh. It was true. He flashed her a dimple, those white teeth, and all the package that he was, and she gobbled him up.

I was her *best friend*. She'd known me for years. She saw through me like I was transparent, but put Caleb in front of her, and she was thinking with her vagina.

"Wow, that's super harsh," I muttered. Movement in the trees caught my attention. I didn't know what intuition came over me, but I knew not to move.

Golden eyes watched me from the trees. My mouth ran dry as I met the stare of a predator.

Warmth at my back let me know Caleb was behind me. I almost leaned into him, but his hand on my shoulder pinned me in place.

"It's okay," he murmured into my ear. "Just a hunter. Don't let it show you are prey."

*What the actual hell was that supposed to mean?*

"Shh," he warned, his voice in my ear no more than a whisper. "I've got you."

The trees rustled once more, and the eyes were gone.

My body was trembling, and Caleb squeezed my shoulder. "It's gone." He moved away from me, and I sagged forward, my heart racing as if I'd just sprinted the hundred meters at the Olympics.

"What was that? A wolf?"

"Maybe a bear," he said with a shrug. He was already walking back to my bedroom.

"Since when do bears have golden eyes?" I snapped, following him.

"I dunno, Willow. Never seen one up close."

"You are so full of shit." His shoulders straightened as I spoke to him, but other than that, he looked unimpressed. "You're a hiker who's never come across a bear?"

"Not so unusual. I've found that the ones who do, have a scar or, I don't know, a *death* certificate to show for their encounter!" With arms crossed and that frown on his face, his stance of aggravation was one I was all too familiar with. "People hike, they don't go looking for bears. If they do, they're stupid." His look was cutting. "I'm a lot of things, but stupid isn't one of them."

"How did you know it was out there?"

"I didn't. I came to see if you were okay." He waved his hand casually over my body. "You tend to faint."

Bristling even more, I was ready to throw down with the asshole. "I am not weak," I growled at him.

"I never, at any time, said you were."

"So, it's a coincidence? You here and a wolf outside." I held my hand up. "Don't insult me by saying bear again."

He sucked his teeth, looking away briefly. "A coincidence? Yes. What do you think it was? Planned?" Caleb's sarcasm was scathing, but I wasn't perturbed.

"You seem very interested in the fact I draw wolves." Pointing behind me to the window, I carried on. "*That* was a wolf. Was it the one I drew?"

Throwing his hands up in the air, he turned away from me. "What kind of question is *that*? Do you hear yourself?"

"Do you?" Stepping forward, I moved closer to him. "You know so much more than you tell me, which wouldn't be hard, you tell me so little. But I know you know what was out there, and why. *Tell* me."

"I have nothing to tell you, except maybe..."

"Maybe?"

"You have a really active imagination."

My sketch pad sailed through the air as I threw it at him, and to my disgust, he caught it easily, packing it with the rest. "This box is full. We should leave soon."

"Tonight?"

"Do you think we did all this so we could nap?" Caleb picked the box up and carried it to the front door.

"For hours, you've said I was too tired to help, and now I'm road-tripping right now?"

Wiping his hands off the back of his pants, he nodded. "Lily had blankets in her truck. I've already made a bed in the back for you. You should be fine."

"You can't take over my life, Caleb."

"For fuck's sake, Willow, I was thinking of you. Not everything has to have an agenda attached to it."

"This whole entire thing, this, this *insanity* that my life's become since I met you, has had an agenda! If I'm suspicious of *everything*, it's *because* you made me this way!"

"No!" He was in my face so fast that I hadn't realized how close he had been to me. "I haven't known you long enough to *make* you anything. If you're suspicious and untrusting, that's on you, not me. Blame me for what you want, hate me, I don't care, but everything that's shit in your life, Willow, it's not on me."

He moved away, walking past me to get to the bedroom, and I heard him collect more boxes. When he came back, he dumped a tote bag at my feet. "Pack. We leave in twenty."

Wordlessly I snatched it off the ground. I didn't snipe at him that he wasted his time bringing it into the living room, because I was a mature woman. An *adult*. Even if he was a tiny-dicked prick who could kiss my ass. I didn't say a word, just packed my tote for a few nights and grabbed my toiletry bag.

When I came back to the main room, he was waiting for me.

"Ready?"

*No.* "Let's get it over with."

"Perfect."

He handed me my house key at the front door, and I again bit my tongue and took it off him, never mentioning the fact he had to go into my purse to get it.

As I opened the door, Caleb's hand slammed against the wood, closing it quickly. He pulled me into his body, his hand over my mouth, his lips at my ear.

"Shhh, we're not alone."

My instinct was to speak, and he must have known that, because he pressed his hand firmer against my lips. I nodded to let him know I understood.

Caleb was still as my panic rose, making me feel like I was coming out of my skin. He didn't react, just holding me tightly. After what may have been an eternity, he loosened his hold.

"Change of plan," he murmured. "We leave at first light."

He turned me to face him. The moon shining through the glass partition at the top of my doorway lit his features. "We'll leave later." He shook his head as he spoke. "We'll rest tonight and head off in the morning. Okay?"

His face was telling me one thing, which was contrary to his words. He mouthed *say okay* to me, so like the puppet I was, I nodded.

"Okay, sounds good."

Caleb pulled my unresisting body to the bedroom and guided us both to sit at the end of the bed. There had been some notebooks he had deemed unworthy of including, and he grabbed one and an old stub of a pencil.

*We wait and then we leave.*

Grabbing the notepad and pencil off him, I scribbled, *What is out there?*

When he didn't take the notebook off me, I shoved it into his chest. With a sigh, Caleb took the pencil off me.

*Danger.*

Wide-eyed, I looked up at him. Was he serious? *That* was his answer and nothing else? He gave me a look of impatience, and I didn't move away when he placed his arm around my shoulders. Was he trying to comfort me?

I should have trusted my instincts and moved away.

He wasn't a comforting man.

When I felt the sharp pain from his hand, I tried to jerk away, but instead, blackness swallowed me whole.

I woke up in the back of the truck, disoriented and slightly alarmed, scared to move.

"It's me," he spoke from the front, and I was at once both relieved and pissed off.

"You knocked me out?"

"You fainted."

"You're so full of shit," I grumbled, sitting up and looking around. "You did some Vulcan trick on me."

He looked at me, using the rearview mirror. "I did what?"

Rubbing the back of my neck and trying to stretch my legs, which had been curled up in the back seat, I still managed to glare at him. "Spock. He used to knock people out with his thumb." The fact he looked at me as if I was an idiot only cemented the fact I knew he had knocked me out. "You can look at me all wide-eyed innocence or confusion all you like, mister. I may know little about you, but I know you're a shady shit and you knocked me out."

Caleb grinned at me. "It's a simple process of knowing the right pressure points."

"It's dangerous. It's not good for a person, and you could mess up and kill me!" Ugh, I needed to walk around. My legs ached.

He gave me a flat stare. "Trust me, if I kill you, it won't be with my thumb."

Shaking my head, I leaned forward and hit him on the shoulder. "You think saying crap like that is reassuring? *If* I kill you? Seriously?"

"Did you have a good sleep?"

Oh my God, at this rate, I was going to kill *him*. "You knocked me out. It's not the same."

"Willow, I put you in the truck last night. You've been asleep for most of the journey. You came to after I put you in the truck, told me I'd be sorry, and then slept for eight hours."

When he saw I didn't believe him, he checked his mirrors and pulled over to the side of the road. Caleb got out of the truck and opened the back door.

"Come on, stretch your legs."

Unfamiliar trees were behind him, but they were still woods, and all of a sudden, I didn't want to get out of the truck.

"I won't hurt you," he grumbled. "Come on, out. You're going to need to pee, I expect."

His tone was so matter-of-fact that I felt stupid for the internal cringe I'd had when he said it. Slowly, I got out of the truck. Caleb caught me and steadied me when I landed on the ground.

"Last night?" It felt about right. My body felt groggy. But also...what the fuck? "How long are you planning on being away? This isn't my truck, Caleb!"

"I may have exaggerated. Day and a half almost." He saw my incredulous look, completely ignoring everything else I had said. "You woke up twice. You were definitely out of it, but the last sleep was a deep healing one. I could tell."

As he spoke, I remembered fragments of conversations, darkness, moving, Caleb telling me I was okay, he had me. Those I pushed far away.

"Okay. We'll talk about boundaries later." You had to know when to fight your battles, and right now wasn't the time. Looking around, I didn't recognize anywhere. "I'm a bit disoriented."

"We're in Colorado," he assured me. "I took a detour."

He didn't expand and I waited until my patience snapped. "A detour? So we weren't followed? Right?"

"Just..." Caleb suddenly looked weary. "Just go behind a tree, do what you need, and come back here, and I'll sanitize your hands." He handed me a pack of tissues.

"Um...I don't think so."

His eyes closed briefly. "Okay, let me make this easier for your current discomfort. It's been a day and a half, and this isn't the first time you've been awake, just the first time you've been extra precious about peeing in nature."

Horror swept over me as I understood what he was saying. "You *helped* me?"

He leveled me with a look. "I prefer the smell of pee on the outside of the truck, don't you?" He shook the tissues slightly. "Now, we can go for round three, or you can hurry this up and go yourself?"

Snatching the tissues off him, I practically ran behind a bush. Looking down, I stared at my jeans and sneakers. He helped me. Oh my God, what did he *see*? Pulling at my waistband, I saw my plain gray panties and felt a ridiculous sense of relief that they were semi-decent.

"What is wrong with you?" I scolded myself, pushing my jeans down. "He had his *hands* on you."

"I didn't."

I screamed in fright and almost fell over due to my jeans being at my knees. "Caleb!" I heard his chuckle. "You're an immature child!"

He was still laughing as I crouched with my ass hanging out my jeans in the woods. "I didn't touch you, not like that," he told me quietly. "I helped you to where you could *go*, I opened the snap on your jeans, and you did the rest yourself."

Swallowing back the lump in my throat, I felt my eyes fill, so desperate for him to be telling the truth. "Promise me?" It was barely a whisper, but I needed this one thing to be true, or I was sure I would break.

Caleb heard me and probably what I hadn't said out loud, for his voice was gentle when he spoke. "On this, I promise you, I didn't do anything to compromise you...or myself."

Closing my eyes, I believed him. "Thank you." My bladder let itself be known, as it had been poised for release for a while now. "Um...go away now and let me do this with some dignity at least."

I heard his snort of laughter and then the truck door opening and closing. "You're free to urinate," he called, and I blushed scarlet once more.

"I swear, just once, I'd love to punch you," I muttered bitterly, pulling one leg out of my jeans. Squatting and being one with nature is not a good look for women. Adopting a low, wide-legged squat, I held my jeans away from my leg in case of splash back, and after some coaxing, my bladder emptied.

When I was finished, and decent again, I emerged and stumbled when I saw him leaning against the truck with a bottle of hand sanitizer. He hadn't been inside the truck?

"Hands."

His eyes danced with laughter as he watched me bite my tongue, literally bite my tongue, to stop from demanding to know if he listened to me. Caleb dropped a generous amount of liquid on my upturned palms and then a little squeeze for himself.

"Hungry?"

Rubbing my hands together, I was about to say no when my stomach answered for me.

Caleb seemed satisfied with that as my response. "Good, me too. Let's eat."

# FOURTEEN

# Caleb

WILLOW SAT ON THE TAILGATE, HER LEGS DANGLING OVER the end, and I thought she was enjoying the freedom of moving her legs after being cramped in the back seat. She was still pale. The black circles under her eyes were faded but still there. I wondered if they ever truly cleared.

She ate her BLT in silence, looking around, her eyes curious as she took in the unfamiliar surroundings. I handed her an open bag of chips, and she ate them slowly along with her lunch.

"Have you always camped alone?" she asked me suddenly.

"Mostly."

Her attention was on the trees. "I wouldn't be able to settle," she told me, offering me the open bag of chips, and I shook my head. "I would hear every unknown sound and be sure I was going to get murdered."

Balling up my trash, I could see it as clear as day. "Yeah, I don't say this often, but I think you should forget camping and stick to hotels."

"Agreed."

She lapsed into silence, content to sit on the tailgate while I checked the truck over. I hadn't had much chance to check it out. It was fairly modern, so there was not much wrong with it. Guzzled gas, but all these vehicles did.

"You like the solitude, don't you?"

Looking up, I realized she'd been watching me. "I'm comfortable in my own company, yes."

Willow's lips curved into a smile. "Loner, it's the same answer."

"I guess it is." I went back to checking the condition of the truck. I heard her dismount from the back, and by the time I'd circled the vehicle, she was tidying up. "You ready or do you need the ladies again?" I jerked my thumb over my shoulder, and she swatted me away.

"I'll hold it if need be."

"Suit yourself, I'm going now." I stepped into the thicket and quickly took care of business. I hadn't lied before; she had been half asleep the other times, but I hadn't touched her or seen anything I shouldn't. I hadn't told her she fell over once, because there was nothing that I couldn't brush off her clothes and she didn't need to know. Fortunately, she'd toppled over *after* she was dressed, which had helped.

Walking back to the truck, I reached in and took out the sanitizer. Willow was frowning at the trees.

"Seal's broken," I told her. "You're better off just going now."

She didn't look my way, but she grabbed some paper napkins from the lunch bag and headed to the trees. Knowing she couldn't see me, I smiled at her back. She was funny with her silliness. My smile faded as I also thought about how frustrating she was at times.

We had a few hours left before I would need to leave the truck and call Alpha Cannon. He'd texted a couple of times, not at all happy when I told him there were wolves in the woods at Willow's house. He, like me, suspected that we would be followed.

Why were we being followed? Neither of us had that answer.

I heard her cursing and fought back the laughter. Willow in the woods was like watching a newborn deer trying to walk on ice. She was so far from her comfortable life it was amusing. I could sympathize in a way. I felt uncomfortable when I was in towns and cities.

Willow emerged from the trees, twisting and turning to check out her ass, and I guessed she'd fallen again.

"Stumbled over a tree root," she explained. When she saw my lips twitch, she glared at me. "Shut it."

Pressing my lips tighter together, I averted my head. "Wouldn't dream of saying anything. You ready?"

"Yeah." To my surprise, she opened the passenger door and climbed in.

"The back?"

"Nah," she said, looking at the back seat. "I spend so much time lying down. It's good to sit."

I could understand. "Okay, but if you need to rest, take the time to do it." She saw I was serious and rolled her eyes at me. "Willow?"

"Yes! I will, okay? Happy?"

"Are we ever truly happy?" I countered. She ignored me

and looked out the window. We drove in silence for a while, and I decided I'd waited long enough. "Any urges?"

Willow had been watching the road but turned to look at me. "Urges?"

"To draw, or paint?"

"Ohh." As she drew her knees to her chest, I almost scolded her to keep her feet off the seats when I remembered this wasn't my truck and Willow probably had a better idea of what Lily allowed in her truck than I did. "No urges." She thought about it. "Nope, all clear."

Was that good? "Good."

Willow bent her head, her chin resting on her knees. "Maybe you were right?"

"Don't sound too surprised." My dry tone caused her to chuckle.

"I actually thought it would be worse, being beside you and in your natural habitat."

My breath hitched at her terminology. "Natural habitat?" I tried to make my voice sound light.

"Yeah, I reckon you hike a lot."

Right, of course. "I do."

"You seem more relaxed in the woods."

*You have no idea.* "I like it," I told her simply.

"What's your job?" she asked me suddenly. "I can't believe I don't even know that."

Looking at her from the corner of my eye, I was skeptical. "Small talk? Really?"

"Well, it's either that or I ask why we're being hunted by wolves...but I was hoping to forget about that mind-fuckery for a while longer."

"Huh." With one hand on the wheel, the other resting on my thigh, I drummed my fingers against my leg. "I have some things that I'm good at, nothing that I can say I excel in."

"So...you're like a jack of all trades?"

"Sure."

"And you what? Move around a lot?"

"Yup."

"You're lying again, aren't you?" She was studying me intently.

"Does it matter?"

Willow turned her head, lowering her legs to the floor, and returned to staring at the empty road instead. "I guess not." Pushing her hair back, she didn't look at me. "I already got in the truck with you."

"You did."

The truck was silent once more, because really, what else was there to say?

***

WILLOW WAS ASLEEP AGAIN, HER HEAD DIPPING TO THE side at an angle that didn't look comfortable, and I contemplated pulling over again and putting her into the back seat. Her breathing was steady, and I envied her the rest. I'd been driving for hours. I may be a shifter, but I also needed sleep.

My wolf was also restless, and I knew I would need to shift soon to rid myself of the feeling of unrest. I couldn't shift when she was with me, though I would prefer to be in my wolfskin if those other wolves caught up with us.

I hadn't recognized their scents, even though admittedly,

few were known to me now. Not since I left that life behind me. An alpha like Cannon? You didn't need to know one to recognize one. And Cannon, he was infamous. An alpha power like his was to be envied, and he came to his power much younger than anyone expected.

No, you didn't need to know his scent before you knew who he was.

We passed through a small town, so small that I missed the signpost telling me where we'd just been, but a few miles down the road, I saw a motel. Glancing at Willow and feeling my tiredness pull at me, I decided to stop for the night.

I locked her in the truck while I spoke to the front desk, and when I returned, she was still sound asleep. Reluctant to wake her, I got the important stuff ready to take inside before I tightened the tarp covering the boxes in the truck bed. I could do it in two trips, Willow included, and I opened the room door to find something to prop it open, but looking in at the room, I hesitated.

A double bed took up most of the small room. Debating about asking for a room change, I heard a buzz and, turning, I saw the "no" had been illuminated over the "vacancy" sign.

"Fuck." With no other option, I dumped our stuff and then went and retrieved Sleeping Beauty from the truck.

She didn't stir as I lifted her and carried her inside, placing her on the bed. With the door locked, I took off her sneakers, pulled one of the blankets from the truck over her, and then used the bathroom to freshen up. After a quick shower, my teeth brushed, I climbed under the covers and went to sleep.

I heard her get up several hours later. She mumbled to herself the whole time about me having an inexplicable problem with not waking her up. She used the bathroom and then I heard her take her clothes off. When she came back out, I pretended to still be sleeping while she rummaged in her tote for her PJs. In just her shirt and panties, it took her a moment to find her nightwear. Hastily pulling them on, she kept looking over her shoulder at me in the dark to see if I was awake.

I was and she didn't have wolf sight, and the less she knew, the better.

The blanket was tossed to the floor, and after another conversation with herself, she pulled the covers back and got into bed. She tossed and turned for a good five minutes, and I was ready to put her back in the truck when she seemed to finally settle down, curled on her side, with her back to me.

"Comfy?"

Willow's yelp of alarm made me smile, followed by a strong curse word. "I'll talk to you in the morning," she muttered. Her threat, like her, was clawless. "I'm going to sleep."

"Mm-hmm." Closing my eyes, I settled in for a few more hours of sleep.

I woke up in the morning with Willow snuggled into my side. I had barely moved during the night, but her side looked like a tornado had wrecked it. Her head was on my chest, her arm across my lower stomach, and her thigh was hooked over mine.

Her warm body was comfortable next to mine, but I was a shifter, and we ran at higher temperatures, so adding her body heat to mine was not pleasant. Given that I knew she wouldn't appreciate waking up in this position, I contemplated fucking with her and waking her up. As I lay there, she pressed closer into me, murmuring as she slept. Watching her, I wondered if she was having one of her dreams or if she was just in a deep sleep.

Listening to her breathing and hearing her heart rate was slow and steady, I relaxed slightly. Moving her off me, I got up and out of the bed. She snuggled deeper into the pillow, a soft sigh escaping her. I watched her for a moment longer, trying to figure her out. She looked like she was resting, properly resting. Not the slumber of before where her body was replacing what it missed when she'd been starved of energy. No, this looked like she was enjoying a good sleep.

I went to the bathroom to get ready for the day. Coming out of the shower and back into the room, I saw she was still asleep, and I used the opportunity to change my shirt.

"You have a strong back," Willow murmured from the bed. "So clean and defined. I'd love to draw it."

As I looked over my shoulder, she saw my surprise at the compliment, and she shrugged before stretching. "I'm an artist; I can appreciate the human body and not be a pervert, you know."

Pulling on a clean navy T-shirt, I turned to face her. "Sleep well?"

Willow nodded, a yawn stealing her reply. "So good." Pushing the covers off, she got out of bed. "I need ten minutes and then we can go."

"Sounds like a plan."

Happy, rested Willow was so much easier to deal with. I made a note to keep her rested for the remainder of the journey. By the time she was ready to leave, wearing a fresh change of clothes, I'd repacked the truck.

Willow stopped in the walkway, her head turned, her nose sniffing the air. She looked at me with expectancy. "Bacon!"

"Already got us a table. You go ahead if you want."

She didn't need to be told twice. Her eagerness for her breakfast made me smile. When I joined her, she was already prepping a teapot, and there was a steaming cup of coffee waiting for me.

"I got us drinks, but the menu's there." She indicated to the menu on the side of the booth.

"Thanks."

We both ordered breakfast with all the works, and while she ate slower than I did, she still cleared her plate.

Sitting back, Willow patted her flat belly. "I feel good," she declared. "I always know, when I wake up hungry and the smell of food doesn't make me nauseous, that I'm going to have a good day."

"That's good." Was it? I had no idea, but she seemed happy, and who was I to ruin that for her when I'd already caused such upset to her normal routine?

"How much longer before we get to your friend of a friend's place?"

"A few hours." I finished my coffee, sitting back and waiting for her next questions. There were bound to be some.

"I know you said he's a friend of a friend, but have you met him before?"

"No."

Willow glanced away and I saw her uncertainty. "How do you know he's going to be any help?"

"I don't," I admitted. "But it's worth a shot." I looked at my empty coffee cup and back up at her. "What do you have to lose?" When she went to speak, I cut her off. "Do not say your life; you're better than that."

She blushed but her eyes crinkled with humor. "Didn't know I was so predictable..."

Saying nothing, I put some money on the table. "You done?"

"Yeah." Willow got up out of her seat. "You don't need to pay for everything, you know. I have money."

"Okay." We held each other's stare for a moment longer until I saw her slight nod.

Leaving the small diner to the side of the motel, Willow stopped and went back inside. The diner had a couple of shelves beside the cashier, offering snacks and magazines for sale. She came back out with a small bag and two magazines. Holding them up like they were the spoils of victory, she declared, "For the awkward silences." She smiled at me impishly as she sauntered past. "There'll still be silences but hopefully comfortable."

I said nothing as I followed her to the truck, but I had to admit it was a good idea.

She got in the front with me again, and after I'd been handed a bottle of water and she was comfortable with her own water and a fashion magazine, I drove us out of the parking lot.

Willow looked up at me and then at the radio. "Do you mind?"

"As long as it isn't country, pop, or shit."

"What's shit?"

"Everything else."

She frowned at me. "That leaves what? Nothing." She looked at me speculatively. "Let me guess, rock?"

"Sounds good to me."

She muttered *figures* under her breath but, in the end, found a classic rock station, and with the music on low, she reopened her magazine, and we fell into a comfortable silence.

Maybe the next few hours wouldn't be so bad after all. The shaman would hopefully have answers, and then Willow and I could go our separate ways. I could go back to my life and forget this ever happened.

Wishful thinking on my part that it would be so easy? Probably.

# FIFTEEN

## Willow

Long drives in the country weren't something I'd ever relished. With Jan and John, my foster parents, the only ones I'd ever used the term "parents" with, road trips had been few and far between. With anyone else, it meant I was being taken back to a care home. Or on my way to another foster family who didn't want me.

So, sitting in the front seat of the truck with Caleb, who took the saying *comfortable with silence* to a whole new level, was...pleasant.

I hadn't expected that.

I hadn't expected to relax, and I most definitely had not expected to enjoy it. I'd put the magazine down a while ago, simply content to watch the scenery go by while 90s grunge rock played on the stereo. I felt myself relax.

I had a desire to stare at Caleb, observing every detail to understand him. However, I knew I wouldn't get the opportunity, and I knew it was impolite to stare.

So I kept my attention on the outside, while I thought about everything I knew about the man inside. I went over every little thing he'd said or let slip. There wasn't much. He was his own special brand of mystery.

I had no clue about where he came from. When he found his way to Whispering Pines, I was completely unaware of his actual destination. It didn't seem to be my town. He was drawn there. Strangely enough, he seemed to be aware of my sketches of him, although he never revealed how he knew. I knew he had been observing me, but I wondered just how long he had been doing so. Was I the reason he came to Whispering Pines? Had he actually been going somewhere else?

Then there was the fact that he hadn't been staying anywhere in town. He didn't have a vehicle, and there was no camping gear with him. Where had he been staying? Had he been sleeping rough? But that couldn't be right. He was always so clean, and he had fresh clothes. He had a backpack. Maybe it held more than I gave him credit for?

"You think much harder, and you're going to have steam coming out of your ears from overheating your brain."

His dry voice caused me to jump. "Wh-what?"

"Your thoughts are very loud." Caleb looked over at me, and I grabbed the opportunity to twist in my seat and give him my full attention.

He had a laid-back approach when it came to driving. With one hand on the steering wheel and the other in his lap, he maintained a relaxed posture. He appeared at ease, with his shoulders loose, head slightly tilted, and his long legs stretched out comfortably. His hair was neatly styled, the longer length suiting him, with a few strands curling under his ear. The stubble on his face wasn't quite a full beard, but it was more than a typical five o'clock shadow. His clothing comprised familiar pieces, including a plaid shirt over a navy tee, worn jeans, and black boots.

He looked like either an extra from *Supernatural* or a logger.

Maybe that's why he'd been in town? Was he a logger? Working at Lily's dad's plant? That would fit.

"Did you work for Lily's dad?"

Caleb glanced at me and shook his head. "Who's Lily's dad?"

"He owns the lumber mill on the outskirts of town."

"A lumber mill." His top lip curled into a sneer. "No, I wouldn't work for people who cut down trees."

He was an environmentalist? "You're a tree hugger?" I couldn't hide the surprise in my voice.

"Rather be a hugger than a feller."

No way. There was no way in God's green earth that Caleb Foster was a hippie.

Biting my lip, I watched him. It would explain the minimal living. The camping outside. Holy shit. "You're a hippie?"

"I am?"

"Okay, hippie may be a stretch too far. You don't give off the bohemian vibes, and you always smell fresh, plus you eat meat."

"I think you need to reassess your stereotypes," he chided me.

"Yeah, probably. Okay, so I suppose I should say that you're an environmentalist."

Caleb seemed to think about it, and I saw the small smile. "Maybe I am."

Leaning back in my seat, I continued to stare at him. "That shocks me."

"You can't see me caring about the environment?" he asked me casually.

"No." I thought about it. "Maybe. Honestly, I pictured something else, like you in a suit wouldn't look amiss." Caleb shuddered. "You have CEO vibes," I declared with a laugh.

"I do?" He appeared affronted by the comment.

"Yeah, you're all bossy and commanding. You give orders like it's second nature to you."

"So, because I have leadership skills, that automatically puts me in a suit amidst corporate America?" He shook his head, but he was smiling. "I knew we weren't friends, but there's no need to insult me."

I laughed at his outrage and got comfy in the seat as I watched him. "You're funny," I told him. "You should show that more often." I sat up with excitement. "Ooh, you're a stand-up?"

"Stand-up what?"

"Comedian! Do you work the circuit?"

"Willow..." He reached over and patted my knee. "Stop. I'm just a guy who likes to travel and picks up odd jobs where he can. Okay?"

It wasn't okay. I knew there was more to him, but I didn't know what it was. "No," I protested, watching the light humor disappear from Caleb's face. "I don't believe you're *just* a guy."

"Well, I'm flattered, but I am."

Once again, silence filled the air between us, but this time, I couldn't tear my eyes away from him, even though he seemed completely disinterested in me. Eventually, I shifted my focus and leaned over to reach into the back seat, grabbing my tote. I pulled out my sketchbook and rummaged through the contents of my bag, finally unearthing my pencil case. With the book open in front of me, I felt the smooth texture of the clean page beneath my pencil as I sketched.

"Really?" Caleb grunted, and I noticed his hand tightening on the wheel.

"I have a captive subject," I teased. "It's not an opportunity I am going to let pass me by." Making strong strokes with the pencil, I drew his profile. The details I could concentrate on later, but right now I wanted to capture the tilt of his head, the way the sunlight lit his features, the way his lips were pressed together in annoyance.

"You're smiling," he murmured, glancing at me.

"You trying not to snap at me is funny," I told him without lifting my head from my sketchbook.

"Don't you have to have someone's permission before you draw them?"

"Do you?" I murmured. "Is it the same permission you need before entering someone's home without their knowledge?" I looked up at him. "Is that what you mean?"

Caleb met my look of feigned innocence with a scowl. "Yeah, something like that," he grumbled.

"That's what I thought." Dipping my head, I hid my smug smile.

I sketched while he drove. There were no more complaints, and the silence became comfortable again. I knew Caleb wasn't completely at ease, but he had no other option but to accept it. I reluctantly acknowledged that he handled that resigned acceptance better than I had.

Deep in concentration, I was adding his eyelashes when the truck swerved erratically. An arm as firm as iron pushed me into the seat, and my sketchbook went flying as Caleb controlled the spin of the truck with one hand.

"Caleb!" The screech of tyres drowned out my scream.

The truck shuddered to a halt. I could smell the burning rubber on the asphalt, and peeling my eyes open, I looked at the man beside me.

Caleb's arm was still on my chest. He slowly lowered it, his attention focused on the road ahead. Following his gaze, I gasped loudly as I saw a large brown wolf in the middle of the road.

He told me to stay put as he turned off the engine. It took a moment for his words to sink in, and by the time I snapped out of my shock, he had already jumped out of the truck, leaving me unable to stop his madness. With my jaw dropped, I watched him walking towards the wolf, and I held my breath, fully expecting it to pounce. However, the wolf simply repositioned itself as Caleb got closer.

Still, I anxiously waited for the wolf to launch itself at him, or at the very least, I expected it to snap at him. However, to my surprise, it remained motionless. A low growl echoed from where they stood in a standoff. Caleb obstructed my view of the wolf's head, preventing me from seeing it fully.

Convinced I'd hit my head off the dashboard, I watched as the wolf suddenly hopped backward as if struck, and then it looked as if it tried to dodge past him. Caleb took a step to the left, and again I heard the growl, and fear tingled down my spine from the menacing sound.

Filled with desperation, I impulsively seized the handle,

fully intending to sprint to Caleb's aid, although I had no clear plan in mind of what to do once I got there. However, my impulse to throw myself between Caleb and a wolf ceased when I saw the wolf run away.

It *ran away*.

I didn't understand what I was seeing. I shook my head, convinced that I must be dreaming. Shaky fingers pressed against my forehead, feeling the beads of sweat on my brow, convincing me I was awake. Caleb remained in the center of the road, facing away from me. His posture was strong, standing tall with a straight back, squared shoulders, and a held-high head, but I noticed his hands clenched into fists by his side.

I didn't know why, but I could sense fury in the air, and a small voice in the back of my head told me it was coming from Caleb.

After a few swallows, some moisture returned to my mouth. Caleb had left the truck door open, and when I called his name, he slightly turned his head to show he heard me, but he didn't fully turn around.

"Caleb?" My voice sounded stronger the second time I called for him. "Come back to the truck."

I saw him rolling his head from side to side, and then he glanced to his left and right. My eyes frantically scanned the surroundings, finding nothing noteworthy, yet I couldn't tear my gaze away from the man in front of me for too long.

Caleb eventually turned around, lowering his head in a way that obscured his features, and headed back towards the truck. I realized there was smoke, and some fragmented part of my brain told me it was from the tyres after Caleb had skidded to a halt.

At the truck door, he scanned the wooded areas again, and then with a grunt, he got back into the truck. He didn't speak as he restarted the engine, nor did he look at me as he placed his arm across the back of the seat when he turned to look out the rear window as he reversed and straightened the truck.

I expected him to leave saying nothing, but instead, he parked the truck on the side of the road. Caleb massaged the back of his neck before finally facing me. "You okay?"

The casualness of his question pushed me over the edge.

"Am I okay?" I screeched at him. "What the *fuck* was that?"

"Willow, calm down."

"Calm down?" I felt as if my entire body was vibrating. It might have been with anger or adrenaline. Perhaps it was both. "I will not *calm* down. Are you *out of your mind?*" I needed out of this truck. As I attempted to exit, he forcefully grasped my arm, yanking me back into the seat. "Caleb!"

"Unless you missed it, there was just a wild wolf on the road. Be smart, stay inside the truck."

My eyes were as wide as they could go. "Unless I *missed it,*" I yelled at him. "I didn't miss the big scary wolf on the road or that *you* got out of the truck and walked up to it and *made it run away!*"

Caleb was watching me carefully, but he was calm. He looked perfectly at ease. "You're hyperventilating."

"Really?" I was panting. "D'ya think?"

"You're in shock."

"Mm-hmm." My heart was racing, and I couldn't catch my breath. The tightness in my chest made me gasp.

"Willow, I need you to relax."

The grunt I answered with was more pain than the derisive snort I was going for.

"Willow." Caleb reached for me, gently cradling my face in his large hands and making me meet his gaze. His brown eyes exuded warmth. "Calm down." His voice was soft and low as he gently instructed, "Take a deep breath with me."

In unison, we breathed in and out, and I sensed the panic releasing its grasp on me. As I attempted to move away, Caleb pulled me towards him, until we were intimately close, and I could feel his breath on my lips. We carried on with the breathing exercises until he moved his head back slightly. "Better?"

I gave a nod. Although I still felt a bit unsteady, the chest pain had subsided, and even though I was aware of my anxiety, I wasn't in a state of panic.

Caleb sat back. "Good." He looked around. "We need to move. There may be more."

A spike of panic jolted me forward. "Wolves?"

"Yeah." He put the truck in drive. "Now that you're calmer, we can talk and drive."

I didn't know where to start, and we'd actually been driving for about five minutes before I found my voice again. "What just happened?"

If I thought my question came out of nowhere, Caleb was ready for me. "A wolf was on the road."

"You got out of the truck and confronted it..." I still couldn't believe it.

"Done a lot of hiking in these parts. They say if you stare the wolf down, it won't attack." His attention was on the road, and he didn't look at me as he drove. "Wolves are pack creatures," he told me easily. "But they have a leader. An alpha. They say that if you stare a wolf down as if you're its leader, they will submit."

"That's stupidity." I couldn't wrap my head around it. "No, that's not stupid...that's absurdity. Madness!"

"Never been accused of being sane." He glanced at me. "It worked, didn't it?"

I was at a loss for words. I wanted to scream at him. I wanted to demand a better explanation because I was sure there was one. Though God knew, I didn't know what. A whirlwind of emotions swept over me—confusion, fear, and an overwhelming sense of *relief* that he was safe. I didn't know which one to address first. The latter reaction won, and I impulsively threw myself at him, despite him being behind the wheel, wrapping my arms around him.

Caleb grunted in response as I fell on top of him, his arm instinctively coming around me as I nestled my head into his neck.

"Willow?" The combination of his hesitant and worried demeanor stirred something inside me, and I burst into tears. "Shit," Caleb muttered, but rather than pushing me aside, he embraced me even tighter.

As I scrambled to move closer, he pulled me into his embrace, offering comfort as I released my shock and fear through my sobs. It had hit me hard to see how unconcerned he was about his rash actions, and I was filled with fear at the thought that something bad could have happened to him.

That I was concerned about him and didn't know how to handle it could be postponed until I was in a better place emotionally. I quickly acknowledged that the level of adrenaline I'd just experienced was not something my body was used to, and the exhaustion that followed caused me to crash sooner than I anticipated.

I was aware of the truck coming to a halt, and Caleb gently moved me away from him. The sound of doors opening and closing didn't fully rouse me from my sudden fatigue, nor did the sense that I was being lifted from my seat by powerful arms. I could feel the cool breeze on my skin before I was gently placed in the back of the truck.

"You're okay." His familiar voice settled me. Caleb covered me with a blanket and gave my shoulder a comforting squeeze. "Sleep."

Once he sat back down in the driver's seat, the truck started moving, and I fell asleep, aware that there was something not quite right about his earlier explanation, though I couldn't quite put my finger on what.

I suspected that Caleb knew a lot more than he was sharing with me. While drifting off to sleep, I made a vow to myself that I would get answers when I woke up.

# SIXTEEN
## Caleb

WHILE SHE WAS IN A DEEP SLEEP, I PARKED THE TRUCK, grabbed my jacket, and locked the truck after I got out.

Cannon answered on the first ring. "What is it? Where are you?"

"I had a welcome committee on the road this morning." The rage I'd kept tempered surfaced white hot within me. "A fucking shifter in the middle of the road! What the fuck is your problem? I told you I was coming!"

"Be careful how you speak to me, Caleb." Cannon's voice was low and calm but with unmistakable authority.

"And if I'm not, then what? Are you planning to send more reinforcements?" I was reckless with anger. "She could have been killed!"

"But she wasn't." He was still calm. His tone grew cold as he stated, "I didn't send anyone. I trust you to come in with her yourself. I take it you did not reveal yourself to her?"

"I'm not stupid," I spoke through gritted teeth. "If not you, who?"

"I don't know."

This was bullshit. "This is Pack Council bullshit," I hissed down the phone at him. "I told you they were fuckers."

"I don't think this was them." I heard him sigh. "Just make it here, and we'll sort things out once you arrive."

My gut twisted. I'd avoided pack for a long time. For good reason. I tilted my head back and gazed at the sky.

She wouldn't be safe there.

Would she be safe anywhere?

"You're driving through pack territory," Cannon calmly stated, as if he could read my mind. "Pack patrol will catch your scent. Did you stop to consider it was *you* that they were checking out?"

I hadn't. I looked back at the truck, feeling torn about what to do. "She's vulnerable."

"More so with just you at her side, Caleb."

My foot bounced as I mulled it over.

"Caleb?" Cannon's low warning was enough for me.

"We're not coming. End of discussion." I hung up on him and quickly turned the phone off. Packs had different ways of operating, but most of them had some members who went to college and worked like humans to earn money for their pack. I wouldn't turn on the phone until I swapped the SIM card since every pack knew about human technology.

I walked back to the truck and opened the back door, being careful not to wake Willow. I grabbed her phone from her bag and switched it off.

I'd need to change this truck. I didn't doubt that Cannon knew what mode of transport I'd picked.

Worry gnawed at my gut as I considered if I was overreacting, but looking into the back seat at the woman who lay asleep there, I was sure I was doing the right thing.

Willow was different from most humans. She was fragile. I had to protect her...even though she was the reason she gained the attention of a powerful alpha.

I got in the truck, made the turn, and went back the way we came. She was gonna see a shaman—she would have to—but I decided to try to find answers on my own first.

The pack was our last option, not the first.

I didn't lack resources on my own. I had some connections. I hadn't talked to them in years, but that didn't mean I couldn't.

Feeling more confident about my decision, I settled into the seat, ready for the long drive. We'd go back to Whispering Pines. The human numbers would be to her benefit. The paintings, we'd put somewhere that Lily wouldn't see them, and I'd stay with Willow, and we'd figure this out together.

Our relationship was not the smoothest, I knew that. She didn't like me, and I hardly put up with her. Yet, she'd cried earlier, and whether it was conceited or not, I think a few of those shed tears were for me. I went against the order of an alpha for her sake, so although we weren't friends, there was more than mere indifference in our relationship. We would learn to coexist until this matter was resolved.

While driving down the empty roads, I was conscious of the occasional presence that sprinted through the woods alongside the truck. Observing another shifter on their territory, the border patrols were content to see me leave quickly and not stay in territories where I was unwelcome. Maybe Cannon had been right; maybe it was me the wolf made a stand for. Either way, I wasn't willing to chance it.

Willow woke a few hours later, and I saw a deeper effect of her ME. Her complexion was ashen, devoid of color, and she displayed signs of extreme exhaustion. She had a sore and swollen throat, and when she hoarsely mentioned needing lozenges, I immediately changed direction and drove to the closest town to find a pharmacy. Throughout the entire journey, she stayed in the back seat, constantly feeling lightheaded and dizzy.

The owner of a small bed & breakfast on the edge of a wood welcomed us. She was curious but respectful with her silence when I carried my *wife* past her and up the stairs to our room. Willow's groans echoed through the room as I gently placed her on the bed, and my gut churned with anxiety until I relented and sought the doctor in town.

I described her condition to him, and after a thorough examination, he reassured me she was experiencing a severe episode and needed to rest and recover. I checked my wallet when he was gone and she was still asleep, finding that I had thirty-one dollars left.

Rooms, food, and doctor visits had severely hit my finances. The latter, I suspected Willow would tell me I hadn't needed, but it was my watch she got sick on, so she could bite me.

"Shit." I flung the wallet onto the bed and sank into the chair. I'd paid for two nights, and because I said Willow was my wife, we ended up with a double bed once more.

Willow was already under the covers, curled up and peaceful. I needed to go find a quick way to make some cash.

I knew what I needed to do. I'd done it before, and looking down at myself, I knew I needed to change clothes first. I found a dark gray Henley at the bottom of my pack. I switched my belt to a custom one with a small knife holder—you never knew when you might need one. I tucked another knife into my boot, making sure my jeans concealed it.

I had a black jacket that I unrolled, shook out, and slipped on. I double-checked that Willow was still asleep, and then I went ahead and opened her toiletry bag and found a little tub of hair product. I took a little and smoothed my hair back with both hands.

There was a small notepad next to the telephone. It was a nice little detail. An actual landline, when was the last time I'd seen one of them? I left a note for my *wife*, telling her I wouldn't be long, and then I snuck out of the lodge without the owner noticing.

The journey into the town was quiet and uneventful, with only a few cars passing by. The drivers who slowed down to check if they recognized me quickly moved on when they realized I was a stranger.

Finding the bar was not difficult at all. Despite the disappointing quietness, the night still held promise. I found a spot at the bar and asked for a beer. Then it was simply a matter of waiting and seeing who I could con.

The clientele remained low-key until around ten o'clock when four loud-mouthed jerks fell through the door. The bar, which was already quite subdued, became even more silent, and I discreetly watched as they aggressively pounded on the counter to be served. I half expected the bartender to refuse them, but although he looked pissed off, he served them four beers and four whisky chasers.

The way they confidently strolled through the bar to the

pool tables in the back made me believe that this night might actually have some potential.

I sat through their profanity-laden conversations and rowdy teasing, which oscillated between playful and outright aggressive, for a good twenty-five to thirty minutes. As soon as the leader of the group, who I had quickly identified as the loudest one upon their arrival at the bar, confidently proclaimed that his friends were all worthless and not worth challenging, I swiftly turned my chair around, ready to get his attention.

"Hey, man, don't," the bartender warned me quickly.

"You looking for a new player?" I shouted across the bar, ignoring the man behind me.

The four men grew quiet, and their leader shifted his focus to me. He had a tall stature, possibly around six feet, with a lean build that revealed some visible muscle. He had both arms covered in tattoos, with some extending to his neck. I saw he even had a teardrop tattooed on his cheek. You had to love the bad boy cliches.

"You good?" he asked with a sneer on his face, though it didn't manage to make him appear intimidating if that was his intention.

"I play." I didn't stand up yet, and I changed my ploy from hustling to playing to his ego. "You decent?"

He looked at his friends, the sneer morphing into a smirk. "I play."

Nodding, I leaned back against the bar. "I'm game, you?"

He licked his lower lip. One of his friends stepped into him, whispering into his ear, "He looks like he can play, Ray."

Ray pushed him back a bit. "A hundred says I beat your ass."

"Two hundred says you don't."

"You can't bet in the bar," the guy behind the bar said half-heartedly, and I got the impression his protest had fallen on deaf ears too many times.

"Let's play," Ray told me.

As I approached the pool table, I didn't pay any attention to his three friends, who were all giving me dirty looks, each one trying to intimidate me in their own way. I wanted to tell them I'd seen pups with more bite than they had.

"Two hundred?" Ray confirmed.

"Too much?" I asked, taking a pool cue from the rack. I shrugged. "Fair enough, drop it to one."

"I got two Benjamins, man."

"Good." He didn't ask me if *I* had the money, which was his first mistake. His second was letting me win the toss.

The bar was so quiet you could hear a pin drop as I broke the rack, and the balls went everywhere. I kept my smile hidden when the first ball went straight into the side pocket. Ray hadn't realized yet that I'd just set the tone for the game. I strolled around the table, acting like I was scoping out my next move. With a seamless stroke, the next ball effortlessly found its way into the corner pocket, and the cue ball smoothly rolled into position to line up for the next shot.

The four boys were now ominously quiet as well. With a controlled touch, I successfully sank my third ball, and as I turned to face Ray, I noticed his sneer disappear as he witnessed me lining up shot number four, which smoothly found its way into the opposite corner pocket.

It left the table open, and with slow measured care, I pocketed my fifth shot.

"Shit," the guy who'd whispered to Ray muttered, and one of the others nodded.

After taking a drink from my beer, I lined up the next shot. Another ball pocketed, leaving just two balls between me and victory. The next ball was positioned at a challenging angle, and with the tension rising from the group of four men in front of me, I pretended to make a mistake, stepping back and sipping my beer.

Ray sprang into action, successfully sinking three of his own balls, but he failed to make the fourth shot. He'd also moved my seven-ball, and I nailed it home with a firm, confident strike. After that, I had only the eight-ball left on the table.

"Name the pocket," one guy demanded.

The tip of the cue gently tapped the farthest corner. I glanced at Ray to see if he noticed, and the swift jerk of his head told me he did.

Taking a deep breath, I lined up for the final shot. With a perfect strike, the cue ball sent the last ball rolling easily into the corner pocket.

The bar was eerily quiet.

"Good game," I said, laying my cue on the felt. "Thanks."

"You cheated."

I anticipated it, yet his predictability still brought a smile to my face. "Did I? How?"

Ray turned to his friends for support, only to find that they all avoided his gaze. "You just did."

With a tired sigh, I shrugged off my jacket, fully aware of how the Henley shirt I was wearing emphasized my physique. "Damn, I was hoping you'd be different."

"What do you mean by 'different'?" It was the friend who

spoke, the one who I suspected was the only one with any intelligence.

"Your friend just called me a cheater, even though we all know I won fair and square. So that means he either doesn't have the green to pay me or he wants to cheat *me*, and I want my money, so I have to kick his ass." I met each of their stares. "I know you won't play fair, so I'll beat *all* your asses. Are we on the same page?"

Ray dropped his cue on the table. "Just give him the money. This place is a shithole anyway. We're outta here."

The friend casually tossed the money onto the table, and as they exited, one of them carelessly knocked over a bar stool. Once they were out of sight, the remaining customers started cheering and laughing.

I gathered the money, placed it in my wallet, and then put my jacket back on. I restored the knocked over bar stool and locked eyes with the bartender at the bar.

"Be careful when you leave," he said while placing a new bottle of beer on the counter. "Ray is someone who doesn't handle losing well." When I went to pay, he shook his head. "Hell no, that was the first time in a long time the little shit's been quiet. You earned that," he said, nodding to the bottle. "Enjoy."

I received congratulations from a few more people before I departed not long after. The bartender reminded me once again to stay safe as I left, and I thanked him for the warning as I said goodbye.

Even without any prior notice, I would have stayed alert as I walked back to the bed and breakfast. Ray and his friends would never win awards for subtlety. The first one jumped me when I rounded the corner, but I was ready for him. While I was in the middle of punching the first one, the second guy rushed towards me. Surprisingly, the third person, whom I'd believed to be somewhat intelligent, jumped from a roof but failed to hit me or his companion. A loud scream accompanied the sound of a bone snapping upon his landing.

Which just left me and Ray.

While one friend was rolling around in self-inflicted pain, the other two were on the ground groaning. I couldn't help but grin. "I'll let you have the first hit," I told him. With my fists raised, I gestured for Ray to approach by opening my right hand and motioning him forward. "Let's do this."

Big Bad Ray caught me off guard for the first time that evening. He turned on his heel and ran. At first, I thought it was a trick and he would come back with more sycophants and minions, but then I realized he'd just run away.

With a smile on my face, I strolled back to the lodge, knowing there wouldn't be any more surprises.

The owner noticed my arrival, quickly covering her initial confusion, and greeted me with a smile. Upon entering the room, I quietly locked the door behind me, careful not to disturb Willow, who was still fast asleep.

Only after I had changed for bed did I notice that she had been awake while I was gone. The notepad had an addition since I left it on the nightstand beside her.

In the sketch, I was in a bar, sporting a confident grin, with my gaze fixed straight ahead. I looked at it, then at her, and ripped the paper off of the notepad, crumpled it, and threw it away.

As I climbed into bed, I couldn't help but let out a frustrated sigh. I had hoped that a couple of beers would help me relax and fall asleep, but seeing that sketch only pissed me off again.

It took a long time for me to fall asleep, and when I finally did, the only thing I could see when I closed my eyes was Willow smiling in her sleep. Like she knew she'd pissed me off and was happy she had.

Which was stupid. It was more likely that she would have no recollection of waking and drawing her little sketch.

Well, that's what I convinced myself before sleep took over.

SEVENTEEN

*Willow*

WHEN MY ME GOT BAD, PROPERLY *BAD* BAD, I COULD LOSE days to my bed, where the never-ending cycle of sleep, fatigue, aches, and pains never lessened. When the cycle began to break, there would be glimpses of light at the end of the tunnel. Sometimes this break would be false hope, and the cycle would gain in intensity. Which this most recent spell seemed to be.

I was aware of Caleb during my bad spell. I knew he was there, but the brain fog and my exhausted state barely let me acknowledge him. My brain was sending signals to my body to let him know not to worry, but my receptors were going through a current mutiny and weren't open to any correspondence.

I was awake in bed but hadn't yet opened my eyes. I felt like shit, but I knew the difference between a ME attack and coming out of a ME attack. The room was silent, and I lay there feeling guilty because I knew I would have been an inconvenience to Caleb, and I felt guilty for taking a moment to appreciate the quiet of the room, the comfort of the bed and...the smell of fresh bread?

Opening my eyes, I looked around the room. Floral patterned wallpaper, white gauzy drapes hanging loose over a six panel sash window. Pushing myself up was an effort, but I managed, immediately looking at the floor. Thick-looking deep-pink plush carpet.

Caleb had said his friend was a *he* that he was taking me to. I knew all about diversity and inclusion, but the person who decorated this room was a woman.

Pushing the covers off me, I tried to get up to find out where we were. I was in a T-shirt and panties. I didn't even want to ask, but I knew if Caleb provoked me, I would.

Opening the door, I came face-to-face with a middle-aged couple coming out of the door opposite me. They were both well-dressed, and I registered the woman's huff of disapproval at the same time as I saw the man's appreciative look at my legs.

"Sorry!" Hastily shutting the door, I waited until the grumbling faded, and then hesitantly opened the door again. Seeing the number six on it, I closed it again.

I was in a bed and breakfast. Going back to the bed, I searched for a note from Caleb to tell me what was happening. Surely he'd left one? When I found nothing, I searched for my jeans.

The door opened and, turning swiftly, I saw Caleb running his eyes over me. Conscious of my bare legs, I jumped on the bed, scrambling under the covers.

Shooting me a quizzical look, Caleb frowned. "What's wrong with you? You see a bug?"

"Where are we? Where's my clothes?"

"We're at a B&B. Your jeans are drying in the bathroom. How are you feeling?" Caleb leaned against the door as he watched me.

"Um...I feel okay." I saw his look. "Okay, I feel a bit wrung out still, but it's to be expected. How long have I been down? Two days?" I guessed.

"Three." He checked his watch. "You think you could eat?" When I nodded, he opened the other door, which I guessed was the bathroom. Leaning in, he came back out with my jeans. Caleb scrunched the waistband a few times. "Feel dry." He tossed them onto the bed. "I'll ask Shelby if she'll hold on before she shuts down breakfast."

"Shelby?"

"Owner, real nice woman." He was watching me again. "Five minutes?" When I nodded, he flashed a brief smile. "Good. See you down there." He'd just left when the door opened again, and he popped his head around the door. "Oh, forgot to say, if anyone asks, you're my wife, okay?" When I stared at him mutely, he seemed to take that for acceptance. "Great. Five minutes, remember."

"I'm his what now?" For the second time, I got out of bed. Picking my jeans up, I took them back to the bathroom, taking it all in as I freshened up. My toiletry bag was spread around the counter and in the shower cubicle. The counter beside the sink and the shower tray had *my* things. The only thing I could see that belonged to Caleb was the handheld toothbrush sitting in a plastic cup with a half-empty tube of toothpaste beside it.

Washing my hands, I noticed my hair was clean if not a little flat. My skin, while deathly white, looked nourished.

"He washed me?" Baring my teeth, I inspected them, and

then holding my hand up in front of my face, I exhaled. Stale breath, not rancid, but still, not three days' worth.

Pulling my jeans on, I quickly brushed my hair and then my teeth. From my tote, I shook out a T-shirt and quickly changed. After finding a hair tie, I put my hair in a ponytail. That took a lot out of me, and I rested my head against the door as the room swam a little. Grabbing my notebook, I noted I'd had a three-day attack and closed it again. I would get more information out of Caleb. When I was steady, I opened the door only to step back when Caleb appeared at the top of the stairwell.

"Thought you may want a hand," he explained as he approached. "Stairs are a little steep."

"You washed me?" I asked him in a low voice.

"Sponge bed bath." He looked at me and then the stairs. "How do you want to do this? Me first so if you fall, you land on something soft? Or you first so if you fall, I can grab you?"

"Tell me they don't believe you're married to me."

"Why wouldn't they?" Caleb ran his hand over his hair. "It's believable."

Squinting at him, I couldn't read his expression, but he looked...slighted? "Are you *insulted* that I'm questioning it?"

He huffed and broke eye contact. "Are you going first or second?"

It took me a moment to understand what he was asking, and then he decided for me by simply stooping and picking me up bridal style. "Caleb! Put me down!"

He ignored my hissed whisper and went down the stairs quickly, barely jostling me. At the foot of the stairs, he put me back on my feet and immediately stepped back. "You good?"

"Ah, there you are!"

Peering past Caleb, I saw an older woman wearing dark gray slacks and a deep-pink lightweight cardigan over a light gray T-shirt. Her trimmed, tidy, shoulder-length hair was clean, with not a strand out of place. She had a round open face, and she looked like a nice lady.

"Shelby." Caleb half-turned. "Meet my wife, Willow."

I was still trying to digest the *wife* word when Shelby stepped around Caleb, holding out her hand. "So nice to finally meet you properly," she told me warmly. "You've had this one here so worried about you."

Caleb cleared his throat, giving me a pointed look, and I realized that Shelby was still holding her hand out to me. Quickly grabbing it, I shook it. "Hi, nice to meet you."

"Now, I was almost finished serving," Shelby told us as she walked away, and my *husband* snagged my elbow so we'd follow. "But when Caleb said you might be up to coming downstairs today for a bite to eat, I agreed to serve past my usual nine-thirty." Looking over her shoulder at us, she gave us an apologetic look. "Of course, it's not what I usually prepare. Some things had already run out, so it is a poor representation of my usual breakfast, Willow."

"It'll be enough," Caleb reassured her, and I gawked at the pleasant, mild-mannered male in front of me. He saw my look and not so subtly squeezed my elbow. "Willow never has a big appetite at the best of times," he added.

Shelby led us into a bright sunroom, and I tried to hide my wince at the sunlight.

"Well, today, let's see you eat more than toast, dear," she told me with a beatific smile. "I'll be back with your tea."

Gently patting Caleb's shoulder, she gave it a slight squeeze. "And more coffee for you, I know."

She left us alone and I leaned across the table to glare at Caleb. "What is this? I feel like I've woken up in the twilight zone!"

He huffed, buttering a slice of toast that was already on the table. Caleb took a hearty bite, even while he frowned at me. "I'm being nice so my sick wife can enjoy a cooked breakfast. You need to eat, and eat lots."

"Why aren't we where your friend is?"

"I changed my mind."

When it was quite clear he wasn't going to elaborate, I tried a different tactic. "So why aren't we home?"

"Because you became ill, and I took a detour." He finished his toast and buttered another slice. Placing it on my plate, he gestured to it with his knife. "Eat."

I recognized that look, so I didn't even try to argue. Picking up the slice, I took a bite and chewed as I tried to remember what I last remembered. "Oh my God, the *wolf*!"

"What about it?" Caleb looked over his shoulder as he spoke. "Your food shouldn't be too long."

Reaching over, I grabbed his hand, bringing his attention back to me. "The *wolf*, Caleb! Why aren't we talking about the big freaking wolf?"

Sitting back in his chair, he watched me. "What do you want me to say?"

"I want to know what kind of crazy person stares down a wolf," I hissed at him.

"I told you, it's not crazy, I read about it."

We were interrupted by Shelby, and Caleb was on his feet,

taking the tray off of her. "Oh thank you!" She beamed at him. "Such a catch you have there," she told me.

Yeah, the stoic, grumpy, laugh-in-the-face-of-danger guy was *such* a catch. "Mm-hmm."

Picking a plate off the tray, she laid down an overflowing plate of food. "Now I hope I got it all right. He was quite adamant on how you liked your eggs." Shelby looked at me worriedly. "Are these okay?"

Two over-easy eggs wobbled on the plate. I almost protested when I saw Caleb's face. "Yeah, really good." Between the bacon, sausage, two pancakes, and slice of French toast, I wasn't sure where to start. "I'll never eat all of this," I told her with dismay.

Shelby was placing a basket of breakfast pastries between us. "Manage what you can. You need your strength."

Once the teapot was down and a mug of fresh coffee for Caleb, she took the empty tray away, leaving me with all the food.

"You like eggs?" Caleb asked me.

"I do. Not like that though," I answered, not giving it much thought.

"Excellent." Leaning over, he deftly lifted them off my plate, onto one of the remaining slices of toast, and when I looked up, he winked just as he bit into his stolen breakfast. "She makes these perfectly," he told me happily, licking the running yoke off his thumb. Caleb tapped my plate. "Eat."

The breakfast was nice, but too much too soon, and I surrendered halfway through, which wasn't a problem because Caleb polished off the rest of the plate.

Shelby was a good host; she didn't hover. I could hear her

banging around in the kitchen, and I guessed she would be cleaning up.

When we were finished, Caleb deftly stacked the plates and carried them through to the kitchen. I heard the raised voice of surprise, and while I couldn't hear what they were saying, I had no doubt that Caleb was charming his new admirer.

Charming to everyone but me.

He didn't come back into the sunroom, lingering midpoint between the living room and the kitchen. "You ready?"

I did feel slightly stronger, and my feet weren't so unsteady, but I wasn't sure when *ready* would be an adjective I used to describe me. When we got to the stairs, I darted in front of him before he got any ideas, and I climbed the stairs, silently grateful for his close proximity in case I tumbled.

Inside our room, he took a chair by the window, and I sat on the edge of the bed. "You've been making friends." I tried to sound lighthearted.

"You were unwell for three days. I had to find some way for the locals to let us stay." He opened his wallet, holding out a twenty. "After this, I'm clean out." Tossing the wallet on the bed, he sighed. "I need to make some money."

"Are there no banks here?" Getting off the bed, I looked outside, seeing only trees. "Where are we anyway?"

"I don't keep money in banks." He stood, crossing to come and stand beside me. "Kettlebridge is the name of the town. Very small, very...involved."

"Nosy?" When he nodded, I didn't tell him I'd already guessed that. "And who doesn't have a bank account?"

"Me." Caleb went back to his seat. "I made two hundred

the first night we got here, but I needed another night here, and the truck needed gas."

"I have money," I assured him. "How did you make money?"

"Won a game of pool."

There was something about his face when he said it that made me decide not to ask for any further details. What you didn't know couldn't hurt you, right?

"I'll give you my share," I told him easily.

"I'm not telling you for that reason."

"I know." We held each other's stare for a moment. I looked away first, picking up my notebook, ready to ask him about my symptoms while I was out of it. "What did you tell Lily?" I asked absently, but when he didn't answer, I looked back and saw he hadn't moved, but his lips were pressed together. "Caleb? Tell me you told Lily where we were?" I was already retrieving my tote, looking for my phone. "Why is my phone off?" I demanded.

"Because you wouldn't have been able to answer it," he told me calmly.

I waited for it to come on, and when it did, it had a message on the screen that I wasn't expecting. "Insert SIM?" Caleb stood up and I looked up at him. "What did you do?"

"Phones can be traced."

"Yes. It's a *good* thing."

He looked at me like I had told him the sky was green. "It's not. Anyone can trace you, and we need to be untraceable, especially when you were incapacitated."

My knees felt weak, and I sank back onto the edge of the bed. "What have you done?"

"I told them I changed my mind." He sniffed. "About you." He held my gaze. "About taking you to them."

"Why? What changed your mind?"

"I don't like it."

"Okay...why?"

"It's hard to explain."

"Try."

Caleb shook his head slightly as he looked away. "Just... It just is, okay?"

"Then we go back to Whispering Pines, right?" He didn't look back at me. "Caleb? We go back, right?" He didn't answer, and I got to my feet. "Caleb! Answer me!"

"I don't know."

Flabbergasted, I watched him. "Okay...well, *I* know, and I want to go home." When he said nothing, I turned around to pick up my phone. "I need my SIM card."

The click of the door had me spinning around, and I realized he'd left me. "Asshole." Dropping to the bed, something fluttered off the nightstand, and stooping, I bent to pick it up.

*Dr. Nigel Hardman, M.D.*

"You called for a doctor." My whisper echoed around the room. "No wonder you have no money left," I murmured as conflicting emotions warred within me.

He'd taken my SIM card. He hadn't told my best friend where I was. He wasn't letting me go back to Whispering Pines, my *home*. He'd called a doctor to a B&B to ensure I was okay, paying the charge without question. He'd found a nice place to sleep, clean and well cared for. I knew it wouldn't be cheap. He was protecting me. From what, I didn't know, but I knew he was.

Or he *thought* he was.

Or...maybe he was a psycho serial killer, and this was his elaborate plan so no one ever suspected him?

The room was stuffy, and I needed fresh air. Slipping my feet into my sneakers, I left the room and went to find my sullen friend-slash-kidnapper-slash-husband.

The front door was open, and when I checked outside for Caleb, I saw Shelby with her back to the door, deep in conversation with someone who wasn't Caleb. Heading through the house, I looked for a back door. Finding it in the kitchen, and finding it slightly open, I pushed it wide as I searched for Caleb.

The backyard was immaculately tidy, and as I admired Shelby's gardening skills, I saw the slightly concealed path. He would have gone for a walk, I reasoned, and with little thought, I followed the path.

Voices drifted through the trees, and I slowed down, not sure who would be out here. Other guests maybe? Townsfolk. Scrambling in my head, I couldn't remember if it was deer hunting season. I had nothing to visibly identify me as *not* being wildlife, and panicking that I was about to be shot, I hurried forward and immediately tripped over nothing, tumbling to the springy mossy ground, which thankfully softened my fall.

With my palms flat against the ground, I prepared to push myself up when movement made me freeze. Turning my head to the left, through the underbrush, I saw the furry paws.

I almost swallowed my tongue in fear as my brain screamed at me to stay still. I didn't know how long I stayed like that. I was sure the wolf had moved on when I heard a sudden crashing, and looking up, I saw the wolf run straight at me.

I scrambled backward, sure I would be today's dinner, when from nowhere, Caleb appeared and tackled the wolf. My yell was drowned out by Caleb's grunt as the two hit the ground. Frantically getting to my feet, I looked up to see if he was okay, and the trees were clear.

There was nothing here. Only me. Turning slowly, I looked everywhere.

"What?" I turned once more. "This makes no sense."

When I turned to go back to the B&B, I screamed in alarm as I came face-to-face with Caleb.

He grabbed my arm, concern on his face. "Willow, why are you out here?"

"The wolf." My chest was tight. "You fought the wolf!"

He was frowning and looking around. "Willow, listen to me, you're disoriented. Let's get you back to bed, okay?"

Shaking my head, I wanted to keep him here and make him explain everything I knew he was hiding. "No. The wolf."

Caleb's arm slipped around my shoulders. "There is no wolf. It's just me and you here," he assured me, leading me back to the house. "Let's get you back to the room, and you can lie down, okay?"

"There was a wolf."

He didn't say anything to contradict me, and I didn't push it. Not here, not in the open. I didn't know how I knew that, but some instinct was telling me not to say anything more out here.

But I wasn't letting it go. One wolf, rare. Two? Something was happening here, and I was going to find out what.

## EIGHTEEN
## Caleb

We walked back to the B&B in silence. Willow was pretending to focus on what was straight ahead, but she was really bad at being subtle, and I kept seeing her looking at me out of the corner of her eye.

"The wind will blow and freeze your face," I joked quietly. "You'll be squinty-eyed for the rest of your life."

Willow huffed out a laugh, and I saw the smile that she tried to hide. "I have so many questions," she admitted. Stopping suddenly, she reached out, took hold of my arm, and tugged me to a stop. "I know you don't want to talk out here." She hurried on when she saw my look. "And I'm *not* going to talk out here," she confirmed.

"But?"

Willow looked up at me in amusement. "There's always a but..."

I nodded. "Yup, always a but."

"But..." She flashed me a smile. "But when we get inside, I want you to promise to tell me everything."

I was already shaking my head. "I can't do that."

Her expression morphed from hopeful to disappointed. "Why?"

"Because I don't know everything." It was true, I didn't. "If I knew everything, I wouldn't have dragged you out here."

We resumed walking and she was silent until we reached the edge of the B&B property. "You must know something," she argued softly. "So, you can tell me that at least?"

I was going to tell her nothing had changed since I put her in the truck, but the look she gave me was ready for that, and I simply nodded. Shelby waved at us as we passed her. She seemed to be checking in a new guest, as there was luggage beside her, and I was halfway up the stairs when I turned back and looked towards the front door.

Every sense was on alert.

"Go upstairs," I directed Willow softly. "Now." I knew she was about to argue, and I not so subtly pushed her ahead of me. "Move."

She did, and I knew I'd get shit for manhandling her later. Turning, I faced the doorway, so when the big ass bruiser walked through it, I was ready for him, and he met my gaze immediately, ignoring the human who had noticed that her guests were in a stare-off.

"Do you know each other?" I heard the tremble in her voice. Her scent changed to fearful, and I knew I should appease her, but I was focused on the male in front of me.

"Not that I know of." I kept my eyes on the shifter in front of me, who was now idling beside Shelby. "You look familiar." He didn't. The only familiar thing about him was that he was a shifter.

"Do I?" He had dark hair, shorter than mine, but still longer than most. He was clean-shaven, his eyes were hard and saw more than they should, and his shoulders were wide, but he wasn't overly bulky. He looked solid, which is why I thought *bruiser* when he came in. Wearing jeans, a flannel shirt, and brown scuffed work boots, he looked very similar to me.

A traveling man who spent a long time on the road. He looked past me up the stairs. "You got someone waiting?"

"His wife has been poorly," Shelby helpfully told him, and I almost growled in frustration.

"That's a pity," the stranger said.

"Yeah." With a nod to them both, I went up the stairs and found Willow pacing the room. "How are you feeling?"

She blinked at me. "What?"

"We need to move, and we need to move soon. How are you feeling? Can we move you? We need to be out of this town."

"What happened downstairs?" Willow stopped pacing, her arms crossed over her chest, her face determined.

"Nothing, new guest. Looks shady." I started packing her stuff. "You look okay," I told her, checking her over again. "But I know nothing about your illness"—or any illness—"so you need to tell me if you need more rest."

"I'm fine." I turned to look at her fully, and she threw her hands up in the air. "Okay, I'm not fine, but I'm better."

That was good enough for me. "Good." Walking past her, I ducked into the small bathroom. "We leave in ten minutes."

"You said we could talk!"

"I say a lot of things, Willow." I dropped her toiletries onto her stuff. When I saw she wasn't moving, I fought back the groan. "You don't trust me fully, I get it, but you've trusted me some. I just need a little bit more. We need to move."

Heavy footsteps sounded outside the room, and Willow watched me with wide eyes when she saw me freeze. Putting my finger to my lips, I watched her nod that she understood she was to be quiet. I knew I needed to throw the shifter outside off the scent of the two of us.

*Scent of the two of us.* It could work...

Willow turned from apprehensive to guarded in a heartbeat. "Whatever you're thinking, don't," she warned in a low whisper as I approached her, her eyes locked onto mine with a mix of suspicion and irritation.

It was such a familiar look from her that I couldn't help but smirk. "Relax. I've got it under control." I pulled her unresisting body into my arms. "Punch me later," I whispered into her ear.

"Wh—"

But before she could say more, I moved, taking the chance. My hand cupped her cheek, and my lips crashed against hers with a force that sent a jolt of electricity through me.

For a brief second, the only thing I could focus on was the intensity of the kiss—the heat, the unexpected softness, the way her scent seemed to envelop me like a warm, inviting cloud. When I kissed her, her body went stiff with surprise, but as I moved my mouth over hers, I felt her loosen. Slowly, her hands reached up and rested on my shoulders. When I pulled her closer, she came willingly. My tongue tasted her bottom lip, and Willow parted for me.

She tasted sweet. Fresh.

I took a deeper taste of her. I felt her hands slip into my hair as she melted against me, kissing me back. Her scent changed, her pheromones letting anyone with that extra sense of smell know she was here freely and hinting that we weren't to be disturbed.

I heard the footsteps move away from the room. I knew the room on the other side of us was already occupied. I'd checked them out the first night, and Shelby's guest book told me they were here until the day after tomorrow. Which meant the shifter was in the room at the far end of the hall.

I heard the door open and close in the distance, my attention split between the woman in my arms and the threat that was two doors down.

Pulling my head back, I broke the kiss. I didn't miss the flushed look on her face or the slight hitch in her breath, but I pretended I didn't see it.

"Um..."

"You did well," I told her, moving away and going to the door, pressing my ear against it. "Thanks."

"Thanks?"

I should have noticed the lack of emotion in her flat voice. Despite my earlier comment, I should have been more alert when I turned around, completely taken aback by the unexpected slap.

Willow glared at me. "You are an asshole! What the hell was that?" she demanded, her chest heaving, a flush creeping up her neck.

Somehow, her indignant glare and put-upon attitude

rubbed me the wrong way. Massaging my jaw, I looked her over slowly, enjoying seeing the flush burn brighter across her cheeks. "A distraction," I replied casually.

"A distraction?" Willow's incredulous hiss sliced through the air, her hand rubbing the sting on her palm that mirrored the dull ache on my cheek. A twisted satisfaction flickered within me, knowing that she had hurt herself slapping me. "A distraction from what?"

"You," I explained, and I could anticipate her next question, so I elaborated. "You were freaking out."

Willow's eyes burned bright with anger as she glared at me. "You're a dick," she snapped.

"Probably am," I conceded, my gaze dropping briefly to her lips before meeting her eyes again, "but it worked, didn't it?"

Turning her back to me, I knew she was still pissed, but I could still smell her arousal from the kiss. I gave her a moment to compose herself. I could hear her heartbeat still pounding.

With her back turned to me, I took a moment to catch up with what had just happened. I could still feel the imprint of her lips against mine, the shadow of the sensation I knew wasn't a good idea to remember but one I wanted to explore more of.

A bad idea indeed.

Willow walked over to her small luggage bag. "Next time," she hissed, refusing to look at me, "warn me before you pull a stunt like that again."

"Where's the fun in that?" I asked, failing to hide my amusement at her presumption that there would be a next time.

She didn't dignify that with a response. Instead, she went into the bathroom and locked the door. I heard the faucet turn on, and I felt a moment of regret, knowing she had locked me out while she tried to grapple with the last few minutes.

I didn't have time to dwell on it. Packing up all our stuff, I checked the room for anything left behind, and when I knew it was clear, I rapped my knuckles softly against the bathroom door.

Willow jerked the door open, her eyes narrowed with distrust. "What?"

"We need to leave," I told her. "This is our window of opportunity. We need to use it."

"Window from who?"

"I'll explain."

"But you won't," she grumbled, reaching to take a hoodie off me. "You say and never do. It's getting old, Caleb."

I knew she was right. I held onto the hoodie as she tried to tug it out of my hold. Willow looked up at me, and I held her questioning stare. "Just a little longer, okay?" With a deep breath, she reluctantly nodded. "Good girl," I praised, letting the hoodie go, and I didn't miss the skip of her breath at the term.

Filing that little nugget away for future use, I hesitated at the door.

I hadn't planned on staying here more than two nights. It was a place to lie low while Willow recovered. But now, knowing there was a shifter down the hall from us, from *her*, I could almost taste the danger. I could feel it closing in on us.

I should have known better than to stay for so long.

"You got all you need?" I double-checked, keeping my voice low as I listened for movement outside.

The floorboards creaked as she moved across the room,

stepping up behind me. "I'm ready." Her tone was controlled, but her scent was a mix of fear and adrenaline.

"I need you to be fast, okay?" I asked, meeting her gaze.

She nodded, slinging her bag over her shoulder, eyes wide and alert. "What's the plan?"

"We're going out the back," I said. "There's a fire escape at the other side of the hall when we go right, past the stairs, okay? Follow me. Keep close. The truck's close. We don't stop for anything."

She swallowed hard but didn't hesitate. I could see the tension in the set of her jaw, the way her knuckles turned white around the strap of her bag. No questions, no second-guessing. That was good. We didn't have time for either.

I eased the door open, wincing at the faint squeak of the old hinges. The hallway was bright with morning sunlight but thankfully empty. We moved quickly, our steps muffled by the thick carpet, but I couldn't shake the feeling that every creak and whisper was giving us away to the shifter resting just a few doors down.

The back staircase was narrow and steep, leading down into a kitchen that smelled of cleaning products and the remnants of this morning's breakfast. My pulse quickened as we reached the bottom step, the anticipation of being seen riding high. I motioned for Willow to stay close, and she did, her breath warm against the back of my neck as we edged toward the back door.

I paused, listening. The silence of the lodge was too perfect, too heavy. It pressed in on my ears, a warning in and of itself. My wolf was close to the surface.

I heard a shuffle, soft and deliberate, just outside.

Grabbing the doorknob, I turned to Willow, holding her gaze with a look that said we had no other choice. Her look was frightened, but she nodded, her hand hovering near mine. *On three*, I mouthed.

One.

Two.

Three.

Yanking the door open, we ran into the warm sunny morning, the heat slapping us in the face in comparison to the air-conditioned rooms. The truck was parked just beyond the old oak tree, less than twenty yards away as we sprinted across the backyard. My heart was pounding, the sound almost deafening in my ears. I could hear Willow breathing beside me, quick and shallow but steady.

We were almost there.

Then, out of the corner of my eye, I caught a flash of movement—dark shapes hiding in the trees, watching us.

"Get in!" I barked, skidding to a stop beside the truck. I threw the door open and shoved her inside, slamming it shut behind her. I could see the figures now, two, maybe three, their faces hidden, their intent unmistakable.

To catch us.

I didn't give them a chance. I vaulted over the hood, my boots hitting the ground on the driver's side just as the first wolf broke free of the forest.

Something barreled into me, knocking me away from the door, and I realized it was the shifter from the inn, still in his human form.

I shoved him off, barely registering his weight, Willow pushed the truck door open, and I clambered inside, jamming the key into the ignition. The engine roared to life, and I floored it, the tyres churning up Shelby's neat graveled parking lot.

The truck fishtailed as I jerked the wheel to the side to avoid the wolf that jumped in front of us as we tore down the road, leaving the B&B behind us. My hands were white-knuckled on the wheel, my eyes darting to the rearview mirror. I saw the shifter was on his feet, watching us drive away, two wolves on either side of him.

They weren't following us—yet.

"You okay?" I asked, glancing over at Willow. She was breathing hard, but she nodded, her eyes still wide with adrenaline.

"Yeah," she said, her voice shaky but strong. "You?"

I let out a deep breath. "I am now."

"What in the actual fuck is going on?" She looked at me, anger, confusion, and fear etched on her face. "Why are they after us? Who are these people? Where the *hell* are all these wolves coming from?"

Her voice trembled slightly, and I could tell she was trying to make sense of something that didn't fit into her world.

That *I* didn't fit in her world.

"Not yet," I murmured. "Let me put a few more miles between us."

The reminder that they were behind us and could be following us made Willow jerk around to check if the road was empty.

We drove in silence for a while, the tension slowly draining away as the distance grew between us and the shifters. But the feeling lingered—the sense that we were only just ahead of the danger, that it was still out there, waiting for us to slip up.

For *me* to slip up.

Tightening my grip on the wheel, I pushed the truck harder down the empty road.

Whatever was coming, I'd be ready. I just had to hope that Willow would be as well.

# NINETEEN

## Willow

As the day wore on, the truck rumbled down the narrow, winding road, its engine echoing through the stillness. Outside the window, the dark trees became a jumbled mess, their outlines blending together. Despite the passage of time since the incident at the B&B, my heart was still pounding, each beat a reminder of the fear that enveloped me when the stranger had launched himself at Caleb. As I tried to make sense of the events, they played back in my mind like a disjointed film, each scene more surreal than the last, leaving me utterly perplexed.

"What happened back there?" I asked again, my voice trembling despite my best efforts to stay calm. I glanced over at him, searching for answers in his profile, but his jaw was clenched tight, his eyes fixed on the road ahead.

He didn't answer right away, and the silence between us grew heavy, suffocating. My fingers curled into the seat, nails digging into the upholstery, as I pushed down my need to demand answers.

"Who were they?" I pressed, hearing the fear in my voice. "And why were they after you?"

He hesitated, his grip on the steering wheel tightening as though he could strangle the truth into submission. The tension between us was building until it was almost unbearable. The air hung thick with unspoken words and secrets Caleb didn't want to tell, but he needed to.

He promised.

"Caleb!"

"I'll explain," he snapped. "But not here. Not yet." His voice was rough, almost reluctant.

It wasn't the answer I wanted, but I could hear the strain in his voice, the way it cracked around the edges.

No matter how hard I tried to tell myself that I was being dramatic, I couldn't shake the feeling that something was coming, something I wasn't sure I was ready to hear.

"When?" I pushed.

Caleb cursed savagely, and I saw that he wasn't just tense—he was on edge as if expecting something to leap out of the surrounding trees at any moment. The man I had known for weeks, who had been cool, composed, and sometimes apathetic, was no longer present.

In his place was someone different, someone dangerous, someone I wasn't sure I knew anymore. Had I ever really known him though?

I was going crazy, and I needed answers and I'd been put off too many times.

"Please," I said quietly, my voice barely above a whisper. "Just tell me what's going on."

His eyes flicked to me, softening just a fraction, but the

tension was still there, coiled tight like a spring ready to snap. He took a deep breath as if steadying himself for whatever he was about to say.

"There are things in this world," he started, his voice deliberately low and slow, "that many people never lay eyes on, things they think are a figment of someone's imagination. Yet, they are undeniably real. And...well, they're not exactly human."

I blinked, trying to process his words, but my brain was struggling to make sense of what he said. "What do you mean, 'not human'? You're talking about that guy back there, aren't you?"

Caleb nodded, his gaze fixed on the road ahead. "They're shifters. They can...change. Become something else."

The words sounded wrong. Shifters? Like something out of a movie or a TV show? I felt the urge to burst out laughing and mock his insanity or hit him for trying to insult my intelligence, but the expression on Caleb's face made it clear that he was deadly serious.

"That's crazy," I said, my voice shaking. "Are you serious?" He nodded once. "That's... How is that even possible?"

"I know it sounds insane," he admitted, his tone softening. "But you saw it, didn't you?" He looked over at me briefly, seeing me hanging on his every word. "You felt it—that instinct, that fear, that there was something different. You knew something wasn't right."

I swallowed hard, trying to push down the rising panic. What he was saying wasn't right, yet...he *was* right.

I *had* felt it at the B&B, that irrefutable sense of fear that told me something was off. That there was almost something *supernatural* happening. And this time, I didn't mean a TV show.

But...to hear it being said? Out loud. It was... *Jesus*. This was too much.

Nausea swept over me. I felt like my world was being turned upside down in a matter of minutes, and I didn't know if I would be able to keep up.

"Why you?" I asked, my voice sounding small and frightened. "Why were they after you?"

Caleb glanced at me quickly, and the squeak of the leather protesting as he seemed ready to crush the steering wheel made me steel myself for what he said next.

"I don't think it's me," he said, a note of regret creeping into his voice. "At least, not *just* me." One hand finally let go of the wheel, and I watched as he smoothed back his hair. "They've been tracking for a while now, keeping their distance. But..." He cleared his throat.

"But?" Fear was clutching at my throat, and I didn't recognize my own voice. "But something happened?" I guessed. At his curt nod, I felt the overwhelming urge to cry. I almost knew the answer, but I asked anyway. "What?"

"Willow..."

"Me?" I wanted to run from his answer, but there was nowhere to go. "How is it me, Caleb?"

His sigh was long and filled with regret. "You know why," he spoke quietly. "What you paint."

Suddenly my artwork that he'd stored in the back of the truck felt like it was looming over me. "My paintings?"

I sounded skeptical. Hell, I *was* skeptical.

"You sound surprised," he murmured, and I saw his frown

as he drove. "I know a lot of what I'm saying is a shock, but surely the fact your drawings are involved isn't one."

"Gee, Caleb, you're right," I snapped at him as I slapped my forehead. "The fact I've been drawing you for weeks and missed the fact that there are *fucking werewolves* in the world is so stupid of me."

"I didn't say werewolves," he grumbled.

"Call it an educated guess." My voice was so full of scorn that he met my anger with his own heated glare. "You and wolves and then *shifters. Wolf* shifters? Am I right?"

"Yeah." Caleb's shoulders were drawn tight. They had been for most of the drive, but it was like the fight suddenly left him, and I watched them droop as he exhaled loudly. "You can't tell anyone."

My burst of laughter surprised him so much that, for the first time, I saw the man beside me actually *react* to something.

"Who in the name of God am I going to *tell*?" I demanded. "Who am I going to tell who isn't going to take my delusional ass right to the nearest mental health facility?"

"You're not delusional," he reasoned.

"*I* know that, but if you weren't here with me and hadn't seen it, would you believe me?"

"Yes."

I scoffed. "No, you wouldn't."

"I would," he admitted. "Because it was you."

My tummy did a little somersault, and I tried to ignore the thrill his words created within me. He didn't look at me, and I wanted him to. I wanted him to look me in the eyes when he told me such fantastical things as werewolves existed or that he would so readily believe me.

Believe *in* me?

"What do they want?" I asked, looking away. He confused me. Looking at him only made it worse.

"You?" He shrugged, drawing my attention back to him. "Me? Both?" Caleb turned his head, meeting my gaze. "I don't know. I don't know how they know about you."

"You told your friend," I said reasonably.

"He would never tell anyone who would want to harm you," he spoke quickly. He started worrying his bottom lip. "He may have told the Pack Council."

"Pack Council?"

Caleb grimaced and I realized he hadn't known he had spoken out loud. "You have your governments, they have theirs."

I stared at him, the weight of his words sinking in. My mind raced, trying to piece together how I had gone from a quiet, uneventful life to being hunted by something out of a nightmare. Shifters? Creatures that weren't even human? It was too much, too fast, and yet here I was, tangled up in something I didn't understand.

"You're saying this like it should all make sense to me," I murmured, more to myself than to him.

He flinched, just a small movement, but I caught it. There was something more he wasn't saying, something that connected me to this mess. My heart pounded as I considered the possibilities, each one more terrifying than the last.

"They're a secret, you say," I continued, my voice rising with panic, not waiting for him to answer. "Why would my paintings matter? What aren't you telling me?"

He kept his eyes on the road, his jaw tightening. "I don't

know," he admitted, his voice low, almost a growl. "But I do know that a woman like you shouldn't be able to *see* me, and that makes you dangerous."

"A woman like me?" I hadn't liked the way he said that, but then he said something even more preposterous. "Dangerous?" My voice cracked, it was so high. "Me?"

"You don't know what it is you paint, Willow. You're a threat to their way of life."

The realization hit me like a punch to the gut. It wasn't *both* of us they were after—it was just me. I hadn't been dragged into this world because of Caleb—a world of dangers and secrets I couldn't begin to understand—he was involved *because* of *me*.

The fear that had been simmering inside me threatened to erupt. "You should've told me," I whispered, my voice trembling. "You should've warned me before it got this far."

"Maybe," he said, and I could hear what sounded like regret in his voice. "But I didn't know it would come to this."

Anger and helplessness mixed within me, adding to my feeling of disorientation. I hadn't asked for any of this, hadn't wanted to be part of some supernatural *reality*. However, it was already too late. I was involved, whether I wanted to be or not, and there was no avoiding the fact that my life would never be the same knowing there were *shifters* out there in the world.

"I didn't think they'd catch up so soon. I'm not sure who's following us."

I locked my eyes on him, struggling to reconcile the man I thought I knew with the person now seated beside me, a man concealing secrets that exceeded my wildest imagination. There was a battle within me, torn between the desire to scream out and demand answers, and the fear of what those answers might reveal.

Caleb seemed to sense that I was struggling. "You okay?"

"No."

He nodded, looking out the window and pressing his foot on the gas a little more as silence filled the small space once more.

The silence didn't help. I wanted answers. So many answers, but where did I start? "So what now?" I asked, my voice barely above a whisper.

"Now, we keep moving," he replied, his eyes hardening again. "I'll protect you, I promise. But we do need to find answers. And maybe I need to think about things."

"What kind of things?"

"Well, I changed my mind about taking you to my friend, but I wasn't expecting others to come after us."

"Why did you change your mind?" I wasn't interested in outside of the truck. Caleb was finally talking, and I had been waiting so long for this that I wasn't ready for him to stop.

He gave a slight shake of his head. "I don't know..." I wanted to tell him that he did know, but he spoke before I could. "I saw the first wolf, the one on the road, remember?"

How could I forget?

Caleb looked over at me and must have read the answer on my face, and surprisingly, I saw the corner of his mouth hook upwards in the semblance of a smile. "Right," he said with a lightness we'd been missing since we left the B&B. "Well, it didn't sit right," he explained. "Shifters don't willingly expose themselves to the human world. But..." He hesitated. "The alpha said that we were traveling through packlands and it wasn't *that* much of a coincidence that a wolf would stop us on the road."

He was using the terms so loosely. Casually. His openness was almost as surreal as the topic he was discussing.

"Alpha." My murmur brought his attention back to me. "You told me about them. Leaders?"

Caleb grunted. "Most packs have one," he explained.

"Are they bad?"

Caleb was already shaking his head. "No, not all of them." A look I didn't recognize passed across his face. "Some are the best of men."

Was that wistfulness? "The one you were taking us to, he isn't?"

Caleb cleared his throat. "I think he's decent enough."

I waited. When he said nothing more, I gaped. "That's it? He's decent? It's hardly a ringing endorsement."

Caleb chuckled. "I don't really know him," he reminded me. "From what I know *of* him, he's okay. I've seen him once before, a long time ago, when he was in his wolf form." He seemed to think about it. "Put it this way. There are ones I would never take you to, so the fact I was taking you to him means I know he's one of the good ones."

"But you didn't take me to him."

He met my look with an unreadable one of his own. "I made a mistake." I watched as he scratched his jaw, the look of determination on his face unsettling me. "I should have taken you there and never detoured, even when you were sick."

Emotion overwhelmed me, and I turned my head away so he couldn't see my tears. "I appreciate that you looked after me." Swallowing past the lump in my throat, I spoke softly. "I appreciate that you got a doctor. You didn't need to. I'm sorry you wasted your money."

"It wasn't a waste," he corrected me quietly. "You were lifeless. I was sure you were at death's door."

I let out a low chuckle. "You sound like Lily. She likes to dramatize it sometimes too."

"I'm not being dramatic." Caleb's snort made me turn and face him. "Knowing that you lose your energy around me, I had no way of knowing if I was causing you harm."

"It was just a bad spell." I tried to offer him comfort. "Trust me, you'll see more." I'd spoken flippantly, but by his look, I knew what I'd said worried him. We couldn't afford for me to be...well, me.

"It may be hard to get to the alpha now," he said, measuring his words carefully.

"I can keep up." Sitting straighter, I tried to look like I was fine. Healthy. *Normal.*

"I don't know if you can," Caleb admitted. "It could be rough, and..." I saw his glance at me, but I stared straight ahead. "We need to walk some of the way."

"I'm capable of walking, Caleb." My voice sounded defensive, but I couldn't help it.

"I know." He wisely didn't argue. He didn't remind me that he had seen me after I'd walked to and from my store and then almost collapsed afterwards. He didn't remind me of the times he had carried me when I was too weak to walk.

"I'll do my best," I promised quietly.

"I don't doubt that." His simple reassurance strengthened my resolve. "I'll help you."

I turned my attention to the darkness that we drove through. "What if they're following us?"

"Then we'll outrun them." He ignored my look of disbelief. "It's unlikely they're following us so quickly," he added, but I could hear the falseness of his assurance.

I nodded, though he knew I didn't believe that those *shifters* weren't on our trail.

Shifters. Who would believe it?

The world I'd spent my whole life in no longer existed. The illusion of *normal* had been shattered by a truth I never expected, and I knew I needed more time than I had to process everything.

Caleb reached over and patted my knee, knowing I was freaking out. "It's okay, Willow. I'll protect you."

His words should have been comforting, but instead, they only deepened my unease. The fact that I needed protection only highlighted how bizarre my life had become, and I longed for the time when I'd never picked up a pencil and drawn Caleb Foster's face.

I longed for the routine of simple days and nights—living my life and managing my ME, without monsters lurking in the shadows. That now felt like a distant memory, almost out of reach.

How did I even return to "normal"? I tried to ignore the voice in my head that warned me that I may never return, but I shoved it away. I'd experienced too much tonight to start thinking like that.

I had enough to deal with *now*; whatever came later could wait.

TWENTY

## Caleb

We had lapsed into silence as the miles lengthened between us and the B&B. I'd told her as much as I could, but as we drove through the darkness, I could feel the tension mounting once more. Willow's eyes were on me often, searching my face for answers that I didn't have, or didn't want to share.

She knew about shifters now, knew that they were real, that the wolves from before were not wild animals cowed by a mere man. No, now she knew there were worse things than a hungry wolf on the prowl. That the wolves behind her were hunting her.

She knew more than a human should. But still...there was one thing that she didn't know.

And I had no idea how I was going to tell her.

My focus was on the road, on putting as much distance between us and the pack that had confronted us at Shelby's. My grip tightened on the wheel as the silence stretched, and I bit my tongue to stop myself from blurting the truth to her. I told myself it was for the best, that I was protecting her.

When I was only protecting myself.

I'd seen the horror on her face at the knowledge of *werewolves*. For her to look at me with that same disgust, I wasn't ready to face it.

Willow moved in her seat, and I realized how long we'd both been in this truck. My own body would welcome the stretch if we stopped, and I had a sharp pang of regret, knowing the toll it would have taken on her. The adrenaline, the fear, the worry, her body would fold in on itself with exhaustion soon.

"We need to stop," I told her, breaking the silence.

Willow looked at me with alarm. "Why? What's wrong?"

Her panic was warranted, but I forced an eye roll, trying desperately to cling to some form of normalcy. "Nothing. I need a break, a chance to stretch my legs, and a comfort break."

She relaxed slightly. "Oh, you need the bathroom."

"I'm sure you do too." Was it only this morning she got out of bed unaided for the first time in three days? "It's been a long day."

Glancing outside, the half-moon, the only light for miles, mocked me. The *day* was long past.

"Maybe a chance to stretch would be nice," she admitted. "Is it safe, you know, to go out there?"

Her concern was also warranted. "We look to be deep in mountain country," I told her. "But there's a town not far from us. It has a twenty-four-hour diner, just off the highway. Popular with truckers."

Willow's curiosity was piqued. "You're a trucker?"

Shaking my head, I smiled. "Nah, been a hitchhiker a few times though."

She watched me before she realized she was staring at me again, and with a jerk of her head, she looked away. "I can see that," she told me quietly. "You have total drifter vibes."

"That's because I am."

We lapsed back into silence once more. I knew she wasn't fully comfortable with the admission or what had happened over the last few hours. I'd come to know her mannerisms, and right now I knew that her mind was in overdrive as she tried to make sense of everything that I'd shared with her.

I had no idea if she still trusted me, or if she'd ever trusted me, and I knew that losing her trust shouldn't irk me as much as it did. I couldn't blame her if she doubted me; I'd given her reason to.

I needed to confess it all. But how the hell did I tell her? How did I tell her that the monsters she feared were the same as I was? That the gift of Luna ran through my blood as much as it ran through theirs. The pack that was hunting us was *my* kind.

The only consolation was that she hadn't put it together herself yet. I didn't doubt that she would. She was clever. The one thing I told myself was that when she asked me, I wouldn't lie.

For now, she hadn't asked, and I decided it was best not to offer. Even so, the weight of my secret hung heavy around my neck. All it would take would be one slip, one careless word, and the truth would be unavoidable.

Would she look at me with the same fear that she'd had in

her eyes when I told her about shifters? I wasn't ready to see that.

So for now, I would keep my silence. Hopefully, a bathroom break, some coffee, and food at the diner would distract her for long enough. As long as the threat to her safety remained behind her, I could keep her safe without her realizing what I was.

Nodding to myself, I assured myself that I was doing the right thing. Still, I could feel the walls closing in on me. The sooner we got to Cannon, the sooner she would understand that not all the *monsters* were the same, and then maybe, just maybe, it wouldn't matter that I was one of them.

Blowing out a low breath, I tried to clear my mind and focus only on the road. Now that I'd alerted my brain to the possibility of a comfort break, my bladder wanted to let me know it would welcome some relief. My empty belly reminded me it had been a while since it was full.

"Are you hungry?"

Willow had been looking out the window at the darkness, seeing nothing beyond her own reflection in the glass, I would guess.

"Maybe?" she answered softly. "Maybe I don't know if I will ever eat again. My stomach keeps rolling every time I think of men being wolves and wolves being men."

"It's a lot to process."

"Is it only werewolves?" she asked me suddenly. "Are there other monsters out there?"

"Shifters," I corrected. "You're imagining men walking on two legs, a cross between wolf and man." I didn't need to see her nod to know I was right. "Shifters are men or women that—"

"There are *female* ones?"

That did earn her a look from me, and she instantly flushed. "Of course there are."

Willow immediately went on the defensive. "Don't 'of course' me. How am I supposed to know? This is brand new information!" Her attention flicked to my hands on the steering wheel. "You're going to break that thing," she snapped. "You've been strangling it since we left the B&B."

Loosening my grip on the steering wheel, I turned to look at her. "Happier?"

Willow stuck her tongue out at me before looking away quickly, hiding her smile. "So, there are women and men shifters," she carried on. "And they *shift* into wolves."

I nodded. "It's only a wolf." I noted her confusion at that and clarified, "They don't shift into any other animal."

"Why?"

Well, that was a philosophical question for someone with more brains than me. Instead, I countered with a "Why not?" causing her to narrow those light green eyes at me.

"What about vampires?" she asked. I shot her an "are you crazy?" look and was rewarded with her flicking me the middle finger. "Zombies?"

"I think you'd notice if there were." My dry comment pissed her off. "It's just shifters."

"Into wolves."

"Yup, shifters shifting into their wolf form."

"So when they're human, they're..."

"Human," I confirmed. Well...a little bit more than human, but I didn't want to overwhelm her.

"It figures," she mused. "I was always Team Jacob."

I didn't understand the reference. "Who's Jacob?"

Willow huffed with amusement. "Only the best-looking werewolf ever."

Now I was confused. "You know a shifter already?"

Willow's peal of laughter filled the truck. "No!" she declared, delighted by my ignorance. "It's a character from a book," she explained. "*Twilight*. You've never heard of it? It's about a werewolf and a vampire in love with the same girl."

I had a dim recollection of a franchise that made traveling through the north of the state of Washington annoying. "Ah, I see. Got it." A weird spark of curiosity lit inside of me. "So...you would be okay with this Jacob person?"

Willow looked entirely too amused by the idea. Her expression twisted into one of speculative longing. "I wouldn't kick him out of bed in the morning, that's for sure."

Interesting.

While Willow proceeded to tell me the entire plot of the series, I let her ramble on, pleased that the silence was broken, and relieved that she wasn't dwelling on the events of today.

As she spoke, I let my mind drift to the heaviness of my consciousness. Willow, animated and excited, was pleasant to experience. I should have been telling her that the books she was praising sounded incredibly complicated and that none of the characters sounded endearing at all.

I didn't. Instead, I was thinking about how she would react when she found out what I was.

It shouldn't matter. Willow and I didn't have the same kind of relationship as these characters in one of her books. We weren't friends. Despite the kiss this morning, we weren't lovers. We were two people who had come together through some weird psychic draw and circumstances.

Nothing more.

Once we got to the bottom of why she was having visions of me, or the few she had of Cannon, then she'd return to Whispering Pines, knowing more about the world than she did when she left, and I would go wherever I went next. It wouldn't be in the same direction as Willow.

We'd separate.

I knew that. I *wanted* that. So why did my gut feel like it was in knots at the thought of her finding out my truth?

As I looked at her from the corner of my eye, she was facing the front, still telling me about the books. She'd progressed to telling me how the books differed from the films, and I let her ramble.

She was so tied up in her retelling and monologue that she was oblivious to my inner turmoil. She had no idea that she was sitting beside a real-life version of a werewolf.

That I was as dangerous as, if not more so than, the ones who hunted us. Hunted her.

It shouldn't have mattered. Not at all.

But it did.

Was it because I'd tasted her? Had I let one kiss twist my thoughts? Was I letting *emotion* get the better of me? How Willow thought of me didn't matter to me, or it shouldn't, because *Willow* didn't matter to me. I was to take her to Alpha Cannon, that was all.

A task.

A job.

I'd already fucked up when I changed my mind, and look what had happened. She knew about shifters anyway.

I didn't care about Willow. Not in that way. She was a job. No, she wasn't even that. She was a *task*.

Grunting at the term, I moved uncomfortably in my seat. That didn't sit right with me, because that was harsh. She was more than that. Somewhere between learning of her illness, looking after her when she was sick, and protecting her when she was in danger, I could admit the line had become blurry.

And now, here I was, stuck between a rock and a hard place. If the rock was the truth and the hard place was admitting that I cared for her well-being.

Her well-being? Thoughts of it being anything else were shoved away quickly. I didn't need to look at that too closely.

*It was just a kiss.*

I was worried about her. There, that was it. It was my responsibility to keep her safe and protect her. The alpha had trusted me with this, and I had accepted it. It didn't matter that I resented the responsibility; a good shifter protected those weaker than them.

Willow was definitely weaker. In strength. I was still on the fence about her mental strength. Despite her reservations about me, she had still trusted me. Still come with me. Sure, I hadn't given her much choice, but I knew I didn't want to lose that.

The thought of her seeing me as something other than the man she thought I was, the man she had trusted to keep her safe and take her to where the answers were, filled me with dread.

I didn't want to see the betrayal in her eyes when she found out the truth.

I didn't want her to hate me.

It was so stupid. Her opinion should have been so irrelevant to me. But it had been a long time since I was entrusted with the welfare of someone other than myself. Was that what this was? My need to prove I could keep someone safe?

If that was the case, then I was more pathetic than I'd previously thought. I didn't need to prove myself to anyone, least of all Willow. She'd hate me anyway.

Cannon? He didn't know me, and I didn't need his approval. He wasn't *my* alpha.

Long buried emotions threatened to surface, and I angrily pushed them down.

"Caleb?"

Her voice drew me out of my inner thoughts, thoughts that lingered too close to old rage.

"Caleb?"

"I hear you," I told her gruffly, seeing the sign for the diner ahead. I hadn't even registered that I'd taken the exit for the highway. I'd been driving on autopilot. Giving myself an internal shake, I tried to clear my head. "Must have zoned out." She didn't hide her reaction quickly enough, and I cursed myself for basically telling her I'd stopped listening to her.

*She doesn't matter. You don't care about her.*

I repeated the mantra, feeling worse within myself the more I said it.

Pulling into the diner, I saw a few cars parked. Lowering the window, I sniffed the air for any trace of a shifter, but all I could smell was fumes, cooking grease, and trash from the over-flowing dumpster.

I parked the truck, and the two of us sat, neither of us moving.

"I feel like if I open the door, something bad will happen," Willow admitted into the quiet night. "It's been a cocoon of safety being in here, and I don't know if I'm brave enough to leave."

She didn't know how brave it was for her to admit that. Swallowing hard, I reached behind us for my jacket.

"You want to wet the seat, or do you want to go inside and use the facilities?" I pulled my jacket through the space between us, catching her eye. "I'd rather you went inside; we've still got a long drive."

Willow gave me a look of exasperation before she turned away, reaching for the door handle. "You're a regular Prince Charming," she grumbled.

Catching hold of her arm, I pulled her back gently. "Wait until I am out."

Willow said nothing, but her eyes widened with alarm as she understood my unspoken caution.

Once I knew it was safe, I took a moment to enjoy the welcome stretch of my legs. The truck was a good enough seat and a comfortable drive, but Willow was right, we'd been cooped up in it too long. The quick walk to her door was the best my legs had felt in hours.

Opening her door, I helped her down. She stayed close as we walked into the diner.

"Toilets are at the front," I told her. "We'll go first and eat after?" She nodded her agreement. "See you in a few."

In the stall, I rolled my head on my shoulders, trying to loosen the tension in my body. I wanted to run and loosen up all the knots and aches, but it would be a while before I was in my wolf form again.

Outside the men's room, I waited for Willow, and she emerged not long after me. I noticed her face was wet and she was rubbing her hands on her jeans. "Splashed my face to hope I looked less like death warmed over," she told me as we waited to be seated.

I hadn't and now I wished I had. "Good call."

When we were seated, armed with menus, we fell into silence again as we surveyed the menu.

"What's good here?" Willow asked, looking up. "You've been here before. What do you recommend?"

"I always take the all-day breakfast." I pointed to another dish on the menu. "Or chicken and waffles."

Her nose wrinkled at the suggestion. "Nope." She perused the menu for a moment longer, looking up just as the server appeared.

I ordered the breakfast and coffee. Willow ordered an egg white omelet, a side of fresh fruit, and toast. She had her usual pot of tea and asked for a glass of orange juice too.

She saw my look as the waitress walked away, and reaching over, she took a straw from the holder, not meeting my eye. "It's definitely my turn to pay."

I wasn't embarrassed that I didn't have the means to pay for the food. Money had never really bothered me, but I knew enough about human men that some would be disgruntled that the woman was paying.

Those men, I called stupid. For Willow, I merely dipped

my head in acknowledgment. Let her interpret that as she would.

It didn't matter what she thought of me. It wasn't important at all. Because if it did matter...then I was already in too deep.

And *that* kind of danger I couldn't afford. At all.

# TWENTY-ONE

*Willow*

THE AIR WAS CRISP AND COOL, FILLED WITH THE SCENT OF pine and earth as we made our way through the dense forest. We'd eaten late, and then after that, we hit the road again. Caleb had parked the truck on a side road I would have driven past, never seeing it, it was so concealed.

He'd made a makeshift holder for my art and was carrying it like one of those big pizza delivery carriers. He'd muttered about some of the boxes, and then he made the call to leave them. I knew he wanted to destroy them, but he saw my look and instead flicked through them and left ones behind that he deemed weren't worthy.

He hadn't said it, but he kept looking at me as if he was expecting me to fall down at any moment. The fact that I was expecting me to fall down at any moment didn't help either.

The towering trees loomed above us, their branches casting long shadows that looked like fingers stretching across the ground as the sunlight started to creep across the sky. The mountains above us were a jagged silhouette against the darkening sky, and the whole place was eerie and throwing off horror movie vibes. Honestly, if I were on the sofa watching this film, I would be screaming at us both for being idiots who deserved to die.

The path that Caleb was following was barely visible. I doubted few hikers used it. It looked more like an animal track than a trail or path.

Caleb moved with a grace that I envied, his movements silent, his body fluid and sure. He looked so comfortable out here, and I didn't doubt that he was familiar with this land like the back of his hand. He was the exact opposite of me. Where he was one with the scenery, I was crashing through the landscape like a bull in a china shop. Every step I took seemed to reverberate through the still evening. I'd tripped and stumbled so often I knew he knew I was struggling to keep up.

When my foot caught on a hidden root, I fell forward, knowing the impact was going to hurt, and I braced myself for the fall. I didn't fall, a strong hand caught me, pulling me back into his chest, waiting while I regained my footing.

"Thanks." I instantly missed the warmth of his hand as he withdrew it, seeing I was steady again.

"Are you doing okay?" Caleb's voice was low, but I could hear the barely concealed amusement. It was quite obvious I was not *doing okay*.

"As we discussed, hiking isn't my thing," I offered with a self-deprecating laugh.

I heard his answering low chuckle, and I caught his rueful smile as he met my gaze. "You're doing better than you think," he offered, and even though I knew it was bullshit and that I was doing as badly as I knew I was, his false compliment made me smile.

Instead of calling him a liar, I dipped my head in acknowledgment while trying to shake off the embarrassment of falling over, again.

Caleb's attention went back to scanning the trees, searching the shadows, and his wariness made my palms clammy once more. He looked casual and relaxed, but I'd come to decipher some of his characteristics, and I could see the tension that he tried so hard to hide from me. He looked so alert, so ready to react to *something*, that I was having a tough time not hyperventilating.

Did he expect us to get attacked at any moment? The idea scared me too much to ask because I didn't want the confirmation that this was exactly what he was waiting for.

As we walked further, the trees closed in around us. The forest seemed even more foreboding as the tall pines formed a dense canopy above us that blocked out what little light was left in the sky. The climb was gentle, but there was no denying that the air was getting colder, and thinner. The unmistakable smell of pine would put me off Christmas for life, I was sure. A shiver ran through me, and I wrapped my arms around myself, wishing I'd had the sense to take a jacket.

When I'd packed, I hadn't expected an excursion through nature. I'd stupidly thought Caleb's friend was *accessible*, and by accessible I thought within an urban area.

I needed to start asking more pertinent questions, and Caleb had to start providing answers. Actual answers, that had information.

Caleb was ahead of me once again, and as I considered him,

I couldn't shake the feeling of unease as I watched him move soundlessly through the forest. I didn't know how he was doing it; it was almost like he was floating over the rugged and uneven terrain. He was wearing heavy black boots, but his steps were effortlessly confident and *soundless* as he guided us along the trail.

"How can you move so quietly?" I blurted into the quiet.

With a glance over his shoulder, he smirked at me. "I'm making noise. You just can't hear it over your crashing."

Okay, *crashing* was harsh. But when a twig snapped loudly under my foot, the sound echoing all around us, Caleb laughed as I blushed scarlet. I fell silent as I followed him, my clumsy steps making me wince as we progressed through the trees.

I didn't know how long we walked, but I knew I was tiring. Caleb knew it too. With an unspoken agreement, he slowed, and soon we were walking side by side. The pace was slow, and no doubt for someone like Caleb, the progress was painful, but he never said a word.

I was just about to give in and admit defeat when Caleb came to a sudden stop, his hand curled around my forearm as he pulled me to a stop beside him. His body was rigid, and my open mouth snapped shut, the question dying on my lips as I watched him. Caleb turned his head up slightly, and I saw him sniff the air.

What could he smell? Smoke? I inhaled trying to smell what he could, but all I could smell was pine and damp earth. I was sure that there were parts of this forest that would never be dry, and the smell of dank, musty vegetation confirmed my thoughts.

My attention was on Caleb, waiting to see what had caused him to stop, what had caused the line of his shoulders to tense.

"Caleb? What is it?" My whisper sounded loud in the quiet, and I could hear how shaky my voice was.

When he said nothing, I felt my heart rate pick up. We were in the middle of nowhere, in the true wilderness, being hunted by *shifters*, and I had the sudden realization I was most probably in the worst position I could be. Just the two of us, alone and defenseless.

What the hell had I been thinking when I followed him into the trees?

Caleb was wound so tight beside me that I knew he was ready to pounce on whatever came at us, but even that didn't ease my panic.

"Calm down," he suddenly said with another look around. "It's nothing." His voice was low and gruff, and with a quick look over at me, he nodded. "Stay close."

Of that, I could absolutely guarantee that I would. Hell, I was so close to him already that I was almost glued to his side. "Okay."

We resumed walking, and even though he'd said it was nothing, I couldn't shake the feeling that he was just saying that to make me feel better. Caleb wasn't acting as if it was nothing. He still felt tense beside me.

I knew I was in danger of freaking out. So I did what I did when I needed to focus: I concentrated on something familiar to me. Right now, that was Caleb.

Strange how it was him, but I was so far outside of my comfort zone, was it any wonder that he was the only familiar thing to me?

I watched him from the corner of my eye as we walked. His steps were sure and steady. He avoided the concealed knots and roots of the forest floor easily as if he already knew where they were hiding. He confidently plowed ahead, sure in his direction. The whole stopping and sniffing the air was strange, but was there anything about this whole scenario that was *normal?*

My steps were slowing even more. We'd been walking for hours, and the tension was growing between us. The thick canopy overhead was thinning, and I could see through the branches now. Night had fallen, and the sky had settled into a deep indigo, peppered with stars that gave no light.

It was getting harder to see, but Caleb had taken my arm a while ago and was guiding me through the fading light. This close to him, I wanted to ask more questions. I knew he couldn't avoid them, he had nowhere to go that wasn't here, and I knew even stubborn, secretive Caleb wouldn't leave my side no matter how uncomfortable my questions made him.

But even so, despite having a captive audience, something still held me back. As I watched him, I'd also seen the number of times that he looked over his shoulder, as if he was waiting for our earlier pursuers to suddenly emerge from the shadows. I'd also watched him try to hide his frustration at our pitiful progress, and maybe it was guilt at the fact I was the reason we were making it so slow that I kept quiet.

Eventually, I had to admit defeat. "Caleb." I slowed to a stop. "I can't."

He didn't argue, didn't protest; instead, his hand left my arm, and I felt him rub my lower back. "You did well," he told me before moving away.

The sudden lump in my throat was hard to swallow past as I struggled to accept the unexpected praise. "I'm sorry it wasn't more," I told him honestly.

"You did your best." He flashed me a quick smile. "I have protein bars." He gestured to a fallen log. "Take a seat."

I was glad it was night so I didn't need to see what manner of creepy crawlies were my neighbors as I sat down. Or which ones I crushed under my ass.

He handed me a protein bar and a bottle of water, and I took both gratefully. I didn't say that I would need a lot more than a protein bar, because the exercise had made me ravenously hungry, so I just ate what he gave me.

We ate our meal—snack—in silence. Caleb remained alert as he crouched beside me. He took the wrapper off me, shoving it into his pack. "You should sleep." He pulled a blanket from his pack, laying it on the forest floor, and I was once again reminded why I hated camping.

"I need the bathroom."

He looked surprised for a moment. No doubt he was expecting to have to persuade me to "go" and instead I was letting him know. With a nod, he was on his feet, his hand held out to help me to mine.

"You'll need to stay close," he told me, leading me behind a tree, and I heard him kicking up the turf. "Try and squat here."

*Squat!* "It's just a...a number one." My face was on fire for having to discuss my toilet needs and for some reason lapsing back to first grade as I numbered them.

"Okay, hover over here and then kick this back over it, okay?"

He knew I didn't understand his bizarre instructions, and

he sighed with exasperation. "You're in the mountains now," he explained. "There's more than us out here."

"Shifters?"

"Mountain lions. Bears. Men." He added the last with a grunt. "We cover our tracks so you don't leave your scent behind."

"My scent?" I quickly realized what he meant before he needed to explain further, and I instinctively covered his mouth with my palm to stop him from telling me that the smell of my urine would invite predators to us.

I was already internally freaking out. He didn't need to confirm it out loud.

In the dark, I was never going to manage to do my business without falling over, especially when my legs suddenly decided to resemble Jell-O. With a low curse, I undressed my bottom half entirely, hoping it was only spiders and mice I was flashing my ass to.

The thought of a spider crawling up my bare ass almost made me shriek. I'd never peed so fast in my life. Caleb had given me a tissue before he stepped around the tree, and I knew he hadn't moved any farther away from me.

"Don't drop the tissue," he told me suddenly. "I have a bag for that." I was going to die of embarrassment. The thought was only cemented when he handed me a plastic food bag. "Drop it in here."

Thank God it was dark and he couldn't see my humiliation as I came out from behind the tree and stood silently as he squirted a drop of hand sanitizer in my upturned palms.

I bit my tongue when he went to my makeshift toilet and I

heard him stomp on the earth, covering my scent, as he called it.

"Get some sleep. I'll keep watch."

*Keep watch?* It all sounded very special ops, but again, I simply did as I was told and lay on the hard, unyielding earth.

The night had gotten colder, and I was sure I would never sleep, and it was with surprise that I was shaken awake.

Barely clear of the fog of sleep, I felt the prickle of unease trickle over my skin. Caleb was beside me, and I instinctively moved closer to him. His large hand clasped mine, and I felt him squeeze it slightly. Maybe in reassurance. Maybe in warning. I didn't know, and at that moment, I didn't care.

I was just so grateful he was beside me, and I knew to keep quiet.

Caleb went to withdraw his hand, and I felt him jerk in surprise when I clung to him tighter, my fingers linking with his, keeping a firm hold on him.

There was a sudden rustling in the dark of night, and me being so far from my comfort zone, I had no idea in which direction it was coming from.

But Caleb did.

I could just make out his outline in the blackness that surrounded us, and I could see his head turned to the left of where we were hidden.

"Stay behind me," he told me, his voice low and commanding and so sudden that I'd jumped with fright.

He didn't wait for confirmation as he rose and took me with him. I felt another squeeze of my hand, and then Caleb gently disengaged from my panicked hold. He stepped in front of me, and I fought the urge to throw myself forward and plaster myself to his back.

The small area we'd been using was suddenly lit with the light of the sliver of the moon that shone free from the cloud cover.

My eyes darted from tree to tree, desperate for whatever had alerted us both to remain in the tree line. When nothing immediately revealed itself, I took a step out from behind Caleb, and for the first time I saw his face.

His chocolate eyes appeared black in the night, and they were focused on that same area to the left with an intensity that caused my tummy to flutter with fear. I couldn't take my eyes off him as I watched him.

I had no words to describe him. He looked completely different from the man I thought I knew. It was like he was someone else. His face looked sharper, tension and danger rolled off of him in waves, and I took a step back. His hand snapped out and caught me. He didn't take his eyes from the tree line, but he pulled me back to his side.

"With *me*," he growled.

My body was refusing to accept that Caleb was my *safe* option as he drew himself up to his full height, and I wanted to put as much distance between us as humanly possible.

*Human.*

He heard my startled gasp and turned to face me, quickly checking to make sure I was okay. Our eyes met, and I saw him flinch.

"Later."

It was a one-word command and held no promise, but I knew better than to ask questions right now. But by God, he *would* give me answers if we escaped whatever was watching us right now.

Caleb rolled his shoulders, and I had the brief thought of a boxer loosening their shoulders before getting ready to fight.

It's what he was doing, I realized. Caleb was getting ready to fight. Almost as if my understanding was the go-ahead to our foe, something lunged from the shadows, and my scream was drowned by its roar as it launched itself toward us.

Everything happened in a blur. Caleb pushed me backward, and then he moved faster than I thought possible *towards* the thing that had attacked us as he rushed to meet its attack.

I heard a snarl, and I saw Caleb tackle the assailant to the ground. I saw fur and claws, and in my haste to get away, I fell backward. My wail as I lost my balance was cut short when I hit the ground with a thump, my head banging off the log I'd used for a seat earlier.

The painful thud of my head meeting solid wood jarred me, and my teeth sank into my tongue, causing me to yelp as I bit it. Looking up, I saw a wolf, its hackles raised, its teeth bared in a snarl, ready to launch, and I didn't see Caleb.

My head swam as dizziness from the collision made everything spin.

I heard an answering growl, low and threatening and so primal it caused the hairs on the back of my neck to stand, and I tried to turn to look, but my head decided that was the exact point that I was out of this fight, and I passed out.

## TWENTY-TWO
### Caleb

THE WOODS AROUND US WERE SILENT, BROKEN ONLY BY MY harsh breathing as I crouched over Willow, who lay unconscious below me. I hadn't seen her fall, a fact I was furious with myself for. I was supposed to protect her, and I *hadn't seen her fall.*

I could guess what happened though from the way her body lay on the blanket she'd been sleeping on when I woke her earlier. I'd investigated the cause of her fall and felt the egg-sized lump on the back of her head. She wasn't bleeding, but given the proximity of the log behind her, I could guess she fell over her own feet and landed via the log on the way down.

Exhaling long and low, I tried to shake off the remaining tendrils of adrenaline that still pulsed through my veins from the fight. Willow lay so still, her normal pallid complexion looking ghostly in the pale moonlight.

I was grateful she was okay, but I was selfishly relieved she hadn't been awake to see my shift. I felt an unfamiliar twist of guilt in my belly as I studied her prone form.

A part of me wished she had seen, and then I wouldn't have this sickening apprehension every time I thought she'd figure my secret out. But for now, I praised Luna that she had intervened one more time to keep the truth from my companion.

Standing, I searched the trees for any more unwelcome *guests*. From my backpack, I pulled out a pair of jeans, a crumpled tee that I'd relegated to laundry, and another flannel shirt. I'd ditched my jacket as I got ready to shift and kicked off my boots, but the rest of my clothes had been shredded in the shift.

I could feel the tension in my bones as my wolf still lingered beneath my skin, eager to be loose once more. I wanted to run, I wanted to finish this journey in my wolf form, but I couldn't do that to Willow. She would never understand, and I shuddered as I thought of her finding out by seeing me shift in front of her.

Tonight had been close, too close. If she hadn't fallen, well, there would be a lot of explaining to do. She would have seen what I was, what I really was. A shifter betraying her trust by not being honest with her. Not telling her that I was the same as the very monster that made her scream with fear.

Looking around, I took note of the signs of the violence that had happened here. Blood stained the ground, and more than turf had been in danger of being unearthed as we fought. I didn't know the shifters that had attacked. There had only been two of them, but two was too many when I had Willow with me.

Both had run from the fight when they knew they were bested, and I didn't chase. I didn't believe in the slaughter of our kind. Hopefully, the lesson had been taught to these two not to cross me again.

I wouldn't be as lenient the second time.

For now, I had to get out of here before she woke up and saw the evidence of a fight no man could survive. We needed to get to Cannon's pack. Stooping, I lifted her, careful of her sleeping form, cradling her close as I once more checked the lump on the back of her head. The fact she weighed practically nothing set my teeth on edge. She was so incredibly fragile and so completely out of her depth that the urge to return her to Whispering Pines and walk away was stronger than ever.

I knew she wouldn't be safe there. Willow had caught more than my interest with her drawings, and I had no way to know yet *how* that was possible.

A howl in the night made me hold her closer. The two shifters had run, but that didn't mean they wouldn't be back, even though I hoped they knew better. That didn't mean there wouldn't be others who thought they could fight me, and I knew we couldn't be here when they arrived.

Holding Willow close, I picked up the paintings, juggling them both until I got a balance that suited me. With swift feet, I made my way through the forest, my steps sure and steady as I moved faster carrying her than I had when she walked beside me. My wolf sight allowed me to check on her as I moved, and she looked to be sound asleep.

Pausing, I lowered the paintings, not caring that they were on the forest floor. I checked her pulse. She'd taken a blow to the head, but I suspected it was exhaustion that kept her in its clutches more than anything to do with her being knocked out. She'd pushed her body today. Exertion like that was foreign to her, and I had admired her determination to keep up.

A few times I'd wanted to suggest I carry her, but I knew

her pride would have resisted. So I took advantage of the opportunity now. Satisfied she was okay, I grabbed the bundle and resumed walking.

About an hour later, she stirred in my arms, a soft moan escaping, and I ignored the way my breath hitched at the sound of her soft sigh of contentment. Focusing on the fact that she was waking up, I prepared myself for the thousand questions she would wake up with.

I made my way faster, hoping to close the distance to where we needed to be.

As quickly as I walked, I knew I wouldn't be quick enough to avoid the questions. Willow was smart and tenacious. She possessed too much of both qualities if I was honest. She seemed to have that moment of clarity about me before we were attacked, and I hoped that her fall had knocked that revelation from her head.

I'd been careful around her. I knew she was suspicious of me, but after this, she'd be relentless. Coming to another fallen tree, I took care not to jostle her too much as I set her down on the trunk. I easily jumped the obstacle and, with care, picked up my fragile cargo. I held her close as she stirred again in my arms, only loosening my hold when she nuzzled into my neck, getting comfortable once more.

Looking down, I noticed how peaceful she looked when she was sleeping. She had an uncanny knack for bringing my protective instincts out of me, instincts I thought I'd left behind a long time ago. My wolf prowled close to the surface too often when she was near.

Shaking my head, I knew I had no right to feel that way towards her. She may have dragged me into her life with her drawings, but that didn't mean I had to drag *her* into mine. She would have been better off never drawing.

She had no idea who I was. What I had done.

I intended to never let her find out.

Looking up, I saw the tip of Blackridge Peak looming ominously in the night. Cannon's pack was close and, hopefully, so were the answers we sought.

As I walked through the night, we encountered no others. The terrain began to change. The forest thinned to open foothills as I began the hike, the incline steadily becoming steeper the further I got.

I knew she was awake, but she hadn't spoken, and I left her to her pretense of sleep, as she took the aid I gave her by carrying her.

The wind picked up and, with it, brought the familiar scent of pack territory. My fingers flexed and I heard Willow's sharp gasp of pain as they dug into her. "Sorry."

"You knew I was awake."

I wanted to shake my head at her. She was unbelievable. She was happy I was carrying her but pissed off that I *knew* she was happy that I carried her.

"Figured you could use the break," I said instead.

"What happened back there?" She drew a shuddering breath as she squirmed for a better position in my arms. I held her tight, denying her the movement she sought.

"A simple skirmish, was over before it began." That wasn't really a lie.

"A skirmish?" She was staring at me, eyes wide and steady. "With *what*?"

"Shifter."

*Look at me, being honest and all.*

"You fought it?" Willow looked doubtful. I tried to keep the blow to my ego in check.

"Had a little bit of help," I lied.

Willow looked around. "Where did the help go?"

"Ahead."

Was that a lie? Technically, help *was* ahead, so...I guess it was the truth.

Willow turned her attention from my face and looked ahead, taking in the peak. "We're going there?"

"Not all the way up it. The place is further ahead, but not as far up as the actual peak." She was back to staring at me. "We aren't that far away." Glancing down at her, I moved her slightly in my arms. "Try to sleep more; you're going to want to feel as refreshed as possible when we get there."

Willow looked down at her hand, which was cradled in her lap. "I can't sleep while you carry me, Caleb."

"Why?" She'd been sleeping halfway up the mountain. "You were managing it perfectly."

"It's not right," she whispered quickly.

Ah, it was her pride talking. "Willow, you've done more than I thought possible. Take the chance to rest." I saw her head dip lower. "I can move quicker with you like this." It was a harsh reality, and she would be offended that I said it out loud, but it worked. She stayed where she was, and soon the slow rhythm of me carrying her lulled her to sleep.

We would be in packlands by early morning, and I hoped Willow was ready for what was coming.

She knew more than most humans, and that knowledge came with a price. Guarding the shifter secret was given to few, and it came at a great cost. Her life would never be the same. She would be watched going forward, and some shifters would always be suspicious of her, doubting her.

But to get her answers, she had to be exposed to shifter life. There was no way around it.

I just hoped she was ready.

***

"We're close," I told her, my voice steady, breaking the silence that had followed us for most of the morning as we climbed the peak.

Willow was walking beside me. I was strong, but some parts of the mountain made carrying a human in your arms nearly impossible. The unforgiving slope of the mountain made it a natural deterrent to most humans.

She'd been on my back for some of it, to let me carry her and her artwork, but when the ground evened out, she'd wordlessly dropped her legs and slid off.

I hadn't argued. She was stubborn and I had too much on my mind to argue with her.

I could feel the tension in my body getting tighter and tighter with every step we took. It had been a long time since I had stepped into packlands, and it was something I had promised myself I would never do again.

"Their home is just beyond this next ridge."

She didn't need to speak to tell me how nervous she was feeling. I could read her easily enough. Her breath was coming more rapidly, her footsteps slowed, and she looked between me and the ridge with growing uncertainty.

Her whole body language screamed unease, and I could smell her fear.

"You'll be okay," I assured her.

"Will you?"

The question surprised me so much that I turned to look at her. "Why would you ask that?"

"I'm scared," Willow admitted, coming to a stop. "But you? You're *terrified*."

"Wil—"

"I can feel it, Caleb," she whispered. She tapped the side of her head. "I don't have my pencils or sketchbook in hand, but I am still drawing it in my head." She looked away. "*You*, in my head...and I can feel how scared you are."

It was my turn to look away, and I focused on the ridge ahead, a rocky slope that marked the boundary of a town that I'd grown up nearby. My home had never been here, but this was the closest I'd been to *home* for a long time.

I didn't know what waited on the other side, but I knew having Willow here didn't make it better. Maybe she was right, maybe I was scared because I didn't know what to expect once we passed that boundary.

There would be questions. From Willow. From the pack. About her. About me.

I didn't have any answers.

As we'd walked closer to the point of no return, the urge to tell her everything had lessened, but here, now, it was back stronger than ever. She should hear it from me first.

Right?

I knew it was right, but still, the words stuck in my throat.

Breaking my stare from the ridge, I looked back at her,

seeing she was studying me again. There was concern in her eyes, nothing else. No suspicion. No wariness. I wondered when she had lost that.

Or had she just seen enough to piece it together? She wasn't dense. She'd been with me for days. She'd seen the way I moved through the trees, the way I'd known when we were being watched.

*She'd seen the wolf at the edge of a waterfall.*

Had her questions fallen silent because Willow already had her answers? She held my stare with no fear, no judgment. Licking my bottom lip, I turned my head away again. "You know."

I turned back to see her pushing her hair behind her ear. "I suspected."

I nodded. "How long?"

"Truthfully?" I nodded again. "Now." She plucked at the sleeve of her hoodie. "I saw it." She once more tapped the side of her head.

"And you have no questions?"

Willow gave a low chuckle. "I have *so* many questions," she told me.

"And you kept your silence?" I mocked. "How unlike you."

"Don't be mean," she scolded. Her voice was low, but I could hear her perfectly. "I have two questions you can answer now."

"Only two?" My voice was a low murmur.

"Why didn't you tell me? You must have known I was suspicious?"

Of course she was; I'd been lying to her from the outset. "I didn't think you would take the news as well as you seem to be."

Willow's lips turned down as she thought over my answer. "You've protected me," she said softly. "There are things out there I wasn't expecting. Things I would never dream of to be true." Burrowing her hands in the front pouch of her hoodie, she didn't look up. "I've been painting things I can't explain. It made sense to me that the two *extraordinary* things would be linked."

"Okay." I saw her surprise at my simple acceptance. "We should keep moving. You're cold and they have tea and coffee." Rubbing my stomach, I added, "And food."

"I'm too scared to eat," she admitted. "And I haven't asked my two questions."

Frowning, I looked back at her. "You asked two."

"They were related questions. I have two *separate* questions." Her bottom lip pouted petulantly.

"Of course." I sighed and she moved closer to me eagerly. "Ask."

"Why are you so scared to go in there?"

My wolf surged upward, and I took a step away from her as my anger lit within me. "There are some things you don't need answers to." Without waiting for a response, I walked towards the ridge, my pace steady and deliberate.

I knew she followed me. She had nowhere else to go except the pack. She was in too far now.

As I crested the ridge, I was met by three males, two that I knew.

Cannon took a step forward when I came to a stop. He looked at me with sympathy and understanding in his eyes as he looked over both of us. "Welcome back to Blackridge Peak. It's been too long, Caleb."

I heard Willow come to a stop behind me. I saw the male that had too much human in his scent study her, and I guessed he was the doctor she'd met before.

I ignored the alpha in front of me, and I spoke to the doctor. "She hit her head, knocked her out. We were attacked on the way here. She's barely eaten, hasn't had enough fluids, and I've carried her for most of the journey."

He waited until Cannon had turned to give him a nod to go ahead, and then he hurried forward to his new patient. I ignored Willow's muttering about me being an ass and turned my attention back to the alpha.

"I don't want to be here," I told him bluntly. "This isn't my life, not anymore. I brought her here." I dropped the paintings between us. "I brought these. There are notepads in the packs." Cannon stayed still as I spoke. "There's a box or three back in the truck. I hid it, but you'll find it. As soon as you figure out how to stop her, I'm gone." I looked between him and his beta. "Am I clear?"

Cannon watched me silently. His eyes flicked over my shoulder and then back to me.

I had a fleeting feeling of regret when Willow walked past me slowly, the doctor hovering protectively beside her.

"I think we all heard you make yourself *very* clear, Caleb," she said bitterly as she came to a stop in front of Cannon. "Hi, I'm Willow. I'm really hoping you can finally tell me what the fuck is going on?"

## TWENTY-THREE

### Willow

EVEN THOUGH IT HAD BEEN HOURS SINCE HE SAID IT, I could still feel the anger and the *hurt* from Caleb's callous announcement. The moment that the words left his mouth, I'd felt the slice of pain as if he'd stabbed me himself. And in a way he had.

My foster mother always said words hit harder than blows, and she was right because, with each word he uttered, I felt like he'd punched me.

My chest still felt tight as I paced the room I'd been put in. My reception to Blackridge Peak, as they called it, had been friendly but *off*. I knew I wasn't welcome here. Not that they were abrasive or unkind—they weren't Caleb—but it was clear that they wished I was somewhere else.

Anywhere else.

And so did I. Did he think I *wanted* to be here? Did he think I *wanted* to know about men that *shifted* into wolves? No one wanted to know this! No sane, rational human being wanted to accept that there was more than *them* in the world.

Humans were at the top of the food chain with their intelligence and opposable thumbs, and to have that challenged by something *supernatural*...my God, the world would implode. Did they not think that I knew that? I completely understood that they were at risk here, by letting me into their world...but that didn't mean I *wanted* to be here.

Swallowing past the lump in my throat, I tried not to think about it. I tried not to think of Caleb's harsh words, but the familiar sting of rejection, of abandonment, was all too close to the surface. I was proud of myself for walking past him, for approaching the biggest man I'd ever seen in my life and introducing myself.

My voice had been strong, my back had been straight, and *I'd* been strong because I would not, under any circumstances, let Caleb see how much his words had affected me. Not when his mind was already halfway down the mountain.

Cannon had led me to a bunker. I'd had a moment of panic, but I felt no ill will from any of the three men. He'd explained that, while I was welcome, I was to be kept apart from the rest of his people. It made sense. I wasn't feeling particularly sociable anyway.

They'd both stayed with me while Mal—he insisted I call him Doc—had taken blood samples from me, and then I'd been given a hearty lunch and a room to rest.

The room was simple in decor. It screamed temporary accommodation, maybe a borderline hint of *retained guest* more than *welcome guest*, but the door was open, which had assuaged any fear of being a captive, and the lighting was adjustable, not interrogatory. Plus, the sheets on the bed were clean. There was a small shower room, which meant I didn't have to share with anyone else or have any need to leave the confines of this space.

I was tired, and the option of a nap would be welcome, but I couldn't help but be drawn to the blank sketchbook and pack of pencils lying on the small desk. They hadn't hidden their agenda at all. They wanted to see what I drew, so eager to make a connection between the supernatural and...me.

There was a first time for everything.

When Cannon walked me to the bunker, I knew Caleb hadn't followed. I didn't know where he went. Hell, he could be back in Whispering Pines by now for all I knew.

"Slight exaggeration," I muttered.

That had been another lie he told me. They hadn't taken blood from him. Doc had looked at me with surprise when I asked how much blood they'd need from Caleb. Cannon had said nothing, but I'd seen the look in his eye when I'd mumbled about my misunderstanding.

"You should rest."

His voice startled me, and I yelped, the sound seeming louder in the sparse space.

Marching to the half-open door, I looked into the hall to see him sitting on the floor across from my room.

"Surprised to see you still here." I was being a snarky bitch, but I didn't care. He deserved it.

Caleb looked away, his jaw clenched. The tension was back in his shoulders, and I hated that I was the reason it was there, that this situation was the reason that it was there.

"You don't understand."

"Then explain it to me, Caleb."

"No." He turned to look at me, and I flinched at the pain I

saw there, but he quickly looked away again. I knew he was hiding something, holding back, keeping his past hidden from me, and I knew I had no right to ask what it was.

We weren't friends. We weren't lovers. Sometimes I wondered if we were even acquaintances. I meant nothing to him. But still, I knew there was something, and I couldn't explain why, but I felt that it was something he *should* share with me.

Or maybe I was just nosy. He'd looked after me, protected me, and was striving to find answers to my paintings, and the truth was, he owed me nothing.

However, I wasn't sure if I accepted that reality.

"So that's it?" I asked, my voice steadier than I felt. "You're happy to let them solve the mystery of my art, and then you just...disappear?"

"Yeah." His voice was muted as if he didn't want to be overheard. "It's better that way."

"Better for who?" When he didn't answer, I wanted to scream, but instead, I tried to remain calm. "Caleb? Better for who? How is leaving me here, with these strangers, how is it better?"

Caleb stood slowly, brushing off the back of his legs. He wouldn't meet my eyes when he spoke. "You'll be safer here," he told me flatly. "Cannon will protect you from whoever is out there hunting you."

"Look at me."

Slowly he raised his head. His eyes were dark, almost black, and they were unreadable. What had I hoped to see? Pain? Regret? Had I forgotten who I was dealing with?

"Who says those shifters are only hunting me?" My question was met with his silence. And more silence stretched between us when he said nothing at all.

Caleb ran both his hands over his hair, the sudden movement causing me to jump, it was so unexpected. If he noticed, he didn't comment. "You should really be resting."

"You should really be staying."

His flat, unimpressed look was the final straw. With a grunt, I turned my back on him and slammed the door to the room closed.

Sinking onto the bed, I dropped my head into my hands. He was right, and I hated that, but I was exhausted. My ME had really done me a huge favor and stayed at a manageable level, almost cooperating, considering the miles I'd walked and the adrenaline that I'd experienced, but now that my brain had accepted that I was safe, my body was catching up to the fact that I'd pushed it too far.

The four vials of blood that the doctor had taken hadn't drained me, but that last encounter with Caleb had.

I knew nothing about shifters. But I remembered that wolf packs were a topic we'd covered in middle school. They were seldom alone, preferring to hunt and live in packs. Clever, majestic animals, I was always sympathetic to them.

Movies made them the villain so often, or they were the dog-like pets that were domestically trained and their wildness tamed. Both scenarios had always bothered me.

Now here I was in a bunker with people who changed into wolves and who were analyzing my blood.

Knowing I was giving in to his suggestion, and knowing I would never admit it if he asked, I lay down.

From what I'd seen of these shifters, they seemed to hunt

and stay in packs, very much like the predator I was taught about. There had been three at the inn. I now suspected that the man who tackled Caleb was one of them. I think there had been two in the forest as we journeyed here, and Cannon and his companions were there in numbers to greet us.

Yet Caleb was always alone. Why? What had happened in his past to make him choose a solitary life? He said he was a hiker. A drifter. What had driven him to never stay in one place? He'd told me he had connections, but I hadn't seen them yet.

He hadn't wanted to come here, but he had for me, and I sensed that was a huge deal for him. Cannon welcomed him *back*; was this his home?

It would make sense that it was. He was reluctant to be here. Maybe his family was nearby? I didn't need to know, and he didn't want to tell me, but that didn't stop me from getting off the bed and opening the door, intent on finding him and asking him.

He was blunt all the time. It was time to do the same to him. I wasn't expecting him to still be sitting on the floor. "Caleb?"

He didn't look up. "The one and only."

"Why are you still on the floor?"

"Why aren't you lying down like you need to be?"

Inhaling deeply, I tried a different approach. "Can we talk?" He looked up, and I saw the familiar mask of indifference. Familiar and so infuriating. "Why are you doing this?" I whispered, the words slipping out before I could stop them. "Why do you try so hard to push me away?"

I thought I saw a chink in his armor when I spoke, but it

was gone so fast I knew it was more likely wishful thinking on my part.

"I'm not pushing," he said, the finality in his tone making my heart sink. "You'd have to be close to be pushed away."

*Bastard.* That stung, he knew it did, but his hard face gave nothing away. "Fine." I hated that my voice cracked. "Then go. Don't sit outside my door to make sure I'm safe. I know that's why you're here. Don't lie to me, not again."

Caleb raised an eyebrow. "So now you *want* me to go?"

I shrugged. "If you want to go, then go. I can figure this out. I have people here who are willing to help me."

Caleb held my stare, his dark eyes black and fathomless, and my heart started to race when I thought I'd finally gotten through to him. His head jerked in a nod, and any glimmer of hope that I had that he would stay was snuffed out with his next words.

"Take care of yourself." His gaze swept over me once. "Doc will be on hand to help manage your ME, but you know your body best. Rest as much as you can."

He was giving me *health* advice? Before I got the chance to challenge him, he turned and walked away. My palm gripped the doorway, stopping me from running after him. He was contrary and rude, but he was *safe*.

He was familiar.

I wasn't ready to face this by myself, but I also wasn't going to be the damsel he thought I was. I wasn't helpless. I *would* find out what my connection to all this was, and I would get through it like I'd gotten through every challenge life threw at me.

Alone.

"Fuck him." I closed the door and lay down on the bed. "Fuck you, Caleb. I don't need you."

---

I'D BEEN HERE ALMOST TWO DAYS. MY SLEEP PATTERN WAS rubbish, but I'd still managed to get some rest. It didn't matter how agitated I was, my brain had been trained to take sleep where it needed it. The morning after my last interaction with Caleb, when I woke up, the room seemed colder and emptier, which was ridiculous since I was the only person there.

But the silence surrounding me served as a reminder that I was alone.

Caleb had left, I knew it. If I opened my door, I wouldn't find him sitting there.

I'd seen the doctor a couple of times since I'd been here, nothing more than what I'd expect from my own healthcare provider. It was an unspoken request that I remain in the room, and I had done so. I wasn't brave enough to go exploring on my own.

Unfolding the cover of the sketch pad, my fingers had a slight tremble in them as I reached for the pack of pencils, and with a low exhale, I began to draw.

While I worked, I couldn't help but notice that the bunker had an eerie stillness to it, which made an overactive imagination like mine jump at every creak that sounded. There was a blanket at the foot of the bed, and while I didn't feel cold, I still wanted to wrap myself in the comfort of a blanket to chase off the chill that clung to my bones.

Before I sat down, I pushed the door open a little for air.

That's what I told myself, but in reality, it was so I could hear anyone approach. After all, these people were strangers. Ones who may turn against me at the drop of a hat, and that just made the fact that Caleb had abandoned me worse.

Gripping my pencil, I knew I had to stop dwelling on him. He had made his choice, and I needed to get over it. My pencil flew across the page, and it was unsurprising that familiar eyes stared back at me.

He was in the woods, and I lay unconscious at his feet. He was naked, not that his state of undress interested me. I was an artist. A professional. I hadn't lingered over the curve of his ass at all. No, sir. Not me.

I was intent on my drawing when I heard the low murmur of voices, reminding me that I wasn't exactly alone, and as the conversation got louder, I knew they were getting nearer.

I pulled the cover of the sketchbook over the drawing and then remembered this was why I was here, so I carefully revealed my drawing instead.

A soft knock on my open door had me turning to see the doctor and another man I didn't know. He reminded me of Cannon, strong, large and bulky. I wondered if all shifters looked so imposing.

"Hi." I hoped my smile looked friendly and not completely intimidated.

"Willow," Doc greeted me, pushing the door open wider as he stepped into my space. "This is Ned. He's here on behalf of Cannon."

"Is he okay?"

Doc nodded. "He has other commitments this evening. He sends his apologies."

It was already evening? Time flew when you were holed up in an underground bunker where no one could find you. "Cool."

We entered into a three-way stare-off until Doc crossed the small space and peered at the drawing. "You're very talented."

"Um, thanks." Leaning back, I made room for Ned to study my drawing.

Doc glanced at me and then back at the drawing. "This was on the journey here?" he asked.

"Uhhh...yes. I think so. I hit my head," I explained as I pointed at my prone figure. "I guess that's me."

"You guess?" Ned was definitely like Cannon, zero tolerance for bullshit. The sharp intelligence in his eyes, while not as intimidating as the alpha's, was still strong. "Why is it a guess?"

"I'm not usually something I draw." It was true and I wanted to point out that few artists painted or drew themselves into their work, but I decided to keep the conversation short.

"It might not be you..." Doc was assessing me and trying to be subtle, but I'd had too many doctors in my life look at me like that.

"How long before my blood work is back?" I was curious as to their facilities here.

Doc waved me off. "Oh, I analyzed it already. One hundred percent human."

I'd never had any doubt. "Right, and this?" I pointed at the drawing.

"Is not something I will learn from blood work," he said with a smile.

"Right." Then why was I here? "So...um..."

"Why are you here?" Ned guessed with a small smile, and it made him seem younger, more approachable. "Doc is one half of the story; you're here to meet the other half."

"There's another doctor?"

"Not exa—"

"Sure," Ned cut Doc off. "Another doctor."

Doc looked away and I sensed there was more that they weren't telling me. When he looked back, he saw my curiosity before he looked around the room. "Can we ask you some questions, Willow?"

TWENTY-FOUR

Willow

"Surprised it's taken this long." I gestured to the bed. "You can sit there if you like?"

Doc sat at the edge of the bed, but Ned remained standing, though he opted to lean against the wall.

I didn't expect the first question to come from Ned. "You know what we are, what Caleb is?"

Swallowing, I nodded, conscious of their complete attention on me. It felt oppressive. Heavy. But I reminded myself this was a safe space. Caleb may have left me here, but he wouldn't have taken me here if I was in danger. "I know Caleb's a shifter, like you," I answered Ned, my eyes then flicking to Doc, "but not you."

Doc gave a thin smile. "No, not me."

"But not like me." It was a guess on my part, but it didn't surprise me when Doc confirmed my guess. I wanted to ask, but it felt incredibly intrusive, and I was already dealing with enough. "I know that you belong in a world that I probably don't belong to, one I didn't even know existed, but I feel that it's somehow tied to me. To my art?" Ned neither confirmed nor denied, and I kept speaking. "Or am I tied to Caleb?"

"Unclear at the moment." Doc looked to Ned, who hadn't moved as I spoke. "There is a danger," Doc began, "a very real one, that you knowing about us, our world as you call it, is a threat." He licked his bottom lip as he considered his words. "The fact you know is made worse by the fact that you can *see* us." He gestured to my drawing. "Not everything you draw is Caleb."

I racked my brain as I thought about what he meant. "You mean the other paintings?"

Doc nodded, still being careful of how he phrased the way he spoke to me. Of how much he revealed to me.

"What are they?" I asked, looking between them both. "They were just landscapes."

Ned snorted softly. "They are far more than that," he told me, and I could hear the anger lacing his voice. "But most importantly, they are places you, a human, should never see."

"Oh." I didn't know what to say. *Sorry I painted some woods and a pond?* "I didn't know they were important."

"You don't *know* anything," Ned snapped.

"It's why I'm here," I reminded him. I wished Caleb was here; he'd have been...actually, he wouldn't have been support-ive. He'd probably be agreeing with Ned.

"Let's dial it back," the Doc's soft voice broke the tension. "How long have you been drawing, Willow?"

"Um..." I shook my head as I tried to remember. "Since I was eight, maybe nine?"

"And what do you prefer to draw? People, landscapes, still art?"

"I like it all," I told him honestly.

"Your website is quite basic," Ned cut in. *Gee, thanks, did I say I was a website designer?* "You keep images of everything you've sold?"

"I like my website. It does what I need." His non-reaction to my defensive statement was all the reaction I needed. "You looked through it all?" They both nodded. "So you know I keep photos of all my work."

"What do you save them on? Laptop? Phone? External hard drive?"

"On the Cloud," I bit back just as rapidly as he asked.

"Good."

Ned looked at Doc, who waved him to the door. "It's on my desk." When Ned left, I knew it was to get a laptop. He was back surprisingly quickly, handing over a laptop wordlessly.

I didn't protest. I simply found the site, logged in, and then turned my gallery towards them. They watched me with interest, and I hated that I was such a puzzle to them.

Ned turned his attention to the images, his face becoming more and more unreadable as he flicked through my portfolio. With a glance at Doc, he headed into the hall. "I'll get Cannon."

"That bad?" I tried to joke with Doc, but it fell flat in the silence between us. Shifting in my seat nervously, I once more wished Caleb were here. I thought I could do this without him, but these people had no clue as to how intimidating they were.

Doc wasn't one to make small talk, and he said nothing as he just flicked back and forth between my paintings.

I heard them as they approached, and then Cannon stepped into the room, his large form making the room feel even more crowded. He went straight to the laptop, flicking through painting after painting.

"I need these to come off of this," he told me without looking up. "Not all of them, but more than a few."

"Okay."

"No argument?" Ned asked me curiously.

"It's not my intention to piss you off." I heard the frustration in my voice as I spoke to him. "If I've painted something that you feel exposes you or your life, then tell me. It'll come down."

"We're going to need you to buy back these pictures you sold too."

Looking between them, I saw they were deadly serious. "I don't ha—"

"We'll pay." Cannon folded his arms across his chest, and it made him look impossibly bigger. "You're part of our world now, whether you want to be or not. You need to protect it."

Like that was a newsflash, I almost rolled my eyes. "I won't tell anyone."

Cannon's look was filled with pity. "You already have." He pointed at the gallery of art Doc was still flicking through. "You've already shared so much."

"Too much," Ned growled.

"Make a list," Cannon ordered. "I want them off by nightfall," he told Ned. "Then I want them here." His attention fell on me. "This is it all?"

"I think so."

"You forgetting all the pieces you've given Lily?" Caleb stepped into the doorway. When no one said anything, he walked into the room, making the cramped space feel claustrophobic. As he leaned over my shoulder, I heard the sharp inhale when he saw the drawing on my sketch pad. Reaching across, he ripped the paper from the book, without looking at me. Stepping back, he turned to Cannon.

"When does the shaman get here? I want her out of my head."

"I'm not in your head," I snapped. "I thought you left?"

Caleb ignored me, his attention on Cannon. "Well?"

I went to speak again, but Doc nudged me with his knee. When I turned to him, he gave a slight shake of his head. Frowning, I heeded the warning and bit my tongue, although I wanted to demand what the hell was wrong with Caleb. Why was he suddenly being so aggressive towards me? Also, who said he could come *back*?

The tension in the air was thick. Ned kept glancing at me like I was some kind of intruder, and maybe I was. Cannon's attention was solely on Caleb and vice versa, and Doc...well, he seemed to be the only one who looked at ease.

"Can you start to remove the paintings?" Cannon suddenly asked me.

"Yes." I tapped the laptop as I spoke to Doc. "Can I use this?"

"Of course." He moved towards the door. "I'll get you the cable to charge in case it loses juice." He hesitated in the open doorway. "Don't think we all need to stay for this, do we?"

It was a not-so-subtle hint to tell his companions to leave, and I was surprised when they all filed out, which left me alone with Caleb.

I hated how he was acting. He had been distant, as if a wall had come between us the moment we entered this territory, as he called it. The easy companionship that we had as we traveled was gone.

I tried to catch his eye, but he avoided my gaze, his jaw clenched tight, so I turned my attention to the laptop. I'd never really been good with awkward silences, and as I clicked "edit site" on the page, I couldn't stop myself. "You came back? What's going on? You're angry and I don't understand why."

"I don't like it here," he said with a grunt. "I didn't want to bring you here, and I wish I hadn't."

"Then why are we here?"

"I had no choice," he muttered. He was pacing the small room, agitated and restless.

Standing, I reached out to touch him, trying to center him. "Caleb, can you just stop?"

He came to a stop in front of me, unnaturally close, bearing over me. Looking down, his eyes flashed with anger. "Why can't you understand it's not a simple case of stopping? This Peak, these people, I hate it. I hate being here."

"Then we'll leave." The only sign he had heard me was the small frown that appeared on his forehead. "I don't know what's going on with you. You're shutting me out and acting like I made you come here, but I didn't. We don't know each other that well, but I like the person you are away from here."

His frown smoothed a little as he listened to me. "You like me?"

"Since we got here, you're making it very difficult to think pleasant thoughts about you, but yes. I don't think we're enemies, are we?"

He turned his head from me with a slight huff, and I wasn't

sure if I'd pissed him off again or if he was amused by my honesty. "This Peak," he began, "it changes you."

"Do you want to talk about it?"

"Never." His voice was tight and filled with emotion, and I sensed that this subject was very raw for him.

"Will it be better if we leave?"

I expected him to agree, but instead, he shook his head, surprising me. "You're already involved." Stepping back, he dug his fingers into his hair, shaking the locks loose in frustration. "I should never have brought you here."

"Then let's go!"

"To where? Whispering Pines?" he scoffed. "You can't go back. They know about you now. I should have kept you away." Walking over to the bed, he sat down, his head down, eyes on the floor. "I should have never met you."

The harsh words cut deep. It wasn't the words themselves but the way he said them. He truly believed this, and at first, I was too stunned to say anything. "You could at least sugarcoat it when you say you wish you'd never met someone," I grumbled, trying to mask the hurt.

His grunt could not be interpreted as an apology, I tried not to stare at him, but something had been bugging me. "You're not from here," I guessed, he didn't look at me, but the way his body suddenly stilled let me know he was listening. "So... where's your mountain? The one I draw, is it close?"

"No."

Ever the conversationalist. "Does it have a name?" I prodded. "One I'd know?"

He gave me a look, the one that told me he knew what I was doing, and he didn't want to play. "No."

"Fine." I gave up. "Keep all your secrets, it's not like I won't ask anyone else." I rubbed my fingers across my forehead.

Caleb raised his head, his eyes meeting mine, and I saw the conflict in his eyes. "Have you been sleeping?"

The abrupt change of subject confused me for a moment. "You're changing the subject?" I asked him wide-eyed.

"The last one was redundant." Caleb turned his attention to the laptop. "Once you've done that, you should rest."

"Who died and made you the boss of me?" I snapped at him and his demanding ways.

He opened his mouth to say something witty I was sure, but he shut it quickly. I almost said *wise move*, but I saw his hands clenched at his sides, and I decided not to push.

Not today.

We were both tired, I reasoned, and ill-tempered. Tomorrow would be better for this conversation.

"I don't remember which paintings he didn't like," I admitted, turning my attention to the laptop.

I heard his sigh and then he was behind me, close but not touching. "I'll show you."

I deleted twelve paintings from the gallery, and Caleb made me go through my uploaded images folder and delete them from there too. I then signed into the Cloud and repeated the motion.

"Do you resent doing that?" he asked me quietly.

"No," I answered honestly. "It's like I told the others, if it puts you in danger, then I want to stop that."

I didn't turn to look up at him, but I could feel him staring at me. "It's kind of you to think like that."

I shrugged it off. "It's not as easy as I'm making it sound," I admitted, but I thought of what Cannon had said about the paintings. "Getting them back will be difficult, but if I have to, then I have to."

"You have to," he confirmed grimly.

Looking up at him, I asked, "Where are they places of? Do you know them?"

Caleb's eyes turned hard once more. "You don't need to know that."

"Right, of course." I heard the bitterness in my voice and closed the laptop. "That's just par for the course now, right? Keep me ignorant and clueless."

"You don't need to know," he reiterated angrily. "It's better if you don't."

"Says who? You?" Caleb moved to the door, and I already knew he was walking out on me, again. "Don't tell me," I mocked, "you're leaving?"

He stopped at the doorway, his head bent, slightly angled to allow him to look back if he wanted, but he didn't move any further. "I did leave," he spoke clearly, his tone devoid of emotion. "I was half a day away from this mountain when I knew I couldn't do that to you. I hate these mountains. I don't belong here, but I remembered something when I was on my way out of here." He pushed the door open wide. "You don't belong here either." His fingers tapped against the doorframe. "Rest, Willow, tomorrow won't be any easier."

"Why would it be?" I mumbled bitterly.

He hesitated. "Shadowridge Peak," he told me, his voice low, tight with emotion. "That's where I come from, where I once called home."

My emotions swelled and I went to speak, but he left without a backward glance, and that made the tears fall faster.

I'd been wrong earlier. Even with Caleb here, I felt alone. I missed my home. I missed Lily.

The sooner this other doctor came, the sooner I would be "fixed," and that meant the sooner I could go home and put this whole mess behind me.

Lying down on the bed, I closed my eyes and hoped to dream of a time when life was much simpler and shifters were nothing more than a figment of my imagination.

I lay there for a long time, staring at nothing, wondering about the secrets that Shadowridge Peak held, before sleep finally came.

TWENTY-FIVE

# Caleb



"You're up early."

Looking over my shoulder, I watched as Cannon approached me. "What do you want?"

"Good morning to you too." He sat beside me, neither of us caring that the ground was heavy with morning dew. We were higher up the mountain, not much footfall at this time of the day. "She didn't sleep well," he told me conversationally. "I admit, I never expected her to stay in the room."

I grunted at the acknowledgment. "I told you, she's predictable."

Cannon chuckled. "It's not always a bad thing," he reminded me ruefully. "Kezia would have been out of the room the moment I closed the door behind me."

"Willow isn't a shifter."

"Well aware of that." We sat in silence for a while, both lost to our thoughts before Cannon ruined it. "Have you been back?"

"No." I anticipated his next question. "Don't bother asking."

I heard his low exhale. "Right." Cannon looked down the mountain to the village that housed his pack. "You should tell her."

"She doesn't need to know."

He was watching me, and I was pretending he wasn't. "Doesn't she? She's in our world, Caleb. She's a human walking over pack territory. When she sleeps, she visits packlands. I think if you told her more about...things, she'd understand."

"You mean if I told her why I have no pack?" My voice was full of bitterness. "She doesn't *need* to know, and she will never need to know. It makes no difference to what she sees or what she paints."

"You don't know that."

Standing, I brushed off the back of my jeans, my toes curling into the grass below my feet. "I know more than you, and I know her." I didn't look at the alpha in front of me. "Tell me when the shaman gets here. I want off this damn mountain." I walked away before he could answer.

A white wolf passed me as I walked towards the bunker. It stopped and looked at me. The intensity of the amber stare would have been unnerving for some.

"He's higher up the mountain," I told her. I kept walking, knowing I probably just pissed off the alpha's mate by not greeting her properly, and no doubt Cannon would say something about it later.

The door to Willow's room was slightly ajar, and I could hear her moving about the small space as I approached. She didn't hear me. She was oblivious to so much, and I took the opportunity to watch her as she got ready for her morning.

Cannon was right. I *had* told them she wouldn't leave the room, and they had doubted me. It had been three days, and she still kept herself contained within the four walls they'd put her in. I appreciated a rule follower—when Cannon said "stay," she'd stayed—but good grief, she'd *stayed* for three days. Why wasn't she curious?

Or was she scared?

Chewing my inner cheek, I watched her and realized that was more likely. Willow had no idea of what was outside her door, and the fear of the unknown was sometimes worse than the knowledge of the known.

I took in her appearance, checking she looked healthy— well, as healthy as Willow could look. She was wearing jeans and a hoodie, and like me, her feet were bare. Her hair was loose, and while pale, she looked okay.

"You lost your shoes?"

Willow's scream of surprise made me laugh, causing her to spin to glare at me, her eyes already narrowed in anger. "Caleb! Don't sneak up on people!"

"I didn't sneak," I told her, pushing the door wider. I gestured to her feet. "Where's your socks?" Willow turned her head away but not before I saw the slight blush on her cheeks. "Ran out of clean clothes?" It was a guess, but her sharp nod made me smile. She was a rule follower, but dear Luna, she was a stubborn woman. "You should have told someone. They'd have washed your clothes."

That earned me a look. "I don't need to bother people. It's bad enough that I'm here invading their space."

"Dear Goddess," I muttered, walking into her room and picking up the tote bag she came with. Pulling it open, I ignored Willow's indignant squawk as I pulled her dirty laundry from the bag.

"Caleb!"

"For fuck's sake, Willow, it's just clothing. I've seen a lot more."

Slim hands snatched a fistful of clothes from me. "I'm sure you have, but these are *my* clothes."

"And I've seen you naked *out* of those clothes," I said, yanking them back. "So why don't you stop being precious and let me get them cleaned."

Willow stepped back, her face on fire. "You've seen me naked?"

The flat look I gave her made her angrier. "You were bedridden. Who the hell do you think did the bathroom breaks? I *told* you I sponge-bathed you!"

"Naked?" Her voice was a high-pitched squeak.

"No, I washed you fully clothed because that's helpful."

"Don't take that tone with me!"

"Then stop being a whiny bitch."

"Morning." We both turned to look at Doc, who looked as if he wished he hadn't spoken.

"Hi." Willow at least tried to be polite.

"What do you want?" I felt an elbow dig into my side and brushed off her unspoken reprimand.

"I wanted to ask Willow what she would like for her breakfast."

As he rattled off the choice of menu, I turned towards her to watch her falter at being the center of attention. "Bacon and egg sandwich sounds good," I cut him off. "I'll have two, she'll have one." Willow turned to gape at me. "I'll take extra bacon." Doc didn't react when I added coffee to my "order." He left us and I knew we had a fifty-fifty chance of getting anything.

"You're rude."

"You're too timid." Dumping the clothing on the bed, I went about piling it and then rolling it into a small bundle, tucking it under my arm. "I'll give these to someone who'll wash them and have them back soon."

"That it? You're ready to leave again?" Willow picked up her sketch pad, suddenly looking nervous, holding it out to me. "I think you need to look at this."

For the first time in a long time, our roles were reversed, and I was the unsure one. "What is it?"

"Look and see."

Dropping the bundle, I took the book, but Willow's finger was acting as a placeholder, so she came forward with it. As I took in the page, I didn't pay any heed to how close she stood to me.

The scene was chaotic. My first impression was that the page was too small to contain everything that she'd seen, as if the paper couldn't contain the turmoil that she'd drawn. Trees, broken and gnarled, framed the page. The trees themselves felt "heavy," like they were weighed down with an oppressive energy, making the whole drawing even more foreboding.

At the heart of the chaos, wolves snarled, their eyes gleaming with a savage intensity. They stood over fallen figures —some in human form, some already shifted into wolves— locked in a struggle so desperate I could almost taste their fear. The fight to survive was being fought on the paper that I held in my hands. My eyes raced across the page, taking note of the fallen and the ones still fighting, not yet ready to accept their fate.

She'd captured the conflict from both sides brilliantly, or perhaps it was my memory that appreciated the detail she could never understand. Wolves clawing at the air or their attackers in a final, futile attempt to survive. Among them lay the broken who had already been embraced by defeat.

Near the edge of the trees, a large cabin loomed, almost overshadowed by the sheer violence that surrounded it. It stood firm yet haunted, serving as a silent witness to the massacre. Every inch of the drawing was filled with intricate details, the lines jagged, almost frantic, as if Willow had been driven by the intense desire to capture each horrifying moment. However, no matter how much was crammed into the scene, it still felt incomplete, as if the true magnitude of the vision was too immense to be contained within a single page of a sketch pad.

"Caleb?" Her voice was soft and gentle, and I had the desire to pull her closer, to take whatever comfort she offered.

"Are there—" My voice cracked, the sound barely more than a whisper. I couldn't believe I could still speak at all. Swallowing hard, I cleared my throat and forced the words out. "Have you drawn more like this?"

Her eyes flickered with something I couldn't quite place, a mix of hesitation and fear. She didn't answer, breaking our stare as she looked away from me, the silence stretching between us, pressing down on me like the weight of the scene in my hand. Blood rushed through me, pounding in my ears as I waited for Willow to answer. "Willow?"

Finally, she nodded, a small jerk of her head, her shoulders tight with tension. "Yes," she admitted. "There are, but, Caleb..." Willow reached for me, a slight tremble in her hand as it lay upon my forearm, the touch delicate like her. "They're not any easier to look at. I don't think you need to see them."

My breath caught in my throat at the words, making me feel exposed. Vulnerable. I knew I needed to see them, should demand to see them and relive the nightmare of my past, but part of me, the part that was almost shaking with anger as she stood so innocently next to me, wasn't sure I could handle seeing it. Knowing that *she* had seen it.

It was too much. These drawings weren't just images—they were a window into my past, a past that had no right to be revisited.

"Show me." My voice was harder, stronger. It was a good thing because I couldn't be weak. "Now, Willow," I snapped at her. "Show me everything."

She hesitated again, and then slowly she reached across to the small desk for another sketch pad I hadn't even seen. "I'm sorry." Her voice was small, *guilty*, and I wanted to tell her it wasn't her fault, but the words wouldn't form because I was already staring at the next sketch, and I felt the room closing in on me as the world shifted beneath my feet.

I think I stumbled—maybe I fell—but the edge of the bed caught my hip as I sank to the floor. A dull ache throbbed from the impact, but it was nothing compared to the storm raging inside me. My fingers gripped the book, the pages creasing at the tight hold, grounding me in the present, reminding me that it wasn't real, even as my mind whirled with the memories of that morning.

Memories I had fought so hard to bury.

But here it was in front of me, the scene where my father lay murdered, his blood spilling around him as life left him.

I didn't know how long I stared at it, but eventually, I made myself turn the page. I flicked through the drawings, each page a reminder of the past, each as sharp in detail as they were unforgiving in truth. My chest felt tight as my gaze skimmed between the images, not looking too closely, knowing each one was more painful than the last.

It was all too familiar and so dreadfully real.

"Caleb." Willow's voice broke through my haze. I hadn't noticed she'd followed me down, sitting on the floor beside me, her eyes wide and her face pale with concern. "I didn't know that it would hurt you like this."

I didn't know if I could speak, caught so fast between anger and sorrow. My voice was gone. My throat was so dry, the words lodged deep somewhere inside me. I didn't know if I could keep my anger at bay—anger at what she had drawn, anger at her for seeing this part of my past, anger at it all. When I finally spoke, the brokenness that I carried within me seeped through as my eyes stung with unshed tears. "How could you know? How could you know that it would hurt?"

Willow moved closer, no doubt wanting to give me comfort, but I moved away, needing the space between us. I knew that I wasn't angry at her, not really. She had no idea what these drawings were or what they meant to me. Or the pain that was unleashed when I looked at them. She didn't know, but it didn't make the pain any less.

"This is what I've been running from," I admitted, the confession surprising even me. "These drawings, *everything* that they represent, I thought I'd left it behind."

She reached for one of the discarded sketchbooks, her eyes taking in the scene, her finger tracing the image of a fallen wolf. "I don't think you can leave something like this behind," she murmured.

Resting my head against the bed, I tilted my head upwards to stare at the ceiling. I didn't want to see what lay before me anymore. "It's like you've been made to draw this as punishment," I whispered, my voice hoarse.

"Punishment?"

"For leaving," I confessed. "For walking away. But these..." I looked back at the drawings, gesturing weakly to the memories confronting me. "These are the past reaching for me, ready to pull me back in."

Willow looked between the drawings and me, her forehead forming that one single frown line that told me so much. "Maybe..." She bit the bottom corner of her lip. "Maybe it's about reminding you that you're stronger now. Maybe you're being shown that you're ready to face this..." She cleared her throat. "Whatever this is."

My snort was loud in the hushed quiet of the room, the words hanging between us, and I could see that she clearly believed them, but the fear I felt when I looked at those sketches, that fear didn't make me strong.

It only reminded me of how weak I had been.

But the memories that had surfaced had done more than just remind me of the past, they had opened a door I'd shut behind me years ago. Now, it seemed that the only way to ever truly put the past behind me was to either step through that door or slam it shut and never look back.

"I don't know if I can do this," I said, more to myself than to Willow.

She leaned forward and placed a hand on the floor near mine, careful not to touch me but close enough that I could feel her presence. "You don't have to do it alone," she whispered. "I'm here. I think...I think we're in this together no matter what." She moved her hand closer to mine, almost touching. "You're not alone."

Looking at her, her green eyes filled with sympathy, her face one of concern, I could feel the emotion from her like it was my own. Willow's hand lifted to push back her hair that had fallen forward, but my fingers reached it first. The soft, silky strands felt so delicate between my fingers as I gently tucked them behind her ear.

She watched me, eyes wide but cautious, trying to read my thoughts. I moved back, breaking the connection as I got to my feet.

Willow's gaze followed me. I could see her uncertainty, and I could almost hear the unasked questions on her lips, but I couldn't stay in this room a moment longer. Too many emotions battled within me, threatening to pull me apart or pull me under.

"I need air," I muttered, the words more for me than for her. My voice was still unsteady, my heart still felt like it was ready to punch through my chest, and I turned away from her, uncomfortable with how much she'd already seen. The need to escape, to put as much distance as I could between the memories and her, was suddenly overwhelming even though I knew that wasn't fair to Willow at all.

Reaching the door, with one hand braced against the doorframe to stop me from bolting from the room, I could feel her eyes on my back. I didn't look over my shoulder, but I steadied my breathing and tried to quell the emotion within me. "I'm not leaving," I told her quietly. "I just need air."

I didn't wait for her response, walking quickly along the hall of the bunker, the cream walls silent as I passed. Jogging up the few steps that took me outside, I gasped with relief when the cold morning air greeted me. Walking a few steps away from the entrance, I relished the chance to catch my breath.

Without thinking about it, I shed my clothing, my form changing quickly from man to wolf. I needed to break free from it all, and the only way to escape was to run.

I wasn't running *from* her or running away; I just needed a chance to regroup. A respite from the sorrow that surrounded me, and a chance to clear my head before I had to face it all again.

As my wolf raced across the bleak mountain, the cold wind whipped through my fur, and I let myself be free. The rhythmic pounding of my paws against the earth was liberating. Being in my wolf form helped me reconnect with myself, and the memories of pain and fear that I had buried deep down inside, while jumbled, were faced as I ran.

The peak stretched around me, the terrain hard and challenging, a reminder of the challenges I'd faced and no doubt the ones to come. With every stride, the weight lifted from my shoulders, the burden of the past a little lighter as my path seemed to be clearer.

For the first time in a long time, I felt something I thought I'd forgotten.

I felt hope.

# TWENTY-SIX

# Willow

I STAYED ON THE FLOOR LONG AFTER CALEB HAD LEFT THE room. I wasn't sure I had the strength needed to stand. The charge of emotion that had spilled out into this room didn't disappear when Caleb did.

I'd seen him react to my paintings and sketches before—a flicker of recognition, a tightness in his jaw, the clench of his fists—but this time was different. The moment he had looked at the first drawing, something inside him had broken. When he saw the next one, he hadn't *just* been silent, he had been ruined as the air around him became thick with emotions I didn't think he'd let surface in years.

All I had been able to do was sit there and watch him as his eyes traced lines of pencil that depicted scenes I could never have known, yet I'd drawn them with surprising accuracy. Scenes that I now knew belonged to him—someone who had lived through the things that I had conjured from...somewhere.

When he had lifted the sketchbook, I had seen the tremble in his hands, the paper crumpling with his grip. His breathing had been shallow and ragged, coming from him in bursts, and I realized he wasn't *just* angry and upset, he was *hurting*. Hurting deeply. The kind of pain that coated your bones and that no time or distance could ever remove.

Or heal.

I had questions—God, I had so many questions—but how do you ask a man who has just shattered in front of you to answer them?

My heart was still racing, and I berated myself for being so incredibly blind. How had I not seen the damage I was doing to him? No wonder he wanted far away from me; every time I sketched him or a scene from his past, I was tearing open his wounds. How was he supposed to heal and move on with his life if I was constantly reminding him of what he had lost?

I'd told him I hadn't known, and he had turned to me, his eyes dark and devastated, and asked me how I could have known. As if that wiped clean the damage I had done.

His words had given me no comfort, and I deserved none.

Caleb's tone had been flat, devoid of emotion, but I hadn't sensed blame, but he *should* blame me, because I *had* known, hadn't I? Not the details, not the horror that I knew now, but I'd seen the haunted look in his eyes, the way he kept himself distant, never fully mingling with anyone. He kept his secrets close, and I'd been so wrapped up in myself, desperate for my own answers, that I hadn't really seen how I was affecting him. But I knew it was more than a man who kept himself to himself.

*I had known.*

I blinked back the tears that threatened to fall, because this wasn't about me or my guilt. This was about Caleb, about the man who fought for me and protected me, all while he carried the weight of a past I may never fully understand.

Would saying *sorry* ever be enough? It sounded hollow in my head, and I knew I could never apologize enough to him. I had dug up his feelings, ones long since buried, and I'd dragged it all to the surface.

My only consolation, and it was a very small one in light of this morning's events, was that his past was never gone. It had all been there, festering within him, and I believed that it needed to be let out, but I didn't think I was the person to bring it screaming into the light.

He'd told me he needed space, and I knew it would take a while for him to process it all before he came back, probably dreading what else I would be ready to show him.

He'd walked out of the room a different man than the one who had entered this morning, and I swore to myself I would do whatever it took to help him through this. He was alone and he didn't need to be.

He had me.

I was all in, and I would do whatever he asked of me to help him face his past. I was sure that wouldn't be a comfort to Caleb, but I knew that he deserved to heal, and I would do whatever it took to make that happen.

Which is why I did the one thing they had asked me not to. I stepped outside my room and went looking for answers.

When I had been brought here, I'd been so angry with Caleb I hadn't paid any attention to my surroundings until I was alone in my room with the promise to *stay* still fresh in my ears.

The hallway looked military. The walls curved slightly,

giving the impression of a cylinder, and I had a fleeting moment of hysteria as I imagined being inside the barrel of a giant gun, just waiting for someone to pull the trigger.

Was the someone me?

It was an absurd thought. I was no one to these people, but still, the feeling that *I* was the danger stuck with me as I walked down the empty corridor.

The fluorescent lights above me hummed with electricity, their brightness causing my tired eyes to wish for sunglasses or, at the very least, a dimmer switch. The hallway had impressive acoustics. Every step seemed to echo, and as I crashed along the hallway, I marveled at how I couldn't hear Caleb or any of the others when they approached my room.

The further I went, the more I told myself this was a bad idea. Was I walking deeper into trouble?

A door opened and Doc came out of the room, looking surprised to see me as I came to an abrupt halt on seeing him.

"Willow? Are you okay?"

Was I? I didn't think I could answer that truthfully. "Caleb's gone for a walk."

Doc looked over his shoulder, and following his line of sight, I saw stairs ahead. "Okay, and you"—he paused uncertainly—"want to go for a walk?"

I was going to say no, I wanted answers, but his question made me pause. Did I want some exercise? I'd been in here for three days. "Yes, I want to go outside."

Doc didn't even blink. He simply turned around and started to walk to the entrance, or was it an exit? Either way, I followed closely behind, the weight of what I'd done to Caleb pressing in on me until I felt like I couldn't breathe.

When Doc pushed the door to the outside open, I practically shoved him aside, desperate for fresh air. I almost tripped over my own feet in my haste to put distance between me and the bunker as I blinked in the brightness, inhaling a deep breath of clean air, relishing the freshness.

Doc hung back, giving me the space I so desperately needed. I walked a few steps from the bunker door. The grass was soft and damp beneath my feet, reminding me I had no socks or shoes on, and my feet were going to protest soon as the chill got to them. The smell of pine and earth mixed with the crisp morning smell, and I breathed in deeper.

"I can almost feel it cleanse my lungs," I told Doc with a smile.

"Was it that bad inside?" he asked me, half joking, but looking over at him, I saw he was as watchful and careful as he always seemed to be with me. "With Caleb, I mean."

I hadn't needed his clarification. Wrapping my arms around myself, I realized there was a chill I hadn't noticed in the air. "Summer will soon be over."

"Willow?" Doc took a step towards me. "Are you okay?"

I nodded vigorously, even though I was pretty sure it was a lie. "I just needed some air," I told him, my voice sounding thin and shaky even to my own ears.

Doc didn't believe me. I could see it on his face, but he didn't push me. He simply took a step back, respecting my need to not talk about it.

I was grateful for the reprieve. For the unspoken acknowledgment that I just needed some space.

Turning myself away from his prying eyes, I looked and saw the mountain for the first time. It was stunning and high, and so damn steep. "I can't believe I climbed this." My voice was barely above a whisper, but I heard the huff of laughter from Doc. "Okay, I didn't do it all myself," I admitted with a grin he couldn't see.

Yet again, my mind turned to Caleb. All I could think about was him. The pain in his eyes as I stupidly showed him my sketchbook. By trying to help, I had only caused more pain. I took another deep breath, filling my lungs with cool air as I steadied myself from the events of this morning.

"Did you eat my breakfast?" I asked Doc suddenly and was rewarded with a guilty flush. "That's stone cold, Doc. Stone cold."

"I'll make sure you get double at lunchtime."

"I'm hungry *now*," I reminded him. I wasn't—the events of this morning had wiped out any appetite I had—but still, you didn't eat someone's breakfast. "I also have questions."

For the first time, Doc looked uncertain. "Now isn't the best time to ask them."

"Why?"

His lips quirked into a smile, but he looked away. "Because I don't have answers for you, girlie."

"Girlie?" I thought about it. "Irish?"

"Scottish," he corrected. "For a very brief spell, but my mum held onto some things and let go of others."

"Like?"

"My dad."

"Oh." Awkward. I changed the subject. "When does the other doctor get here?"

"Later."

Right, well that was helpful. "Until then, we do what?"

"You want to tell me more about yourself?" he asked me, and I wasn't surprised when he plopped down on the grass.

"Aren't you cold?"

"Nah, I have hot blood."

"You're...mixed?" I hoped he wasn't easily offended. I knew there was a better way to ask that question.

"Yeah, I get some perks, not them all." Doc eased back on his elbows as he watched me. "Did you ever find it strange that your foster parents never adopted you?"

*Wow.* "Um...no." The truth was I'd been grateful I had a home and people who cared for me, so I'd never really thought about it.

"You were with them for six years." His head tilted to the side, his eyes searching mine like I was a puzzle. "It's a long time."

"I guess." I heard the defensiveness in my voice and tried to hold back any emotion. "Not everyone gets adopted, you know. Being in the foster care system isn't like being in a rerun of *Annie*." Rubbing my hands on my jeans, I felt the chill even more, or maybe it was because I was feeling exposed that a shudder ran through me.

"They were bad to you?"

I gasped at the thought. "No! They were wonderful people." Pushing my hair behind my ear, I knew I was glaring at him. "They did their best, and that's all I could ask for. They loved me."

"Well..." He shrugged. "I'd have asked for the adoption papers to be signed."

"Says the guy who's never been in the care system."

"Caring and *committing* are two different things." Doc's

words hung in the air between us, heavy with meaning that I didn't want to investigate further. But I knew it would keep me awake tonight... "Did they ever tell you why?"

I opened my mouth to respond but found myself at a loss for words. The honest answer was that they hadn't. It was a question I'd never thought to ask. I'd accepted it, convincing myself that it held no significance. Yet, as he scrutinized me intensely, I began to understand it held a little significance.

To me.

Had it always? Jan and John loved me, cared for me, gave me a home... Did it matter they hadn't fully adopted me?

"I never asked," I admitted quietly. "Maybe I didn't want to know the answer."

He nodded slowly as if he understood more than he was letting on. "The answers we often shy away from are the ones that have the most profound impact on our lives."

He may as well have punched me in the gut.

His statement rocked me. I'd told myself that it didn't matter, that I was fine with how things had been. But maybe I *wasn't* fine. Maybe I had just buried those questions so deeply that I'd forgotten they were there, festering.

*Like Caleb had.*

I looked away, the weight of Doc's words settling over me. "What's the relevance?"

"Because it matters," he said simply, his voice gentle. "And because I think you deserve to know why they didn't make you a permanent part of their family."

I swallowed hard, feeling the sting of old wounds being reopened. "And what if the answer isn't one I wanted to hear?"

"Then at least you'd have known," he replied, his eyes softening. "And knowing is the first step toward healing."

I stood there wondering if what he said was true and how that made me feel, but I remembered my foster parents, remembered how they had cared about me. So I wasn't adopted, but it didn't mean they hadn't loved me. Yes, maybe it had bothered me when I was younger—this morning's conversation suggested it still did—but my mind thought back to the sketches in my room. Knowing that someone had lived through *that?* The fact I wasn't adopted was irrelevant. There were more important things to deal with, ones that brought me here in the first place, that I needed to focus on.

"So, my drawings?" I watched Doc straighten a little. "That's why I'm here, right?"

I watched as a small smile played on his lips. "Yes, it is."

"Then why am I waiting?"

"We need one more person here for you," Doc reminded me. "He isn't here yet."

"Right...the doctor."

"Yeah." He looked uncomfortable, and I wanted to push, but I didn't. "Has it only ever been Caleb you've drawn in advance before meeting them?" Doc focused on me. "I think there was a better way to phrase that."

"The only person? Yes, I think so?" I thought about it. "He's the only one I ever turned around and found facing me," I added ruefully.

"What was that like?" he asked, his gaze unwavering.

"Unnerving. I thought it was weird, and then I realized I must have seen him before."

"But you hadn't?"

"But I hadn't."

"And did it strike you as odd?" He sounded more intrigued than skeptical, which was nice, but still, it was uncomfortable to be talking about it.

"Did it strike me as odd that I was drawing a man into existence?" I asked him with a flat look. "Yeah, it freaked me out." Blowing out a low breath, I tried to rein in my frustration. "You think that I don't know how weird this is?" I considered him and thought about it. "But then you're a descendent of someone who can *shift* into a wolf...maybe this is normal for you?"

Doc laughed at me, giving me a half shrug. "You got me, but even for someone like me, living somewhere like this"—his hand gestured to our surroundings—"you're still weirder."

His playful comment made me laugh, the tension easing. "Yeah," I agreed, my smile fading. "When I drew Caleb and then *saw* Caleb, it...yeah."

"It's not something you ignore." Doc's voice was quiet.

"No. So I walked up to him and accused him of following me."

Doc stared and then burst out laughing. "I don't know him well, or even at all, but I can just see the look on his face!"

"He called me conceited and arrogant, I think it was."

"I think you'll find it was desperate and pathetic," Caleb said as he walked around the corner of the bunker and joined us. He was pulling his T-shirt over his head, and I looked away before anyone could accuse me of checking out his abs. Which I didn't at *all*. Not for long anyway.

"Hey," I greeted as he came to stand beside me. "Are you okay?"

"Went for a run. Needed to clear my head."

He didn't look at me, but I didn't sense any ill feelings towards me either, and I felt myself relax a little. "That's good. Doc was asking me about me drawing you."

Caleb looked at the doctor, his look shrewd and assessing. "Were you? Without Cannon? Or me?"

"I don't need the alpha's approval," Doc said, coming to his feet.

"You sure about that?" Caleb's voice was low, a warning in his tone, and I saw Doc flush and look away.

"It was just general questions," I spoke up, defending the other man. There was a strange tension, so I carried on. "It's why I'm here after all, right? To get answers." I tugged on Caleb's arm. "You don't get answers without questions."

He turned to look at me, his eyes running over me quickly, checking I was okay, but still, it gave me a small thrill that after everything from this morning, he still was making sure I was good. "Yeah, it's been three days, and I haven't heard any answers yet." His voice was low and gruff, a gravelly quality that my body seemed to appreciate too, so much so that I hoped I wasn't blushing.

Caleb's attention flicked past me, looking over my shoulder, and I turned to see Cannon coming towards us. He took the three of us in with one look, and I noticed the look he exchanged with Caleb.

"Okay, you want answers?" Cannon asked as he came to a stop beside us. "Let's go get them. He's here."

TWENTY-SEVEN

## Willow

I DIDN'T KNOW WHAT TO EXPECT, BUT CALEB HAD BECOME tense beside me, even though his gaze was trained on Cannon.

"Let's go," he spoke suddenly, startling me a little and making me jump, which he never commented on if he noticed.

Cannon had already turned away, and Doc quickly followed, both knowing I hadn't moved yet and Caleb hadn't either, even though he was the one who had told us to move.

"You good?" He didn't look at me as he asked. "Ready for this?"

My heart was racing. I wouldn't lie and say I was fine. I was far from fine, ready to lie down and hide under a blanket rather than face what was coming next. Instead of admitting that, I lied after all. "I'm good."

Caleb smirked but didn't call me out on my lie. Instead, his fingers circled my wrist, and he tugged me forward. "Come on, this is why we're here."

We followed the others and soon I was distracted by the small town that was uncovered as we descended the short distance. Looking back over my shoulder, I saw the bunker was hidden.

"Clever, isn't it," Caleb commented. "They used the mountain's natural elevations to conceal what's in plain sight from hikers who will stick to the trail that naturally leads them away from here."

"They built this?" I asked, taking in the range of houses.

"Nah, old mining town. When it was abandoned, the pack just moved in and expanded a little."

A little? It was a proper *town*. It wasn't a few scattered homes; it was streets and deliberate town planning. I'd expected...I wasn't sure what I expected. Shacks? Huts? Neanderthals that lived in caves or dens?

"You were thinking log cabins, right?" Caleb's suggestion was a lot kinder than what I'd actually been thinking, so I agreed with his assumption rather than admit my ignorance. "Because of what you drew earlier?" he asked curiously, cautiously.

Remembering the large log cabin in the sketch, I went with it. "Sure."

If he thought my answer was short, he didn't comment, but his grip tightened fractionally on my wrist. "You don't need to keep hold of me. I won't run away," I told him softly.

"I might."

The low admission made me look at him in surprise, but he was staring right ahead, and when I pulled my wrist free, lacing our fingers together, he didn't look at me. He didn't even blink, but he let me hold his hand, and that said more than words could.

Cannon took us through the street, and as I looked around,

I noticed there was no one else on the street. Instinctively, I knew that was because of me. I was human and I was a threat to these people just by knowing they existed.

The house Cannon took us to had three simple steps that led up to it. The door was open, and I thought it was strange but also suited this town. The house had wooden floors, and that was all I noticed before I was led into a room that looked like a library.

Caleb led me to a couch, and I sat, but he remained standing. An older man was on one chair. His eyes had a coating, like heavy cataracts covered them, but his focus was on me despite his impairment.

"You smell of fresh air," he told me simply.

"Um." I was blushing and I wasn't sure why. "I was just outside," I told him.

He smiled widely, teeth white and even. "So light," he murmured. His attention shifted to Caleb, who was still standing. "Still dark."

Caleb's top lip curled into a sneer. "Still shit at using full sentences," he snarked back at him.

The old man laughed, and I saw Caleb relax and smile too. "Caleb," he said fondly. "It's been too long."

"I didn't know it was you that they asked for," Caleb told him casually.

"We thought you may not have come if you knew," Cannon said, his tone light, but I saw his eyes held a warning.

Caleb sniffed, looking away. "Never knew Blackridge and Anterrio had such a close connection." He looked between them. "Your mate?" Cannon nodded once and Caleb sighed. "I bet that's a story," he murmured.

Unexpectedly Cannon laughed, the other two males in the room smiling too. "You have no idea."

Caleb looked down at me. "That's a definite sign to never ask." His tone was trying to be light, but I think he was deadly serious.

Caleb talking to me brought the older man's attention back to me, and I shifted under the weight of his stare.

"I've looked at what you draw," he told me bluntly. "You have a gift."

Was he telling me I was talented? "Thanks."

He frowned, letting me know I'd misinterpreted. "It's an honor and a curse," he clarified.

Of course it was. Why would it just be a good thing?

"And how do I give it back? This gift?" I asked him. He considered the question, and I hoped I hadn't offended him. He seemed nice, a little quirky, but he was polite and seemed harmless.

"Well, that's why I'm here," he told me. "I shall ask Luna and see what the Goddess has planned for you."

I choked on the word *Goddess*, but he seemed completely at ease blaspheming, and the others all appeared to become more serious when the word was bandied about.

"Luna's your, um, Goddess?"

Out of the corner of my eye, I saw Doc's frown, but he said nothing to contradict anything.

"We are children of the moon," the old man said. "Luna rules us."

A random thought from folk tales and TV shows blurted out of my mouth with little thought behind it. "Like the moon controls you to shift? Like werewolves on TV and in the movies? Full moon and you go all furry?" I wasn't sure which one I insulted, or maybe it was all of them, because three very hard stares centered on me. Except Doc, who was covering his mouth, and I knew he was trying not to laugh at my ignorance. "No?" I guessed. "Sorry?"

"Furry?" Caleb shook his head slightly. "We can change at will," he told me. "The moon has very little influence over us."

"But the moon's your Goddess..." I'd heard of sun worshippers, and honestly, put me on a white sandy beach with a frozen margarita, and I'd happily join the flock.

"Not *the* moon," the older doctor corrected. "It's figurative, and the moon has a lot of influence over us." The latter was said for Caleb's benefit, I was sure of it.

All I knew was it was making my head hurt. "Can we just accept I don't know anything about you people, and I think it is better if that continues. I just want the visions to stop. I want to stop pouring my heart and soul into a painting only for Caleb or one of you to rip and burn it."

"'You people,'" Cannon commented. "So judgmental."

"Our people," the older man spoke clearly, "are a gift from the Goddess. Humans with a little more *magic* in them," he said with a wink. "We are stronger, healthier." His eyes took on a knowing look as he spoke to me. "We age differently, we rarely get sick."

Sounded like they got more than a *gift*, it sounded like bliss. "Rarely sick?" I asked, and I knew why no one was surprised when I asked it. "Then why do you need doctors?"

It was Doc's turn to shift in his seat uncomfortably. "They don't really need me," he explained. "I rarely get to treat anyone here, but Cannon allows me to work here, test some theories."

Test? My mouth dropped. "You test on *them?* When they are animals?"

"The ethics of it are simpler than animal testing," Caleb of all people spoke. "It's consensual and the test subjects can use their voices to relay results."

I didn't like it, but I said nothing. It wasn't my business. My attention moved back to the other man. "And you?"

"I'm a conduit for our Goddess. Like your men and women of faith."

"He's a shaman," Caleb said to me. "Through him, Luna speaks."

Religion. A *believer* wasn't something I would have pegged Caleb for being. "Theology wasn't my major," I muttered. "And I don't have the brain capacity for this conversation even if it was." Looking at the four of them, I sighed. "So, what did she say? How do you fix me?"

The shaman said nothing as he considered me, then turning to Doc, he asked a question I already knew the answer to. "Definitely human?"

"Yes."

The shaman shook his head. "I smell it, but I don't believe it." He studied me some more. "This illness they tell me you have—"

"ME," I corrected. "I have chronic fatigue syndrome."

"It makes you tired?"

"It's more than that. Just think of me as permanently exhausted." My tone must have been more bitter than I realized, because Caleb dropped his hand to my shoulder, giving it a slight squeeze.

"A mask, perhaps?" the shaman mused. "You've had this all your life?"

"No, I got it when I was a teenager."

His gaze sharpened, which was remarkable for a man with impaired sight. "What happened?"

"I got an illness. ME's an aftereffect of that." I felt the weight of Caleb's stare. "Maybe," I added reluctantly.

He sat back in his seat, considering. "Your parents died?"

"Foster parents, yes." He looked up at Cannon in question, and I explained. "I was left," I told him. "I don't know who my parents were. Or if they're alive. I was in the care system, John and Jan fostered me, and they gave me a home for six years." I avoided looking at Doc as I spoke.

"Did you have your illness before or after?"

"I caught glandular fever after they died." I saw his look and elaborated. "They were killed in a car crash. I went back into care."

"John and Jan..." Cannon spoke for the first time.

"McLeod."

"Not Harper?" Caleb asked.

"No, Harper is from the home I was in, Harper's Home for Girls."

"You took your name from the orphanage?" he asked me with surprise.

"It's the name I was given when they found me," I murmured, aware of the scrutiny from the others in the room.

"You lived in an orphanage, you were fostered by the McLeods," Doc summarized quickly, "they died in a car crash when you were sixteen, and you took ill and developed ME after it. Right?"

"All you're missing is the big red book," I grumbled. Seeing the blank faces, I shook my head. "*This Is Your Life?* No? Okay. Forget it. It *is* old, I suppose." Seeing them all look at me, I shrugged. "Sorry."

"What age are you?" Cannon suddenly asked me.

"Twenty-six."

"Ten years," he mused, his gaze locked on Caleb's. "Coincidence?"

"What is?" I asked, looking between the two of them. "What's a coincidence?"

Caleb's lips were pressed together in a thin line. "I think so," he said, ignoring my questions and Cannon's skeptical look.

"It's not a coincidence," the shaman said. *His* attention had never left me, and I would have welcomed the relief of him looking away. It was unnerving. I felt as if he was seeing much more than just my physical body in front of him. "Nor is it random."

"Luna?" Cannon asked doubtfully. "Why?" He sounded as bewildered as I felt.

"I'm human," I reminded them. I felt that someone had to point my humanity out to them. "I don't interest your God."

"Goddess," three voices corrected immediately.

*Oh-kay.* "Right."

The shaman turned his head, his attention moving to the man who still stood beside me. "It's been ten years, Caleb."

What had?

"You're stretching." His voice was tight with controlled fury.

"Am I?" The old man leaned back in his chair, so unassuming, but as I watched him, I realized something I hadn't picked up from him before: he radiated power.

Now that I had noticed it, I couldn't take my eyes off him. A fact he noticed, because his gaze fell back on me. "You see it now?"

I didn't know what *it* was, but I knew whatever it was, I did, I could see it. I wasn't one for talking about auras or any of that mumbo jumbo—that was more Lily's thing, telling me about burning sage and stuff. But sitting here, in a room full of supernaturals, I could feel their presence as more than just four men in a room.

"I don't..." I blew out a breath. "I don't know what it is, but it's something."

That earned me a small smile from him. "You've been brave," he suddenly complimented me. "A lot has been thrown at you, and you have taken it in your stride."

I coughed out a laugh. "I wouldn't say that. Caleb had to deal with my bedridden ass for three days and then carry me up this mountain."

"Yet you are here," the shaman said. "You. Not anyone else."

I didn't have a comeback. Instead, I said nothing, knowing my cheeks were burning from the praise and the attention.

"So..." Cannon's voice drew the shaman's attention away. "We're right, they're linked?"

The shaman nodded. "Undoubtedly."

"Why?" Caleb's voice was hard.

"Well, I have my suspicions," the shaman confessed, talking

over Caleb's demand to know what they were, "but first, I need something from you, Willow."

"No."

Looking up, I saw Caleb glaring straight ahead, having spoken for me. "What is it?"

The shaman ignored him. "I need your blood."

It threw me, but it wasn't *that* strange a request, but I pointed at Doc. "He has it."

The shaman gave me a smile that was borderline patronizing. "I need it fresher."

Fresher? Did he mean... My stomach rolled in understanding. "You want to bleed me?" I looked around the room. "Leeches?"

Cannon looked surprised at the question but said nothing. Doc, however, had leaned forward. "You've had that before?"

"One of the care homes I was in, she was a little more... natural with her medicines." She'd been a proud Wicca and knew that the kids, including me, called her a crazy witch.

"Not leeches," the shaman confirmed. "Alpha?"

No one moved and then Cannon held out a knife. I didn't know where it came from, and that made it even more unnerving when a knife suddenly appeared in his hand.

I was even more confused when the shaman ignored it. Could he not see it? Cannon's hand dropped and still the shaman waited.

No one spoke.

Why was no one telling him that Cannon had the knife in his hand?

"*Alpha.*" The shaman was looking at Caleb. The reprimand in the shaman's voice was strong but also disappointed.

"I don't answer to that." Caleb's jaw was clenched so tightly that I was surprised he could talk at all.

Alpha? *Caleb* was an *alpha*? What had he called them? Leaders? I knew my mouth was hanging open.

"It matters not what you *answer* to," Cannon growled. "You *are* what you are."

"A murderer?"

The two words had my eyes widening even more. Murderer? What? "What the hell is going on?" Every pair of eyes fell on me, and I didn't care that I had their attention, but I was sick of being looked down on, so I stood. "Caleb? Explain?"

"Later."

*Later*? No. "I think when you call yourself a *murderer*, the time for *later* is now," I hissed at him.

"Your blood, child?"

Turning, I looked at the shaman in disbelief. "Oh my God, can you wait *one* minute?"

"Caleb." The shaman's tone was non-negotiable.

With a sigh, Caleb grabbed my wrist, deaf to my cry of protest. In his other hand was a small knife, and it was only when the swell of blood appeared on my skin that I realized he'd cut my wrist.

"What the fuck!" I tried to jerk my arm back, but his grip held me tight. When the shaman appeared beside me, I bit back my scream of outrage as the old man dipped his head and licked my blood like it was completely *normal*.

When he stepped back, Caleb let me go.

A wad of gauze was handed to me wordlessly by Doc, and I had it pressed against the wound as I looked around at them all, not understanding what was happening and, for the first time, feeling scared.

The shaman picked up a cup and took a drink, swirling it in his mouth. He spat back into the cup. In disbelief, I watched him as he focused on the contents of the cup.

"Human," he confirmed. I opened my mouth to tell him he already knew that, but a look from Cannon silenced me. "Luna's influence is light, but it's there." He looked up at me, frowning. "Alpha." He held his hand out.

With wide eyes, I watched as Caleb cut his wrist smoothly, holding his arm out like the request merely inconvenienced him. He didn't flinch when the shaman repeated the motion and licked his arm.

I was wrong before. These people *were* crazy.

I started to tell them that when the shaman looked at Caleb with so much sadness that tears rushed to my eyes, and I couldn't explain it, but I suddenly felt overwhelmed with sorrow.

"Caleb," he breathed. "No."

Caleb's black stare could have cut him in two. "Enough," he commanded. "It ends *now*."

The shaman shook his head. "I don't think it can," he told him softly. "She's tied to you, Alpha. Luna deems it so."

"Sever it," Caleb spoke through gritted teeth.

"No. I couldn't and...I won't. This is what Luna wants." The shaman looked between us both. "Your hate and rage..." He shook his head again in sympathy. "You know the path you are on, Alpha. Luna demands you turn back."

"I'm *fine*." His voice was like stone, and I almost, almost joked he sounded anything *but* fine, but I wisely kept my mouth shut.

"You're spiraling," Cannon spoke, looking down at Caleb's hands, and I stepped back in shock when I saw the long, curved talons that had *sprouted* from his hands.

"What the—"

Cannon stepped between us. "If you care about anything... about her...leave. Now."

Care about her? Did he mean me? I tried to step around the giant in front of me, but a firm hand pushed me back.

"*Go* now."

I heard a crash, and after a few moments, I saw Cannon's shoulders drop. I darted around him and saw the doors standing wide apart.

Caleb was gone.

"Caleb?" I ran to the door. "*Caleb!*"

"You won't catch him," the shaman said tiredly as he sat down, halting my leaving.

Turning back to them, I didn't think they appreciated how fucked up all of this was. "Where is he going? What happened?" Pushing my hair back, I felt tears spill over. "What is *happening*? I don't understand. *Tell me* what just happened?"

"He's gone." Cannon looked at me with sympathy.

"I can see that!" I snapped at him in frustration, trying to calm my racing heart. "Will he come back?"

He exchanged a look with the shaman. "I can't answer that."

"Then find me someone who can!" I yelled wildly, knowing

that fear was riding my senses. I glared at the shaman. "*You!* You have all the answers, don't you? Will he come back?"

Silence was my answer.

"What have you done?" I whispered, sinking into the couch.

Something solid but flexible was pushed into my hands, and looking down, I saw a sketch pad. Doc handed me a pen.

"Show us, Willow," he told me. "Show us what we've done."

With trembling fingers, I took the pen. My heart, oh my God, my heart was beating so fast. Pounding. I dropped the pen, my hands were shaking so badly.

"Breathe, Willow," Doc spoke quietly, pressing the pen into my hands once more. "Focus."

I didn't hear him. I remembered the night in the truck with Caleb. The night I had a panic attack, and he breathed with me, calming me down. I saw his dark chocolate eyes, kind but full of secrets. I remembered how close we had been, breathing each other's air. I remembered how it felt when he kissed me in the B&B. How I'd felt safe when he carried me up the mountain.

Steadying me.

I needed to calm down. This was for Caleb.

*Focus.*

I began to draw.

Epilogue

THE WIND SWEPT PAST ME AS I RAN, MY PAWS PUTTING the distance between me and the ones behind me. I felt like I couldn't run fast enough, far enough, to escape from them.

*Running.* It's what I was best at. I started running ten years ago, and I'd never intended to stop. Keep Moving was my motto. *Why* had I stopped? For *her?*

When I kept moving, I could keep it all at bay. Keep the shadows in the dark. The mistakes could be forgotten if you didn't stop and dwell.

But I had felt a pull. An urge. A compulsion to go to a small tourist town at the foot of a mountain and look for answers to questions I'd never asked.

And I'd found *her. Willow Harper.*

She was different from other humans I'd met. Living amongst them for ten years had made me more familiar with them than my kind usually was. But she was unusual. She should never have caught my attention. She was completely unremarkable.

Slight. Frail. Fragile.

But *I* was the one who was breakable when I was near her. She found holes in my carefully built walls. She made me remember. She made me feel things that I thought I'd buried deep enough that no one would ever find them.

Not even me.

I'd spent ten years by myself. I'd perfected the art of being alone, shutting out everyone, not letting anyone *in* and not letting myself *out*. But with Willow...those walls had lowered.

And it *terrified* me.

And now? After today, how could I look at her again? I'd scented her fear. It was thick and cloying, suffocating me as she looked at me with wide-eyed terror when my claws had come out.

I was the monster she feared.

The others were just as bad. Forcing me to be there, to listen to that bullshit. Luna didn't give a fuck about me. She hadn't ten years ago, and she sure as shit didn't now.

Cannon, once someone I may have called friend, had given me one last chance, and he had told me to go, and I had *run*.

As I flew across the mountain, I angled north, knowing where I was going and accepting my destination. This was my path. It had *always* been my path, and I was taking it without looking back.

I'd had a moment of weakness. Hope? What the hell did I know about *hope*? A falsehood. A dream. Nothing more than an illusion of weakness. I didn't deserve the chance to be anything other than the fragment of my broken past that I was.

The mountain blurred around me as I raced down it. The

night air was cool, the emptiness welcoming. The void inside me opened wider, embracing me.

It was better this way. For both of us. She didn't ask for any of this, and she didn't deserve to be saddled with me. I was nothing.

Worthless.

All I did was bring pain, and she'd had enough pain in her life.

The shaman had said she smelled of fresh air. She did. She smelled of clean air after a light summer rain. Willow was *pure*. Untarnished. She didn't deserve to be dragged into my darkness.

We were linked, and part of me knew that leaving her was unfair, but it was the only way I knew to protect her. I may never be able to escape her, and maybe they were right, maybe she was part of me now, and I her, but I could damn well try.

Memories of her and my past mingled together, crashing around me as I escaped, and I fought them as I ran.

I didn't need to see anymore.

I didn't need to remember.

*Because I could never forget.*

I didn't need to face the truth. I knew what I was deep down. I'd always known. I ran for hours, and hours turned into days.

At the base of the mountain, I held myself back. Blackridge Peak lay behind me, along with the last glimmer of light in my life. What choice did I have? My paws took that step onto the soil as emotion surrounded me, and I hesitated, my head hanging low to the ground.

*Weak. Pathetic.*

*Murderer.*

Voices of the dead whispered around me. My demons had me in their grip now, pulling me deeper down. Panting, I fought to hold on, and then I had a moment of clarity.

*Why was I fighting?*

Lifting my head, I faced the blackness of the mountain I knew so well. Through the darkness, I climbed upwards, my footing sure on ground that I'd walked many times before.

I felt their touch as I ascended the steep climb. The ghosts reached out, gathering me back into the shade. I could almost feel the cold fingers running through my fur as I moved closer to the place I still called home. Each step was heavier than the last, as part of me still clung to what I'd left behind, that promise of something more.

Willow's face flashed in my mind, pale but vivid, full of life, a contrast to the world I chose to return to. I saw the way her eyes softened when she looked at me, the way that one frown line creased her forehead when she was biting back her numerous questions. The way she sometimes checked me out when she thought I didn't see.

But my ghosts knew there wasn't anything left in me to save. They whispered in my ear, reminding me of the lives lost, the things I'd destroyed.

They knew the darkness was where I was meant to stay.

A light breeze swirled around my feet, and I could feel her touch as sure as if she were there, soft fingers tugging me back, urging me to turn around.

I shook my head, willing myself to be free of *all* the invisible touches as I walked on.

*This* was what I wanted. *This* was who I was.

Packless.

Alone.

*Rogue.*

---

# Acknowledgments

Thank you to my Mr. M for being the best, most supportive partner that I could ask for. Your encouragement means everything.

To my editor, thank you for arguing with me over the smallest details. I'm serious here... Your dedication to thoughtful debate helps refine my process, makes me question myself, and ultimately strengthens my writing to create a better story (but I'm still keeping tyres.)

To Renée & Julie, I can't thank you enough for reading the first seventeen chapters and not complaining once when I never gave you the book's second half. You girls are ACES.

To Anna, my cover designer—girl, you blow me away with your talent.

And finally, to you, my readers—thank you for being simply the best. Your support feeds my passion for storytelling! Thank you for reading!

Until next time.

**Eve L. Mitchell** is a USA Today Bestselling author of Contemporary Romance, New Adult Romance, and also enjoys writing Paranormal Romance. If you're a fan of morally grey alpha-holes, chances are Eve has your next book boyfriend waiting to be claimed.

As an avid reader since childhood, Eve still considers herself a reader first. She believes there's nothing quite like the thrill of getting a new book, whether on her e-reader or in her hands. The thought of sharing that excitement with fellow readers fills her with wonder. Writing under a pen name helps keep her "Secret Agent" status intact.

Eve resides in the North East of Scotland with her three coffee machines and her significant other, Mr. M. When she's not writing, she enjoys NFL football, playing music loudly, and having long conversations with the voices in her head that often turn into the stories she creates.

# *THE WATCHER SERIES*

The Watcher Series is a paranormal romance trilogy that will take you on a journey where you will get lost in a world that will hold you in its depths. With a blend of steam, humour and angst, be ready to buckle up for the ride.

With demons, devils and one sassy, clueless witch, what more could you ask for? Join Star as she gets a crash course in what not to do when you get involved with the Watchers.

An enemies-to-lovers story that has all the emotions packed between the pages as the heroine deals with love, betrayal, loss and so much more.

This series is a trilogy and must be read in order. If you love cliffhangers, this series is for you. If you hate cliffhangers, don't worry, the next book's already written.

The series includes **A Glow of Stars & Dust**, **A Flame of Stars & Midnight** and **A Blaze of Stars & Dawn**.

GET THE SERIES

WWW.EVELMITCHELL.COM

## *THE AKRHYN SERIES*

Creatures of evil roam the shadows - the Drakhyn. They may look like humans, but their taloned hands and razor-sharp teeth serve one purpose only; killing.

A Sentinel's purpose is to patrol and protect. They are highly trained soldiers with superior skills and abilities. Whether they be Vampyres, Lycan, Castors or gifted Akrhyn, their purpose is the same; hunt the Drakhyn and rid the world of their evil presence.

This fantasy trilogy covers tropes of chosen one, fated mates, good vs evil.

The series includes **Into Darkness**, **Lost in Darkness** and **From the Darkness**.

GET THE SERIES
WWW.EVELMITCHELL.COM

# *THE DENVER SERIES*

The Denver Series is a three-book mafia romance shared world series. Each book is a standalone, featuring cameos from the other books. Although it is recommended that the books be read in order, it is not necessary to do so.

The series covers tropes of opposites attract, enemies-to-lovers, and forbidden romance (stepcousins).

The Denver Series is a steamy contemporary romance series that dabbles in the mafia romance genre, with book one hinting at it and the other two exploring the darker side of this much-loved genre.

A complete three-book series where sassy heroines meet and fall for their dark alphahole heroes.

The series includes **Her Greatest Mistake, Beautifully Broken** and **Keeping Harmony**.

GET THE SERIES
WWW.EVELMITCHELL.COM

# THE RUTHLESS DEVILS SERIES

A college sports romance series following twin brothers and their cousin. Three football stars who have it all: looks, money, talent and the world at their feet. No one messes with the Devils. Each book deals with a different Devil and their love interest who will either make them or break them.

The series covers tropes of enemies-to-lovers, second-chance romance and forced proximity.

This is interconnected three-book series with an underlying story arc that carries through from book one to book three, and therefore the series must be read in order. The series deals with some elements that sensitive readers may find triggering.

This series includes **Ruthless Heart**, **Ruthless Desire** and **Ruthless Charm**.

GET THE SERIES

WWW.EVELMITCHELL.COM

The Torn & Broken duet is a duet with a twist. You can read either book as a standalone. *Torn by Grace* was written first and one of the female side characters in that book is the main character in *Broken by Faith*, however, you don't need to know what happened in *Torn by Grace* to enjoy *Broken by Faith*. There is a little bit of crossover, but no spoilers.

*Torn by Grace* is a second chance, enemies-to-lovers, brothers-best-friend romance.

*Broken by Faith* is an enemies-to-lovers, forced proximity, fake relationship romance.

The series includes **Torn by Grace and Broken by Faith.**

## *THE ORDER OF THE RAVENS SERIES*
### *written as Ava Speirs*

The Order of the Ravens Series is a traditional epic fantasy series where the focus is on action and adventure.

Bastian dal'Leif is a Knight of the Order, an Order that has fallen into distrust. The Order of the Conclave which were once seen as warriors of the Gods and a beacon of hope, are now cast in shadow.

Bastian and his men remain true to their Order but are forced to become mercenaries, selling their swords for coin.

In the halls of his Order, Bastian is entrusted with a mission. A mission he is reluctant to accept.

The mission is so dangerous and deadly only a fool would take it...and only a coward would reject it.

The series includes **Knight of Sword & Shadow, Knight of Sacrifice & Shade, Knight of Dagger & Darkness, and Knight of Trials and Twilight.**

www.ingramcontent.com/pod-product-compliance
Lightning Source LLC
Chambersburg PA
CBHW030556170726
48283CB00002B/348